CW00860447

Call It Pretending

Frances di Plino

"Delve into the dark side... Well-constructed with an unflinching plot. Satisfying enough for the most discerning crime reader."

Ruth Dugdall

Winner of the CWA Debut Dagger Award

"di Plino's assured and fluid writing style truly brings characters and scenes to life on the page. Her dark psychological thrillers will have you gripped from page one."

Rachel Abbott

No. 1 Bestselling Author of
Only the Innocent and *The Back Road*

CROOKED
CAT

Discover us online:
www.crookedcatbooks.com

Join us on facebook:
www.facebook.com/realcrookedcat

Tweet a photo of yourself holding
this book to **@crookedcatbooks**
and something nice will happen.

This novel is dedicated to David and Michelle.
I couldn't be any prouder without bursting.

About the Author

Frances di Plino is the pen name of Lorraine Mace, humour columnist for Writing Magazine.

She is also a deputy editor of Words with JAM, writes fiction for the women's magazine market, features and photo-features for monthly glossy magazines, and is a writing competition judge for Writers' Forum. Winner of a Petra Kenney International Poetry Award, she has been placed in numerous creative writing and poetry competitions.

Lorraine, a former tutor for Writers Bureau, is the author of the Writers Bureau course, Marketing Your Book, and the co-author, with Maureen Vincent-Northam, of The Writer's ABC Checklist (Accent Press).

Lorraine writes the D.I. Paolo Storey crime thriller series under a pen name because she is also an author of children's fiction and wants to keep the two genres separate.

She is a member of the Society of Authors and the Crime Writers' Association.

www.francesdiplino.com
Writing Critique Service
www.lorrainemace.com
www.flash500.com

Acknowledgements

Thank you to June Whitaker, Derek Mace and Maureen Vincent-Northam for reading early drafts of this novel and helping me to improve it. A big thank you to Dr Robert Lefever for putting the idea of insulin murders into my head. You were a great help. Deepest thanks to Dr Catriona King for forensic advice. If I got it right, it's because of you – if I got it wrong, that's down to me. I would also like to extend my thanks to all at Crooked Cat Publishing for allowing D.I. Paolo Storey this third outing. He's very grateful for the opportunity – and so am I.

Call It Pretending

Also featuring Det. Insp. Paolo Storey

Bad Moon Rising
Someday Never Comes
Looking For A Reason

CHAPTER ONE

Week One – Friday 25th July to Thursday 31st July

In the lift, aware of the security camera overhead, the pretender kept his head down and his eyes on the envelope he held in his right hand. In his left hand was a laptop case, but there was no computer inside. What it did contain would come as a surprise to the man he was about to call on. The lift finally arrived at the top floor and the doors slid silently open to allow him to step into a marble-panelled vestibule with ornately gilded mirrors on the walls to his left and right. He didn't bother looking at his reflection; he knew what he looked like and so, too, would the police by this time tomorrow. Much good that would do them.

Opposite the lift was a single door. Privileged entrance to the only apartment on the penthouse floor. He briefly wondered what it must feel like to be rich, but shrugged off the thought. He wasn't interested in money. All he wanted was to achieve his goal. And today he'd take the first step.

He walked across the vestibule and pressed the buzzer.

The door opened and the woman whose movements he'd been watching and timing for the past month stood on the threshold.

"Professor Edwards is expecting me," he said, handing over a visiting card.

The woman glanced at it and then gave it back. "Yes, Mr Buchanan. The professor is waiting for you in his study. I'll show you the way."

He slipped the card into his jacket pocket, inwardly smiling at how easy it was to fool someone with no more than a rectangle of cardboard he'd had made up in a quick print store. Concentrate, he told himself, this is no time to lose focus. He followed her along the hallway. Tastefully decorated, he thought, looking around at the bronze sculptures, watercolours and oil paintings adorning the walls. But then Professor Edwards was a very wealthy man, so he shouldn't have expected anything less. They passed closed doors on the left and right, but no windows. He wondered where the light was coming from and looked up. A massive skylight filled most of the space above his head. He wondered if you'd ever get tired of looking up and seeing the blue sky above instead of having your view limited by a ceiling, like most of the world. Was Professor Edwards immune to the view from his wonderful home? It didn't matter, one way or the other. The professor didn't have much time left to enjoy being rich enough to afford a penthouse apartment in the most prestigious apartment complex in Bradchester.

They reached a door at the far end of the hall and the woman knocked before opening it and going in.

"Mr Seth Buchanan from the *New York Times* is here to see you, Professor."

"Show him in, Mary, and then bring us some coffee before you go home. I won't need you until tomorrow."

"Yes, Professor," she said.

"Come in. Don't stand in the doorway. You'll have to excuse me not getting up to greet you. Gout keeps me trapped in this chair most of the day. Take a seat."

The pretender forced himself to walk across and shake the hand the professor held out to him, before sinking down in the comfortable armchair his host had pointed out.

"You remind me of someone, but I can't think who."

"I think I have one of those generic faces."

"Must be, because we haven't met before, have we? This is a turn up for the books. Fancy the *New York Times* realising my importance to the field of psychiatry and deciding to feature me in their series on great men. I won't say I'm not flattered, because I am. It's a pity our own press haven't seen fit to recognise me in the same way."

And so you should be flattered, you arrogant prick.
Anger surged through the pretender, but that was good.
He'd need the rage to carry him through to the end.

"Have you been following the series?"

Professor Edwards laughed. "To be honest with you, it's
not a paper I generally get, but when I received your call, I
sent Mary out to get me a copy with the latest interview in
it. You're going to put me in some very illustrious
company."

The professor was interrupted by the arrival of his
housekeeper with the coffee tray.

"Put it down there, Mary, and then you get off home. See
you tomorrow and don't be late. I like my breakfast on time,
not half an hour after it should have arrived."

The woman looked as if she wanted to say something,
but bit her lip before speaking.

"I'll be away in a few minutes. Can you see yourself out,
Mr Buchanan?"

He smiled. Exactly as planned. "Of course," he said. "I
would imagine I'll be here for about an hour or so."

The door closed behind the housekeeper and the
professor pointed at the tray. "How do you like your coffee?
I see Mary has put out some cream. Don't take the stuff,
myself, but I know you Yanks like it. Not that you sound
American. Not at all."

Shaking his head at the offer of cream, the pretender
stood up. "I'm not American," he said. "I'm British through
and through, but with the ease of internet communications,
you don't have to live in a country to work for a publication
based there. I travel all over the world conducting
interviews. Do you mind if I look at your books. I find I get
a sense of the man from the books he keeps closest to him."

He crossed the room to stand next to the bookshelves
lining one complete wall of the study.

"Interesting collection you have here. Are they all first
editions?"

"Not all," the professor answered, looking
uncomfortable as he twisted around in his seat and peered

over the back of the chair. "But many of them are. As you can see, I have a passion for history."

"What is your favourite period?"

"The Tudors, without a doubt. From a psychiatric perspective they make a fascinating study."

Keeping his eyes on the titles on display, the pretender edged his way along the bookshelves, moving out of the old man's line of sight. He stopped when he was sure the professor could no longer see him and waited. Then he heard the noise he'd been listening out for – the front door closing behind the housekeeper.

The professor was droning on about the connection between megalomania and syphilis. The pretender gave the occasional word of encouragement to keep the man speaking, although he probably didn't need to, as the professor clearly loved the sound of his own voice.

He reached into the inside pocket of his jacket and pulled out a face mask and a plastic bag. Placing the mask over his mouth and nose, he opened the bag and took out a piece of material. From another pocket he took a small plastic screw top bottle. Working quickly, he undid the top and soaked the material with the liquid. Replacing the cap, he dropped the bottle into the plastic bag and slipped it back into his pocket.

He strode back to the professor's chair. The old man had briefly stopped talking and was in the act of drinking his coffee. He waited until the professor replaced his cup in the saucer and then put his arm around the chair and held the cloth firmly over the professor's nose and mouth. The old man kicked out and clawed, trying to drag the cloth from his face, but he gradually stopped struggling. The pretender held the cloth in place for a few seconds longer and only removed it when he was sure the professor was completely immobilised.

Fishing the plastic bag out from his pocket, he put the cloth and bottle into it. He removed the mask and walked over to his seat. As he sat down, he was annoyed to feel his body trembling. This was going exactly as planned. Now wasn't the time to get squeamish. He reached down for the laptop case and laid it across his lap. Unzipping it, he fished in his pocket for the plastic bag and mask and threw both inside. Taking a deep breath and telling himself he had right on his side, he took a syringe and a vial of liquid from inside the case.

He filled the syringe and made sure there was no air at the top. That made him smile. Considering what he was about to do, worrying about putting air into the professor's body seemed a bit redundant.

Okay, it was time. Standing up, he walked across to the old man, immobile in his drugged sleep. His hands shook. Get a grip, he told himself. *You've waited bloody years for this; don't stuff it up now.*

He managed to get his tremors under control by deep breathing and repeating the mantra he'd been living by for the last year. Time for justice!

Stabbing the syringe into the old man's leg, he depressed the plunger, shooting the deadly liquid into the professor's bloodstream.

Not as steady on his feet as he would have liked, the pretender staggered backwards and sat down again, waiting for the insulin to take effect.

As the old man's body went into shock, trembling and twitching like a leaf in a gale, he wished he'd been able to leave the professor conscious, so that he was aware of his suffering. Maybe for the next one, that's what he'd do.

"Sorry to disappoint you," he said, "but the *New York Times* doesn't even know you exist and my name isn't Buchanan. You ruined my life. You destroyed me and felt nothing as you did it."

The professor's body jerked and shuddered, his feet kicking over the small table and sending the coffee cups and pot flying. Finally, he lay still as a pool of urine darkened the material of his trousers.

You didn't even recognise me properly, you bastard, the pretender thought, tears streaming down his cheeks. *If I'd used my real name you probably still wouldn't have realised who I was.*

The pretender took one last look around the room. There was only one thing he had still to do before he left. He placed the envelope in the middle of the floor, propped against the fallen coffee pot. He knew he'd left fingerprints behind which would enable the police to catch him one day, but not before he was ready for them to take him in.

CHAPTER TWO

Paolo added his rucksack to the pile of suitcases already stacked by the front door. He turned to Lydia, who was leaning against the stairs, and grinned at her.

She shrugged in response. "We can't say we didn't give it a fair trial this time," she said, smiling.

Paolo could hear the relief in her voice matching the way he felt. "Six months, almost to the day," he said. "Well done, us, for lasting that long. But at least we're friends now. The first time I left you swore you never wanted to see me again."

Lydia laughed. "What makes you think this time is different?"

"Because I'm a great bloke you once loved and now really, really, *really* like, even if you don't want to be married to me," he said.

He stepped up to her and opened his arms. She didn't hesitate, moving into his embrace.

"You're right. I much prefer you as a friend to a husband," she murmured against his neck.

Paolo hugged her. "You know, I swear there's a compliment in there somewhere," he said. He let her go and turned to Katy coming down from her bedroom to join them.

Even after living back at home for six months, he still couldn't believe how well Katy had recovered from last year's trauma. To look at her, it was impossible to credit the nightmare she'd been through. As a family, they owed everything to Jessica Carter, Katy's psychiatrist.

"You off now, Dad? Want a hand with the cases?"

"No, you stay inside. It's chucking it down out there and

there's no point in both of us getting wet. I should have left yesterday; it was blue sky and sunshine all day."

"Ah, but yesterday you were working at chasing bad guys," Lydia said. "That's a sunshine job. Leaving home is definitely something that should be done in the pouring rain."

"You reckon?" Paolo asked. "I think I'd rather chase the bad guys in the rain than shift this lot outside in a monsoon."

He opened the door, grabbed a couple of cases and made a dash for the car, only realising when he got there that he didn't have a hand free to press the remote unlocking device. Why didn't Britain have normal summers, like other countries? he wondered, shuddering as rain ran in rivers down the back of his neck.

By the time he had all his bags packed in the boot, he was soaked through to the skin. He just hoped his new landlord had switched on the water heater as he'd asked. A hot shower and he'd be ready to put his feet up and relax for the rest of the day. Katy was coming over the next day to wield a paintbrush with him, but he intended to do nothing other than loaf around today.

He splashed back to the house and couldn't help returning the grins of his ex-wife and daughter as he stood on the doorstep, water cascading from his face and hair.

"You look like you need a snorkel," Lydia said.

"Thank you, your sympathy is much appreciated."

"I offered to help," Katy said. "You decided you wanted to be all he-man macho."

Paolo grinned and took a step towards her. "A hug for your dad?"

She laughed and jumped back. "No way. What time shall I come over tomorrow?"

"At about ten? I'll treat you to lunch. Restaurant of your choice as long as it doesn't have a Mc in its name."

He waved goodbye and squelched back to his car, slipping behind the wheel. Dripping water everywhere, he wondered if the seat would ever dry out. Oh well, that was a problem for another day. He started the engine and headed off to his new home.

Two hours later he'd showered, unpacked his clothes, switched on the television and stretched out on the couch. It was strange to be on his own again, but this time it felt right. He and Lydia were at peace with one another, Katy was okay with him moving out and he felt ready to move on.

Ah, bliss, the rest of the day to himself, he thought, just as his mobile rang. The tune told him it was Dave Johnson and he was almost tempted to ignore it. But he couldn't. Dave would only call on a Saturday if it was serious.

He picked up the phone and slid the bar to answer.

"Paolo here," he said. "What's up?"

"Looks like we've got a murder on our hands, sir. It's a Professor Edwards, apparently an eminent psychiatrist. His housekeeper called emergency services, but it seems the professor was dead long before she dialled 999."

"What makes you think it's murder?"

"The killer left a piece of paper in an envelope on the coffee table. The computer printed message says: 'one down – five to go.'"

"Shit! I don't like the sound of that. Where are you now?"

"On my way to the professor's apartment," Dave said.

"Give me the address. I'll meet you there as soon as I can."

By the time Paolo arrived at the professor's penthouse, the forensic team were already in place.

"Who's in there?" Paolo asked Dave, slipping on white overshoes so that he could enter.

"Barbara Royston and she's not in a good mood."

Paolo took his eyes off the shoes and looked up, almost losing his balance in the process.

"Maybe she was having a nice relaxing weekend like me and resented being called out," Paolo said.

Dave shrugged. "Could be. I'm just saying, be careful. She bit my head off just for asking a question."

Paolo grinned. "That's normal behaviour for Barbara. Come on, let's go in and see what we can find out."

He saw the forensic pathologist leaning over a figure sprawled in a deep armchair and headed towards her.

"I hope you've covered up," Barbara said, without even looking round. "I've got enough to do without worrying about contamination."

"Hello, Barbara. Happy Saturday to you, too."

She glanced back at him and gave a half smile. "Sorry, Paolo, this call came in at a particularly bad time." She shrugged. "Sometimes I wonder why I do this job."

"Because you're good at it," Paolo said. "What can you tell me?"

She glared at him. "If that half-hearted compliment was meant to soften me up so that I'd answer questions before I've had time to make a proper examination, you've wasted your breath."

Paolo took a step back. "Whoa, calm down. I don't know what's eating you, but whatever it is, I'm not the cause."

Barbara shook her head as if trying to rid her mind of an unpleasant image. "No, I know you're not." She nodded towards the body. "He's been injected with something. I won't know what until I can do a proper tox screening, but there's a faint smell on his face, which makes me think he was given something to render him unconscious before the injection was administered. There's very little sign of struggle other than the table being knocked over. I think someone came at him from behind."

"Thanks, Barbara. When will you do the autopsy?"

"I'm not going to be able to get to it until Wednesday morning. I'll let you know what time."

Paolo nodded his thanks. "I need to speak to the housekeeper. I'll come back and fill you in if she comes up with anything that might help you."

Barbara smiled and Paolo was horrified to see tears forming in her eyes. He stepped in closer so that nobody

12

would be able to overhear.

"What is it, Barbara? Can I help?"

She shook her head. "No, it's something I need to work out for myself."

"Okay, but you know where to find me if you change your mind."

She nodded and Paolo turned away to leave the study, stopping when Barbara called out to him. He turned back, eyebrows raised in question.

"Thanks," she said.

"Any time."

Paolo caught up with Dave, who'd been chatting to one of the forensics team in the hallway.

"Nothing to help us so far, sir," he said. "There are plenty of prints, though, so we might get lucky when they are tested against the database. Did Dr Royston have anything to say?"

"Not much. You know what she's like about giving information before she's had chance to test every aspect of the body. He might have been knocked out before receiving the killer injection. That may or may not be useful. We'll have to see what else comes up. I'm looking for the housekeeper. Do you know where she is?"

"In the kitchen, sir. She's with a WPC."

"Right, let's go."

As they approached the kitchen, sounds of giggles drifted along the hallway. Paolo had expected the housekeeper to be distraught, but she seemed to be in the middle of telling a joke when he and Dave walked in.

"...and the man dropped his trousers," she said, followed by gales of laughter, hers and the WPC's.

"Thank you, Constable. Detective Sergeant Johnson and I will take over now."

The WPC stopped laughing mid-chuckle and straightened up.

"Yes, sir. This is Mary Prentice, Professor Edwards's housekeeper," she said.

13

Paolo nodded and waited for her to leave the room before addressing the woman who was still wiping away tears of laughter.

"Please, take a seat, Mary," he said, pointing to a chair at the head of the kitchen table. He pulled out one of the chairs and sat down. Dave sat opposite and took out his notebook, ready to record the interview.

"You don't seem very upset at the loss of Professor Edwards."

Mary stopped laughing. "I'm not particularly sad, to be honest. He wasn't exactly the most likeable of people. I'm more upset about losing my job than anything else."

"He wasn't a good employer?" Paolo asked.

"The pay was good, better than good, but he was an arrogant pig who'd throw something at you as soon as look at you. I'll be glad to move on."

"Could you tell me the exact sequence of events, starting from the last time you saw the professor alive to the moment you called in 999?"

For the first time, Mary looked serious. "Am I in trouble?"

"No, why would you think you were?"

"Well, I let the reporter in. I didn't know he was going to kill the professor though, did I?"

"Reporter?"

"From the *New York Times*. He'd only phoned to set up the meeting a few hours earlier. The professor was beside himself with pride. Thought he was the bees' knees, he did."

Paolo exchanged a glance with Dave. This was getting interesting.

"Okay," Paolo said, "let's start at the very beginning. When did the man phone and what did he say?"

"The phone call came in the morning and the man asked to speak to Professor Edwards. I asked him who he was and what it was about. I have to, you see. The professor won't... wouldn't speak to just anyone. He felt he was far too important for that. Anyway, the man said...hang on, I have it written down on the pad over there."

She stood up and walked over to the kitchen phone, picking up a notebook before returning to sit down again. She opened the pad and showed it to Paolo.

"See, here it is. Mr Seth Buchanan from the *New York Times*."

"Do you know why he wanted to interview the professor?"

"Do I know? If the professor had been able to find a town crier the whole of Bradchester would have known! The paper is running a series on important men of the world, or some such, and they decided Professor Edwards should be included. If they'd been looking for selfish, nasty, bigoted egotists, I'd have put his name forward myself, but that man was only important in his own eyes."

"You really didn't like him, did you?"

She shook her head. "No, but then you find me one person who did. The man hardly ever went out, but he still managed to upset nearly all the other residents in this apartment block. If he wasn't complaining about the neighbours' pets, it was their children. He didn't think the doorman did a good enough job, the cleaners weren't up to his standards, the lift didn't run as smoothly as he thought it should. You name it, he found fault with it."

"Would you be able to give me a list of people who bore him a grudge?"

Mary laughed. "I'd need a few notebooks to put down all the names. It'd be quicker to say who didn't bear him a grudge. That would be anyone who hadn't met him. He collected grudges like no other man I've ever known."

Paolo smiled. "Still, it would help if you could write down all those you can think of who bore particular animosity towards him. Now, to get back to the reporter. You took the call and passed it along to the professor. Then what?"

"Professor Edwards called me back into his study, told me he was going to be in the *New York Times* and sent me out to get a copy of the latest edition."

"And the journalist seemed on the level?"

"I don't know. The professor didn't discuss it with me, except to gloat about how all his colleagues would be green with envy."

Paolo glanced over at Dave scribbling furiously in his notebook. Dave looked up and nodded. He was keeping up.

"Let's move on to the journalist arriving. Could you describe him for us?"

"Oh, that's easy. He had on those wire-rimmed glasses, you know like the ones John Lennon made famous? Um, let's see. Light brown hair, but now I think about it, it could have been a wig. It's amazing the number of men who worry about being bald."

"What makes you think that? Did it not fit properly?"

Mary put her head on one side. "No, it wasn't that. It was his eyebrows," she said after thinking for a while. "His eyebrows were too dark for his hair. Although I suppose some people do have dark eyebrows and light hair. Just look at that politician, the one who reminds me of a panda with his white hair and black eyebrows."

Paolo hid a smile at the thought of one of the previous government ministers being thought of as a panda. "Anything else? How tall was he?"

"I'm not good with heights," Mary said, "but he was much taller than me."

Paolo had mentally assessed Mary's height at about five feet, so most men would be taller than her. Not much help there. He stood up.

"My height, would you say? Or taller?"

Mary stood next to him. "Yes, about the same as you, give or take an inch."

Paolo sat down again and waited for Mary to do the same. "Eye colour?"

She shook her head. "Sorry, I didn't notice."

"Was there anything else the reporter said that you can remember? It doesn't matter how trivial it might seem."

She glanced up at the ceiling, as if seeking inspiration. "Not really," she said. "Oh, hang on. What about this? The professor asked me if I'd been on the phone all week. When

I said no, he didn't seem to believe me. Apparently, when he asked the reporter why the interview was being set up at such short notice Mr Buchanan told him he'd tried to call several times during the week, but couldn't get through. He was in the UK for a fortnight to interview several people for the series and our phone had been engaged each time he'd dialled, but I think that's a lie. We hardly ever get calls here. As I said, the professor wasn't exactly in demand socially."

"But the professor accepted what the reporter had said?" Paolo asked.

"Yes, because he believed all the flattery the man gave him over the phone about being so relieved he'd finally been able to get through. Besides, the professor would never miss out on a chance to get his name in the paper."

"Would you be prepared to come to the station on Monday to describe the journalist in detail? We might be able to put out a sketch from your observations."

"Oooh, I've seen that done on the television. Yes, I'd be happy to give it a go."

Paolo stood up and handed Mary his card. "Give me a call Monday morning and I'll let you know what time to come over. It will probably be in the afternoon. In the meantime, if you remember anything else, anything at all, feel free to call me."

"I will, but I don't suppose I'll have reason to call. I've told you everything I know."

Paolo waited until Dave had finished his final note taking and the two of them headed back into the hall.

"Blimey, she really didn't like her boss," Dave whispered as they reached the front door. "Just goes to show. Maybe you're not so bad after all."

Paolo returned the grin that accompanied Dave's comment. "Any more from you and your career prospects are going to go into a deep decline. Come on, let's get to the station. It's at times like these I wish George was still with us. No one could beat that man at digging up facts."

Dave shrugged. "Sorry, sir, I know he was useful, but I don't miss him about the place. I can never forgive the fact that he took money and sold us out to the press."

Rummaging for his phone, Paolo ran through a mental list of people he could call in on a Saturday to run some background checks. There were a few uniformed officers who showed promise and were looking to move over into CID. When he got to the station he'd see who was up for some overtime. In the meantime, he wanted his best people on duty and that meant getting Cathy Connors to come in.

"I'm going to get CC to meet us at the station, Dave," he said. "If the professor is the first of six, we need to work fast to find out who might be next on the killer's list."

CHAPTER THREE

Paolo replaced the receiver on his phone. He hadn't been surprised to learn that the real Seth Buchanan had never left New York and that Professor Edwards wouldn't have been considered for the series he was writing in any event. The professor hadn't done anything outstanding and the series was based on men of merit. He stood up and wandered to his office door. Leaning back against the frame, he looked out over a largely deserted office. Apart from three uniformed officers, there was only Dave and CC at work. Dave was hunched over at his desk, phone in hand. From the way he was furiously scribbling, it seemed he was getting plenty of information. CC had been similarly engaged, but she replaced her receiver and looked up at Paolo.

"It's weird, sir. All the people he mentored, right up to the point he retired, were male with one exception. You'd expect there to be a more even split considering psychiatry is one of the professions where there is a large number of female practitioners. Anyway, you'll never guess which name has just come up as his only female specialist registrar while he was the consultant at Bradchester General," she said. "Our friend from the child prostitution case, Jessica Carter! She trained under Professor Edwards, but they had a falling out some years back. Mind you, from what I've been hearing, so did just about everyone he came into contact with."

Dave put his phone down. "I've been getting the same message. If we're going to interview everyone who had it in for this guy, we'll need to draft in half the forces in the country. Disliked doesn't even come close. The man was loathed wholesale."

Paolo sighed. The housekeeper hadn't been overreacting.

"Okay, sadly, we don't have enough manpower to call on everyone straight off. We need to concentrate on the most likely candidates at this stage. What've you got, Dave?"

"I've got plenty of neighbours he upset, but it's not likely to be one of them because surely a neighbour would have been recognised by Mary Prentice, if not the professor himself. Other than that, everywhere he practised, all the institutions and hospitals, seem to be full of former colleagues who would struggle to find a good word to say about him. But then again, if it was someone the professor knew from the past, surely he'd have recognised the man as an impostor."

Paolo shook his head. "Not if the man was heavily disguised."

He looked over at CC.

"Same here, sir. So many people disliked him; it's going to be hard to narrow it down."

"Do your best," Paolo said. "Have you got a list of those Jessica Carter might know? Pass it here and I'll give her a ring to see if she can come up with anyone with a greater than usual reason to hate him."

Paolo went back into his office and shut the door. He tried to tell himself he was only interested in calling her to find out about her connection to the professor, but he knew he was lying. Before Lydia had asked him to move back into the family home, Paolo had been close to asking Jessica out. He knew she liked him as much as he liked her. It could have grown into something, but he'd chosen to give his marriage another try. He hadn't spoken to Jessica for six months.

Should he mention he was now free again or just keep things on a professional footing? Jessica most probably had someone in her life by now. Of course she would. A lovely woman like that wasn't going to be single for long.

He'd say hello, but keep the conversation to questions about the professor. If she was still interested in him, she'd let him know. It would be better that way. He didn't want to put her in an awkward position.

He glanced down as he dialled her number and was amused and exasperated to see his hands trembling. Like a teenager, he thought. Let's hope I don't end up tongue-tied like one when she answers.

The ringing stopped abruptly as she answered. "Paolo? It is you, isn't it?"

"Yes, how did you know?"

Jessica laughed. "The magic of modern technology. I've never taken your details out of my contact list, so your name came on the display."

There was a brief moment of silence as Paolo thought about the fact that she hadn't erased his name, but he tried not to read too much into it. After all, he had names in his phone that were no longer needed. It might not mean anything.

"How are you?" she asked. "And Katy, how is she doing?"

"Fine, thank you. We're both fine. Um, this isn't a social call exactly."

"Oh."

Paolo heard ice forming on the single syllable.

"That is, it's not just a social call. I…you know I…how are you?"

He heard her laugh and wondered if he sounded as stupid as he felt.

"Before you get any more tongue-tied, what can I do for you, Paolo?"

Relieved to be able to get back on track, Paolo got to the reason for his call. "The news hasn't been released yet, but your former mentor, Professor Edwards, has been murdered. We're compiling a list of possible suspects."

"And I'm on it?"

"No, not at all, but your name came up and it seemed to me you might be able to fill in some background detail on people who were close to the professor or working with him at the same time as you."

He heard her sigh. "Close to him? I doubt anyone could be described as close to him, but read out the names and I'll see if I can help."

"Before I go through the list, CC pointed out that you were his only female specialist registrar, was that deliberate on his part?"

"You mean not having females working under him? Yes, it was. He didn't agree with women in the professions – any of the professions. He was very much of the school of keeping females at home and out of the world of men."

Paolo reflected that the more he heard about Professor Edwards, the more he could understand someone wanting to do away with him. But there were five others on the killer's list, so the motive might not even be connected to personality type.

"So how did you come to be on his team?"

Jessica laughed. "I was foisted on to him by the hospital and he never let me forget it. He made my life pretty miserable, which was why I left Bradchester for a few years. I took a position in a London teaching hospital to get away from his sphere of influence."

"He sounds like a charming man. Anyway, let's see who you can remember from that time." Paolo looked down at the piece of paper CC had given him and started at the top. "Andrew Manning?"

"I only knew Andrew for a couple of months. Level headed, good sense of humour, fell in love with an Australian nurse working over here. They married and settled in Australia. I still get cards from them at Christmas."

"Michael Sergeant?"

"Hmm, fiery personality. Often clashed with the professor, but on a superficial level. He went up north somewhere to open a private practice. I can't see him coming back to commit murder."

"Do you know where up north?"

"Newcastle, I think, but I'm not one hundred per cent on that. These are names from over ten years ago."

Paolo scribbled Australia next to the first name and Newcastle with a question mark next to the second.

"Only a couple more to go. Patrick Kirkbride?"

"Patrick? Patrick? I don't remember a Patrick. Oh, hold on, yes I do. We only overlapped by a few weeks. I'm sorry, I don't recall too much about him. Can't help you on that one."

"Right, last name. Conrad Stormont?"

"Wow, now there's a name from the past. Poor Conrad. I haven't thought about him in a long time."

Paolo picked up on the sadness in her voice. "Sounds like there's a story attached to him."

Jessica sighed. "There is. It's a long one. Again, this was shortly before I transferred to London. Professor Edwards went on vacation and his outpatient cases were split between me and Conrad. A young man, I can't remember his name, Jon somebody, came in for a routine check and renewal of prescription. According to Conrad, the professor left him instructions on how to deal with the patient, including a change of medication."

"According to Conrad?"

"Yes, the professor claimed otherwise in court, of course. The patient, I wish I could remember his name, anyway, the patient had a psychotic episode due to taking the wrong medication. He was driving at the time and caused an accident that resulted in the death of a woman. His younger brother, who'd been in the passenger seat, was paralysed from the waist down in the crash. The young patient was arrested and tried, but found not guilty of dangerous driving or driving under the influence. I'm surprised you don't remember it. It was quite a big thing in the press for several weeks. A true cause celebre."

"Why?"

"Because the professor wanted to make sure he couldn't be held accountable for Conrad's actions. He spoke to every journalist within a country mile."

"So the patient was acquitted, but had to live with knowing he'd killed someone and caused the paralysis of his brother?"

"That's right."

"Poor man," Paolo said. "What was he suffering from?"

There was silence for a few moments, then Jessica spoke.

"Normally I wouldn't tell you, but you could find it in the trial transcript if you searched for it. The professor was treating him for dissociative identity disorder."

"What is that in language I could understand?"

"In lay terms it would be better understood as having a split personality."

"So being prescribed the wrong drug would have had serious consequences?"

"Yes, absolutely. Basically, the medication he was given did the complete opposite of what he needed. He literally wasn't himself while behind the wheel of the car. He wouldn't have been able to tell you what happened or why. After the accident he would have had no conscious memory of his actions."

"Okay, can you remember what happened to Conrad Stormont?"

"He was struck off. Professor Edwards stuck to it that Conrad had made an error and hadn't followed his written instructions."

"Your voice tells me you didn't agree."

Jessica sighed again. "Conrad insisted he'd followed the professor's notes to the letter. I hate to say this, but I always wondered if Professor Edwards doctored his notes when he realised what had happened. Conrad was conscientious and not at all the type to go off and do his own thing. He used to drive me to distraction because he would check and double check instructions before doing anything. It just wasn't credible to me that he would have made a mistake like that. But the Medical Council believed Professor Edwards."

"Did Conrad accept their findings? Did he have no right of appeal?"

"He seemed to lose heart afterwards. When he lost his licence to practice he tried to commit suicide – slashed his wrists. If it hadn't been for his wife coming home early from a girl's night out, he would have bled to death. Fortunately she knew what to do to staunch the bleeding and got Conrad to the hospital in time to save him." She sighed. "As I say, I haven't thought about Conrad for years. The last I heard he had a bad drinking problem. When the door slams on the only thing you want to do in your life, some people find it hard to move on to other jobs. Conrad took it really badly and fell to pieces, but I've always thought the blame lay at Professor Edwards's door."

"Do you know if Conrad Stormont is still in Bradchester?"

"As I said, I haven't thought about him in years. I have no idea where he is now. I'm sorry, Paolo, I'm not being much help."

"There's nothing for you to apologise for. You're wrong, though, you've been really helpful. Thank you."

"You're welcome. Regardless of what I thought of Professor Edwards on a personal level, I hope you catch his killer."

"I intend to," Paolo said.

"Okay, bye then," Jessica said.

It's now or never, Paolo's mind yelled at him. "No, wait!"

"Sorry, I thought we'd gone through all the names."

"We have, but...would you like to have dinner with me?"

She kept quiet for such a long time Paolo feared she'd ended the call.

"Aren't you back with Lydia?" she asked after a lifetime of silence.

"I was, but not anymore. It didn't work out. Don't worry; we've parted as friends this time. I moved out this morning into a place of my own."

"And Katy? How did she take it?"

"She's fine about it. Lydia and I gave it our best shot, but even Katy could see it wasn't right for either of us."

Jessica went quiet again. Paolo felt as if his future

hinged on the next few seconds and could almost hear each one ticking away. Face it, he thought, you had your chance just before Christmas and you blew it. You need to accept that she's no longer interested.

"Jessica, I—"

"Yes, I'd love to have dinner with you," she said.

CHAPTER FOUR

Jon opened his flat door and listened. He began counting silently. One, two, three, four, five, six...

"Jon? That you? Where've you been? You're late."

Jon's fists clenched and he forced himself to wait before answering. Just once, he thought, just once I'd like to get to ten before Andy started his whining. He shrugged off his jacket and hung it on the hook by the door. Taking a deep breath, he held back until he was sure he could speak without letting his anger come through.

"Yeah, it's me." He just stopped short of asking who the hell else it would be. "I'll be through in a minute. I'm just putting my bag and stuff away."

He slung his work bag in the hall cupboard and walked through to the lounge. Andy was sprawled out on the couch, beer cans scattered around the section of floor in front of him. His thumb on the remote control was flicking through the channels so fast, it was impossible to work out what the programmes might be. Jon sighed and moved forward to pick up the cans.

"You're in my way. I can't see the television."

Jon clenched his lips. He wasn't going to rise to it again. Andy was bored and wanted an argument. That's all there was to it. He straightened up, arms full of empties.

"You want a cup of tea before we eat?"

"I'd rather have another beer."

Jon looked at the cans in his arms and then down at his brother. "Don't you think you've had enough for today?"

"What else have I got to do?" Andy snarled. "I'm stuck here in this dump while you're out all day. If I don't drink I've got fuck all else in my life."

Jon walked through to the kitchen without answering. He dumped the cans in the bin and flicked the switch on the kettle before going back to Andy.

"You could go out if you wanted to, but you choose to stay inside."

Andy glared at his wheelchair. "Yeah, outside in that thing. You've no idea what it's like for me. You don't care."

"Oh, please, Andy, not this again. How many times do I have to hear it?"

"Yes, this again. You fucked up my life, Jon, so why shouldn't you have to listen to me?"

"Because it was years ago, Andy. Years and years ago. And it wasn't even my fault. Fuck it; you know that as well as I do."

"*It wasn't my fault*," Andy whined. "That's all I ever get from you. *It wasn't my fault*. But what about me, hey? I'm the one stuck in a wheelchair. I'm the one who has no bloody life. What have you ever done to try to make it up to me?"

"You mean apart from spending every penny of *my* compensation money buying this flat and getting it fitted out so that you can move about in it? And making sure you've got every mod con you need? You mean apart from that?" Jon yelled.

"Yes," Andy yelled back. "I mean apart from that. That's just money. What have *you* done for *me* to make up for putting me in this fucking state?"

"Oh, it's just money, is it? Really? I notice you don't feel the same way when I point out the repairs that need doing around here. *Your* compensation money is sitting in the bank earning interest. You aren't so keen to dip into it when the plumbing gets fucked up, or the heating needs servicing. No, then it's down to me to work in a job I hate to make sure the bills get paid and you can afford to drink yourself senseless."

Andy laughed. "It really bugs you, doesn't it? Well my money is staying in the bank. I'm going to need it when you're dead and I'll have to get someone in to care for me."

Jon felt his fists bunch. He wanted to punch Andy's face until it disappeared into a mass of bloodied flesh.

"Every night we go through this," he said, trying to calm down. "Just once, Andy, I'd like to come home and not get into a screaming match with you. I've had the shittiest fucking day at the hospital. That bastard Montague was on my case, just because I took a few hours off on Friday, I don't need your crap on top of it."

"What do you mean, you took a few hours off? Where did you go? Out on a jolly? How come you didn't take me with you?"

Too late, Jon realised what he'd said.

"Nowhere. I didn't go anywhere. I just wanted some time to myself, that's all."

Andy heaved himself into a sitting position. "Well, fuck you, Jon. Fuck you to hell. Try thinking what it might be like having *too much* time to yourself. You leave here first thing in the morning, get home as late as you can in the evening. I know what it's like to have time to myself. I never have any other fucking kind!"

Jon could feel the heat rising. If he stayed here he'd end up doing Andy a serious injury. At least he had a plan in place to change the way he felt. He'd taken the first step on Friday, but he needed to keep that to himself.

"Enough, Andy. Let's call a truce for tonight. I'm going to the White Horse," he said. "You want to come with me?"

Andy's face changed so rapidly it was as if a switch had been flicked. He grinned at Jon, almost as if he was content now that he'd pushed all the right buttons and got the reaction he wanted. "What's in it for me?"

"I'll treat you to a steak as long as you promise not to moan for the rest of the night."

Andy held out a hand. "Deal. Help me up."

Jon helped Andy into his chair. Not that he needed to. Andy could shift himself in and out when he wanted, but Jon knew Andy liked to take every opportunity to remind him not only that he'd been driving when the accident happened, but that he'd only been in the car because Jon had insisted. Andy had planned to stay home and study that night, but Jon had convinced him to go out. Jon got his way and Andy ended up paralysed from the waist down as a consequence. No wonder he was determined not to let him forget, but Jon would willingly exchange a year of his life to live through a single day without having it thrown at him.

Jon manoeuvred the wheelchair down the ramp outside the front door of the Victorian terrace and turned towards the pub, just as Gordon came down the steps from the flat above theirs. Shit, Jon thought, this evening is turning into a nightmare.

"Hi, Gordon," Andy called out. "We're off to the pub. Wanna come? Jon's paying."

"Shut up, you moron," Jon hissed. "Take no notice of him, Gordon. He's just playing silly arseholes. He knows I'm skint."

Jon couldn't put his finger on what it was about Gordon that bugged him, but whenever the man got within a couple of feet Jon always felt like rushing back indoors and having a good scrub. It wasn't that the man smelled, or even looked unclean, but there was something grubby about him. Something that made Jon want to keep him at a distance.

"It's okay, Jon. I'm off to fetch a DVD from my mate. It's a good 'un, he says. Hot. You and Andy can borrow it after me, if you want. I'll try not to get any stains on it," he said with the laugh that made Jon want to throw up.

Jon returned a non-committal answer and pushed the wheelchair away before Andy could say anything. The idea of coming home one night and finding Andy and Gordon watching porn wasn't something he wanted to think about.

"Oi, you," Andy said. "I might have wanted to see the DVD. I'm not a fucking baby being pushed about in a pram."

Jon said nothing, just kept walking as fast as he could. The more distance he could put between him and Gordon the better.

They reached the pub a few minutes later.

"It's a nice evening. Inside or outside in the garden?"

"Garden," Andy said.

Jon pushed the chair through the side gate and saw with relief that a couple of people they knew were there. At least they'd have someone else to talk to. Maybe they could get through the evening without another fight. He edged the chair through the tables and stopped at one next to where the two men were.

"Right, a pint and steak and chips, yes?"

"Yeah, but tell Bradley the chef overcooked my steak last time."

Jon nodded and headed into the pub. The restaurant side wasn't very busy. Lots of empty tables, but the bar was packed. He edged his way through and managed to attract the barman's attention.

"Brad, I'll have the scampi and chips. Andy wants a steak, cooked medium, he said it was too well done last time. And two pints of lager."

He handed over his credit card and waited for Brad to run it through the machine. He looked along the packed bar.

"Have you got someone to bring the food out? You look a bit run off your feet."

"Yeah, one of the kitchen staff is doubling up as a waiter," Bradley said, handing back the card. "Hang on, I'll pour the drinks."

Jon struggled back through the crowd with the two pints and settled himself next to Andy in the garden.

"That barman is bloody good," he said. "He's only been here five minutes and he's already got the place under better control than the last idiot the landlord had in charge."

Andy reached out and took a long pull on his pint. Jon watched him out of the corner of his eye. At least his brother seemed happier now. Thank God it was a nice night, not like Saturday where it had poured until the early hours. Jon relaxed.

Andy put his pint back on the table.

"So, you going to tell me where you went on Friday or not?"

CHAPTER FIVE

On Wednesday morning Barbara Royston murmured into the Dictaphone as Paolo and Dave stood by, watching as she went about the business of cutting up the professor. Paolo thought she was paler than usual, making the birthmark on her neck stand out, livid and raw looking. Her face was drawn, as if she hadn't been sleeping very well. They hadn't discussed it, but he was fairly sure there was someone serious in her life. Maybe the path of true love wasn't running too smoothly. And what's that got to do with you? he asked himself. *Nothing, so keep your nose out.*

Barbara stood back from the body and ripped off her gloves.

"Let's go through to my office," she said. "There's something odd about this."

Paolo and Dave waited while Barbara washed her hands and then followed her out of the autopsy room and along the corridor to her office. Taking one of the chairs opposite her, Paolo held off on his questions until Barbara and Dave were also sitting down. When Barbara thought something was odd, it was always worth listening to what she had to say.

While he waited, he had a surreptitious look around. The fancy coffee maker from her friend, as she'd put it with the emphasis on *friend*, was still in place. But then, it wasn't like a ring, was it? Do you give back coffee making machines if a love affair breaks down?

"Paolo!"

Startled, he turned back to find Barbara glaring at him.

"I've spoken to you three times, but you seem to be more interested in the coffee machine than this case. What is it? Withdrawal? Not getting enough caffeine?"

"Sorry, Barbara, I was miles away. Admiring your machine and wishing I had one in my office. Now, what is it you wanted to tell us?"

The scathing look she gave him clearly showed that she hadn't believed a word he'd said.

"From my examination and the evidence the body presented at the scene, I would stake my reputation that he died as a result of insulin overdose. He wasn't diabetic, so the overdose was probably administered by his mystery visitor. What I don't understand is why the killer drew attention to the fact by leaving the note."

Paolo sat forward. "But wouldn't it have been obvious even without that?"

"No," said Barbara, "and that's what makes it so odd. Insulin overdose is the easiest way of killing someone with a better than average chance of it going undetected."

Dave stopped writing. "I don't follow," he said.

"Because it's a naturally occurring substance it is difficult to spot, unless the forensic pathologist is specifically looking for it in overdose, as I was today. Your killer knocked the professor out with an anaesthetic, so he could have injected him somewhere hidden, such as between the toes. It's highly likely he could have tidied up the room and made it look like a natural death, but he didn't go that route. He made sure you knew it was murder by leaving the chaos behind, not to mention the note. What I don't understand is: why? Why use something that is often overlooked in autopsy and then draw attention to it?"

"Because he is sending out a message," Paolo said. "That's the only thing that makes sense. What the message is and whether it is intended for us, or to the other five he has on his list, we'll only know in due course. The most important thing right now is to work out who the other five might be." He stopped and thought for a moment. "So does the fact that he used something to knock him out and insulin point to a doctor, or at least someone in the medical profession? That would narrow it down a bit."

Barbara shook her head. "Sorry to disappoint you, but

no. Insulin is freely available on the internet. It shouldn't be, in my opinion, but it is. Chloroform, on the other hand, isn't so easy to get hold of. It used to be, but it is fairly tightly controlled now. I've run a tox screen and I'm fairly sure it will come back with something easily accessible to the general public via one of those online medical supply sites. Good luck with trying to find out which site sold the insulin. There are hundreds of them and they are situated all around the globe. It's something that really worries the medical profession here, but we are powerless to do anything about the situation."

"Bloody internet causes more problems than it solves," Paolo said. "When someone is targeted through twitter or Facebook, the public gets up in arms, screaming something should be done, but as soon as a solution is suggested and they realise it will impact on their own use of social media, it suddenly becomes fascist to suggest putting curbs on what can and cannot be done online."

Paolo stopped and glanced across at Barbara. She was grinning at him.

"Want a soapbox?" she asked.

He heard Dave give a snort of laughter, then cover it up by turning it into a coughing fit.

"Sorry," Paolo said. "Katy says the same thing to me when I get into one of my rants. Anyway, that's not what we're here to discuss. When do you expect to get the tox screen back?"

"Not for a couple of days yet. I've put it down as urgent, but that's not saying it will get done any quicker. The lab is overworked and understaffed. Too many cuts—" She broke off, laughing. "Now you've got me started on my pet peeve."

Paolo turned to Dave. "Your turn. You want to have a quick rant about anything?"

"No, thank you, sir. Happy and contented soul, that's me."

"Right, in that case, go on back to the station and bring CC and the others up to date. I want to have a word with

Barbara about Katy."

Dave stood up and said his goodbyes. As the door closed behind him, Barbara turned to Paolo with a questioning look.

"What's wrong with Katy? How can I help?"

Paolo smiled. "Nothing's wrong. I wanted an excuse to stay behind and talk to you without Dave knowing what it was about. I knew he'd accept it if I said it was to do with Katy."

"Sounds ominous, but I'm glad Katy is okay. So, what do you want to talk about? If it's marital advice, you've come to the wrong person." She softened the words with a smile. "How are things at home?"

Paolo shifted uncomfortably in his chair. "I'm not living with Lydia. We decided it wasn't working out and I moved into a place of my own on Saturday. But that's not why I wanted to talk to you, either."

"Okay, not Katy, not your marriage, what then?"

"It's you, Barbara. I'm worried about you." She opened her mouth to speak, but Paolo put up a hand to stop her. "Hear me out, please. We haven't been involved on a case together for a couple of months and I was surprised at how much weight you've lost since I last saw you. You look sad and drawn and I'm concerned."

Barbara stood up. "Well thank you for telling me I look a mess."

"I didn't say that," Paolo spluttered.

"Not in those words, but yes, you did say it. I may not look my best at the moment, but the reason why is none of your business."

"I thought we were friends."

Barbara laughed, it wasn't a pleasant sound. "Did you? Did you really? Paolo, friends keep in touch outside of work hours, or didn't you know that? As you say, we haven't seen each other since the last case we worked on together. That doesn't sound like friendship to me. I like you, Paolo. I used to like you in a different way, but that passed. Now I just like you and would love to be friends with you, but at the moment that's not what we are."

Paolo felt like he'd been drenched in a bucket of water. "Then what are we?"

"We are friendly working colleagues. Friends have the right to ask personal questions. Friendly working colleagues don't. Was there anything else you wanted to ask about the case?"

Feeling like a four-year-old caught stealing another child's chocolate, Paolo shook his head and stood up.

"Sorry, Barbara, you're right. I overstepped the line. But I don't look on you as a friendly working colleague. I honestly think of you as a friend. If you change your mind and need someone to talk to, call me. I'll come over like a shot."

He leaned down and lightly kissed her cheek, then turned and walked to the door. When he looked back, she hadn't moved and seemed to be staring into some distant space. He went out, gently closing the door behind him. As the lock clicked, he heard the sound of sobbing. He opened the door again.

"Barbara, I..."

"Go away," she hissed. "I need to be on my own."

CHAPTER SIX

Jon hated Thursdays. Nothing good ever happened on a Thursday. The day always seemed to drag, with Friday and the weekend to follow just out of reach. He pulled up his jeans and slipped on a tee shirt. At least the weather was still good. Better than usual for July. Maybe he could convince Andy to get out a bit more. If he had something to occupy his mind he might not be so ready to moan all the time.

"Jon! Jon! Come here. Quickly, you'll miss it."

Now what, Jon thought, walking through to the lounge where Andy was already stretched out in front of the television.

"Quickly, for fuck's sake. It'll be gone by the time you get here."

"What will?" Jon asked, but fell silent as the screen filled with Professor Edwards's face, then panned back to the newsreader.

"A police spokesperson says the professor was murdered last Friday afternoon. No reason has been given for why the announcement of the professor's death has been held back until today. However, the police are now appealing for anyone with information to call the number at the bottom of the screen. Professor Edwards, a respected member of the psychiatric profession, was last seen alive by his housekeeper…"

The television presenter's voice fell silent. Jon realised Andy had switched the set to mute.

"Turn the sound back on. I want to hear this," Jon said.

Andy grinned at him. "No way. Did you do it? Is that where you went on Friday? Is that why you won't tell me what you were up to?"

"What? Me? Don't be bloody daft. Why would I do something so stupid?"

"Because he fucked up our lives, that's why," Andy snarled. "If I could walk, I'd have gone round there and killed the prick long ago."

"It wasn't him that gave me the wrong drug. It was the doctor taking over while Professor Edwards was away."

Andy snorted. "You've always believed that, but that woman at your trial, she didn't sound so sure, did she?"

"What woman? What are you on about, Andy?"

"The woman who worked with Professor Edwards and the bloke who gave you the wrong drugs. If it wasn't for her, I wouldn't mind betting you'd have been put away. I mean, you killed that woman and look at me, stuck in this chair—"

"Oh for God's sake, Andy, not again. Please, can't we get through one day without you going on and on and on about the accident?"

Andy held up his hands in mock surrender. "Okay, fair enough. I'm just saying, like, you should be glad the bastard's dead. I am. Whoever did him in deserves a fucking medal as far as I'm concerned."

"Yeah, right, maybe so, but I didn't do it. I'm off to work."

"What about my breakfast?" Andy said. "You haven't left anything out for me."

Jon forced himself to stay calm. "All the cupboards in the kitchen are at wheelchair height. There's nothing to stop you from getting your own breakfast ready for a change. In fact, why don't you get dressed, get in your chair and go out for breakfast? It would do you good to start getting out and about a bit more."

"Really? You think it would do me good to drag my useless body outside? It's fine for you; you can walk, can't you! You don't know what it feels like, stuck in a chair—"

Jon banged his hand on the wall. "Enough! Andy, you're like a stuck bloody record! I...what's the use? Fuck you!

I'm out of here."

Jon stormed out without looking back. He knew exactly what expression he'd see on Andy's face if he did – it was the one that would trigger his guilt complex all over again. He patted his pockets as he reached the front door to make sure he had his medication for the day ahead. No way was he coming back at lunchtime today. Andy could stew in his resentment, or get over it. Enough was enough. Jon swore as he slammed the door behind him that he wasn't going to wear sackcloth and ashes any longer. Ten years he'd carried the guilt. Well, not any more. He'd show Andy and everyone else who thought he should still be paying for the fallout from that accident that he was ready to move on and they needed to move with him, or be put to one side.

He reached the bus stop just as his bus pulled in and jumped on, barely acknowledging the driver as he flashed the man his pass. His mind was boiling over with fury. He'd show them. He'd show them all.

By the time he reached the hospital, he'd managed to calm down a bit, but his rage exploded again when he went into the changing room and found his locker door open.

"Who the fuck's been in my locker?" he yelled at the other porters.

No one answered, but a couple of the men briefly glanced in Iain's direction. Jon hesitated. Iain had been picking on him for a few months and the only time he'd squared up to him had ended in a reprimand for Jon. Their boss, bloody Michael Montague, thought the sun shone out of Iain's arse.

"Iain, any idea who opened my locker?"

"How should I know?" Iain answered, stepping forward and towering over Jon. "You're not accusing me, I hope. I see your padlock is open. Maybe you forgot to lock it when you left yesterday."

From the smile on Iain's face, Jon knew the bastard had somehow worked out the combination. He vowed to buy a new padlock at lunchtime, but there wasn't much he could do right now other than accuse Iain outright. None of the others would get involved. Iain held too much power with Montague and none of them could afford to lose their jobs. Not that he picked on anyone else. He saved his spite for Jon.

"What have you got in there to get all protective over?" Iain asked. "You're only supposed to use it for work stuff. Got any good porn tucked away at the back?"

"No, I bloody haven't. There's sod all in there to interest you."

Iain laughed. "I didn't say I was interested. Keep your grubby mags private; we don't want them flashed around in here, do we boys?"

No one answered. Jon could see a few of them were squirming with embarrassment, but most of them looked more amused than anything else.

"I don't have any porn mags in my locker," Jon said. "I don't need to look at them."

"Why not?" Iain asked. "Fancy little boys, do you? No taste for tits?"

Jon snatched his porter's jacket from the locker and walked out without answering. Whatever he said, Iain would twist it into something disgusting.

Jon got off the bus at the stop outside the White Horse and hesitated. He should go straight home, but that would mean walking into a barrage of moans from Andy and the day had been crap enough as it was. Iain had seen him replace the padlock after lunch and made a big thing out of Jon not trusting his workmates. A few of the blokes in the locker room, the ones who hadn't been there to see the morning spat, started giving Jon evil looks. He'd tried to explain, but no matter what he said, Iain put a different spin on it. Jon had long since given up trying to find out what it was that set Iain off. All he could do was stay out of the bastard's way as much as possible.

He looked at the sign gently swinging in the warm evening breeze and made up his mind. One quick pint before going home. Pushing open the door, he peered inside. The place was almost empty. There were a couple of old men nursing half pints in the table nearest the door to the garden. A workman with less expression than a zombie was feeding pound coins into the machine on the opposite side of the room. Apart from the low murmur from the television above the bar, occasional jingling noises from the machine and the thwack of the man's hands slapping at the controls, it was quiet. It couldn't be better. He'd be able to relax and calm down a bit.

Making his way between tables to get to the bar area where Bradley was wiping down the surface, Jon looked up as the television news came on. Professor Edwards's death seemed to be the main feature on the local news. He wondered it if would make the national programme. Was he a big enough name? Maybe he was, but only if nothing major came up to occupy air time. Jon smiled. He hadn't wanted to get into it with Andy, but the professor getting murdered was justice, pure and simple.

Brad smiled as Jon settled himself on one of the stools. "Usual?"

Jon nodded and pulled out the right money to give Brad when he'd finished pouring the pint of lager. The barman took the coins and dropped them in the till. As Brad closed the drawer, he looked over at Jon.

"Bad day?"

Jon laughed. "Yeah, you could say that."

"So offload. I've been told that bar staff and hairdressers were put on this earth for that very reason. We get special training for it you know. Learn how to pull a pint with one part of the brain and listen to the woes of the world with the rest of it."

"I don't suppose you do a side-line in murder, do you?"

Brad looked horrified. "What, like poisoned pints? Razor blades in the pork pie? We'd be out of business in no time. To say nothing of the extra work cleaning up the dead bodies. That's better," he said, as Jon laughed. "Come on, then, what's got you so down tonight?"

"Where to start?" Jon said.

"Is it to do with your secret mission on Friday?"

"No, that worked out all right, but you mustn't say anything to Andy when he comes in next."

Brad laughed. "Did I not just say secret mission? So it went okay, then?"

"Sort of. When I got there someone had cocked up the interview time and I ended up hanging around for four hours before they could fit me in, but other than that, I think it went well."

"When will you find out?" Brad asked.

Jon shrugged. "They didn't say. Just that they would be in touch."

"So, if it's not that, what's rattled your cage?"

"It's just some arsehole at work making my life a misery and then Andy at home doing the same. Sometimes I feel as if my head is going to explode with all the shit that goes on inside."

He looked up to see Brad looking shocked.

"What?" Jon asked. "Why are you looking at me like that?"

"Nothing. I mean, no reason. It's just that you looked as if you'd like to kill both of them."

Jon smiled. "Believe me, Brad, if I thought I could get away with it, I'd wipe both of them out without even thinking about it."

"What about guilt? Wouldn't that eat you up afterwards?"

Jon swallowed the last of his pint and stood up. "Guilt? Fuck that. I've put up with Andy ramming guilt down my throat for years. No more guilt for me," he said. "Whatever I do from now on, I couldn't give a shit what effect it has on anyone else."

CHAPTER SEVEN

Paolo sat at his desk and glared at the papers on it, trying to make sense of the few facts they had in the Professor Edwards case. That old saw about the first forty-eight hours being crucial was actually true. The more time that passed between the crime and following up on leads, the less likelihood there was of solving the case. The professor had died last Friday and it was now Thursday. They were well outside the magic forty-eight hours and were still no nearer to a possible suspect. The most promising, Conrad Stormont, appeared to have disappeared without a trace seven years back. CC had managed to track down a photo of the man from that time. Paolo had also downloaded an image of the real Seth Buchanan of the *New York Times*. Looking at the two men side by side, it was possible to see a slight likeness between them. He tried to picture Conrad a few years older than he was in the photograph and with a light brown wig. Did that make them look more alike? Maybe a little, but not enough. There was only one way to find out for certain and that was to show both images to Mary Prentice. She might see a connection that was eluding him.

He stood up and went through to the main office.

"CC, I want you to find out all you can about the Medical Council decision that led to Conrad Stormont losing his licence."

She looked up and nodded. Paolo had stopped himself from commenting when she came in this morning, but couldn't help himself this time.

"I've got to know, CC. When you went to the hairdresser, what colour did you ask for?"

She grinned at him. "Incandescent Cerise, sir. Do you like it?"

"I don't think it would suit me, but it…it's…it's…"

"Striking?" she asked.

Paolo laughed. "Yes, that's exactly the word I was searching for. Any news on the fingerprints lifted from the crime scene?"

"Forensics picked up plenty of clear prints, but no matches on the database, unfortunately. Looks like our man hasn't been in trouble in the past."

"Hmm, we can also rule out all those professions where fingerprinting is compulsory. I suppose even negative information is better than none at all."

He looked around the office. "Where's Dave? I want him to come with me to re-interview the housekeeper."

CC beckoned Paolo towards her desk and lowered her voice to a whisper. "He's in the corridor with Rebecca. She came in a few minutes ago and asked him to go outside with her."

"Really? That's interesting."

Paolo settled down on the edge of CC's desk. If there was a chance Dave and Rebecca could get together again, the interview with Mary Prentice could wait for ten minutes or so.

In the end, it didn't take that long. Just moments later, Dave came in looking as if Christmas had arrived early.

"Will you just look at the soppy expression on his face?" CC whispered, grinning at Paolo. "There'll be doing nothing with him until he comes down off that cloud."

Paolo laughed and whispered back. "It's good to see him looking happy again."

"I'd say dazed was more the word, sir. Dazed, but in a good way."

Dave wandered over to his desk, but Paolo called out to stop him from sitting down.

"Don't bother getting settled, Dave. We need to go and re-interview Mary Prentice." He turned back to CC. "I could put a string on his ankle and he'd float to the car like a helium balloon."

Paolo heard CC's soft laughter as he and Dave headed for the door. He had no intention of prying into whatever Rebecca had come to say. If Dave wanted to share, he would. Not that Paolo needed to be told the reason for her visit. It was obvious from the look on Dave's face.

They walked down the stairs and out to the car park.

"You drive," Paolo said. "We're going to Mary Prentice's home address. Parking's difficult in that part of town. We might need your luck with finding a space."

"Right you are, sir," Dave said, patting his pockets for the keys, finding them in the last place he tried.

"Why do you always do that?"

"What?" Dave asked, opening the car door.

"You put your keys in your right-hand pocket, but pat every other one before you try the place where they are going to be."

Dave grinned. "Habit. I never used to be able to find my keys, so I started putting them in the same place each time, but when my mind is on other things, I forget and go through the whole searching for them routine."

Paolo pulled open the passenger door. "Well, do me a favour; make sure your mind isn't on other things while you're driving. I happen to have a date tomorrow night and I don't want to miss it because you've driven me into a brick wall."

Dave got in and started the engine. "Really? A date? Who'd have thought it!"

Paolo grinned at him. "That's enough of that from you."

After negotiating his way into the traffic, Dave glanced across. "Seriously, sir, I'm pleased for you. Everyone should have someone in their lives."

Paolo felt a butterfly of anxiety flutter, but he suppressed it. Things would either work out with Jessica, or they wouldn't. He wasn't going to try to force the issue.

After twenty minutes they arrived at Constellation Road. A row of identical terrace houses, all with cars parked outside, stared back at them. The only sign of personality the houses expressed was in the different colours of the front doors. It seemed to Paolo that every shade of the rainbow, and all those in between, had been used by the residents. Funny, he thought, how we strive to be different, while also trying to fit in.

"Looks like even your luck isn't going to get us a parking place," Paolo said.

"Oh, I don't know, sir. Look!"

Paolo glanced over to where Dave was pointing. The reversing lights shone from a car parked on the other side of the road. As they watched, the car was manoeuvred out of the space and driven away. Dave drove across the road and reversed in.

"I don't know why I'm surprised," Paolo said, shaking his head. "You do it every time."

Mary Prentice must have been looking out for them because her door opened before Paolo had time to use the gleaming ornamental brass knocker.

"Come in," Mary said. "I've just put the kettle on for tea."

She pointed to a door on the right-hand side of the small entrance hall.

"Go into the lounge and make yourselves comfy. I won't be a minute," she said, disappearing along the hall to the back of the house before Paolo could refuse the offer of refreshments.

As Paolo had expected, the lounge was tiny, but what came as a surprise was the choice of artwork on the walls. Images of a much younger Mary Prentice filled every available space. In most of them, clothing appeared to be an optional extra.

He and Dave settled into armchairs facing each other and Paolo was amused to see Dave's attempt to look anywhere but at the walls. Paolo couldn't decide whether Dave was relieved or mortified when Mary Prentice eventually came into the room, carrying a tray laden with cups and what looked like a homemade angel cake.

She smiled and nodded at the wall containing a massive

blow-up of a naked woman reclining on a bed of crimson silk. "That's me in my former glory days. You won't believe it now, but I was much in demand as a model back then."

"I'm sure you were," Paolo said.

He glanced across at Dave who had turned a stunning shade of puce. *If he went and stood next to the photograph, his face would disappear into the background silk,* Paolo thought. He'd never have put Dave down as a prude.

Mary cut slices of cake. "Help yourselves," she said as she sat down on the sofa between the two armchairs. "It's a bit cosy in here, but it suits me fine now that I'm on my own."

"It's very nice," Paolo said, reaching for a plate. "As I explained on the phone, we have some images we'd like to show you. We have reason to believe the man you saw was impersonating the journalist, but we'd like you to tell us if he resembled the real man in any way."

He put down his plate on a small side table and took the images Dave held out to him.

"This is the real Seth Buchanan," he said, passing the photograph to Mary.

She studied it for a few minutes before giving it back. "He did look a bit like him, but it wasn't him, if you know what I mean."

Paolo nodded. "Yes, I understand. Can you tell us what was similar and what was different?"

"He had the same sort of hair and glasses, but the face wasn't the same at all."

Paolo took out the earlier image of Conrad Stormont.

"This was taken about ten years ago. Would you say this could be a younger version of the same man?"

Mary reached out for the image and concentrated on it. Eventually, she sighed and handed it back.

"I'm sorry, I really don't know. I suppose it could be, although I wouldn't want to swear to it. But I've remembered something about the man who pretended to be the journalist. Or, at least, I think I have. I'm not sure."

Paolo waited while Mary collected her thoughts.

"I think he might have been following me, but not when he looked like he did when he came to see the professor." She shrugged. "Sorry, I'm not putting this very well."

"You're doing fine," Paolo said. "Just relax."

She smiled and Paolo caught a glimpse of the younger Mary who adorned the walls.

"It's like this," she said. "When I opened the door to him, he looked familiar but I didn't think much about it. Back in the day, when I was modelling, I met so many people that faces tended to blur after a while. But now that I've had time to think about it, I'm pretty sure I'd seen him before. I've tried and tried to think where I might know him from, but there just isn't anywhere. I don't know him at all, but still his face seemed familiar in some way. The only explanation I can come up with is that he'd been watching me and I'd spotted him without it registering. Does that sound insane?"

"No, not at all," Paolo said. "I think you could be right. He might have been keeping the professor's apartment under observation for a while to see what time you came in and left. Checking for regular movements."

"The really annoying thing is that whenever I try to picture someone hanging around, there's no one specific I can bring to mind."

"Don't worry. Something might come to you later. If it does, call me," Paolo said. "The information you gave to our photo-fit man was very helpful. It seems the killer went to great lengths to impersonate Seth Buchanan."

Mary opened her mouth, as if to speak, and then closed it again.

"You wanted to say something?" Paolo asked.

"Not really, but yes, I suppose so. I feel guilty because I can't bring myself to be sorry the professor's gone. Is that bad of me? I know it is, but he was just such a horrible man to work for."

Paolo stood up, signalling for Dave to do the same. "From what we've discovered so far, you're not alone in thinking like that. I wouldn't lose any sleep over it, Mary.

He certainly didn't inspire affection in those who came into close contact with him."

A look of relief flashed across her face. "Thank you."

"For us, though, it doesn't matter what type of person he was, someone has to be held to account for killing him. If you think of anything that might help, no matter how insignificant it seems, call me."

Back in the car, Paolo turned to Dave and grinned.

"Did I see you getting hot under the collar in there?"

"Blimey, sir, everywhere I looked, there she was, naked as the day, or near enough."

Paolo laughed. "Whatever happened to my detective sergeant who used to love 'em and leave 'em? Surely you must have seen a few naked bodies back then?"

As soon as he saw the stricken look on Dave's face, Paolo wished he'd kept his mouth shut.

"There never was any of that, sir. It was just me talking big. I thought you knew that."

"I did, Dave. Sorry, I was teasing you. That was out of order, but…"

"It's okay, sir."

Dave hesitated and fiddled with the car key for a few seconds, then inserted it into the lock, but he didn't start the engine.

"I don't know if you noticed," Dave said, "but Rebecca came in to see me today."

"I knew, but didn't like to comment. I know how you feel about her."

Dave grinned. "We're sort of back together again. I took your advice and let her in on my issues."

Paolo waited. If Dave wanted to tell him more, fine, but he wasn't going to pry. The silence lengthened and then Dave shrugged.

"I couldn't tell her face to face and it's not the sort of thing to talk about over the phone, so I sent her an email. It took me the best part of a week to get it right, but I told her all about what happened when I was a kid and how it made me feel. I also told her about being in therapy and all that."

He turned to Paolo.

"I thought she'd run a mile, but she didn't. She says she's there for me if I need her. I can't believe it."

Paolo smiled. "Dave, you deserve someone special in your life. We all do," he said, thinking of his Friday night date with Jessica. Tomorrow night, in fact. It took all his willpower to prevent himself from doing a high five in the air like a kid.

"Right, before we get any deeper into our imitation of characters from a 'new men' novel, let's get back to work."

CHAPTER EIGHT

Week Two – Friday 1st August to Thursday 7th August

Paolo ripped off his shirt and tie and added them to the pile of clothes littering his bed. What to wear? He now had more clothes out of cupboards than he'd left hanging up. What did people wear these days on dates? He hadn't been on one since he was seventeen and had fallen in love with Lydia. Had things changed that much in the intervening twenty-three years? Did it matter what he wore?

He sighed and sat on the edge of the bed. With an hour to go before he needed to leave there was no need yet to panic, but there would be if he carried on like this. He felt like a fool. Forty years old and incapable of dressing himself to go out.

The littered clothes testified to half an hour already spent in indecision since he'd arrived home. It was just as well he'd left the station early. He stood up and chose a maroon sweatshirt at random. Would this be okay? What with? Jeans? Too casual? Probably. The shirt and tie he'd just taken off were too formal. He couldn't go out as if he'd dressed for work.

As he sank back down onto the edge of the bed, admitting defeat, his phone rang. He hesitated before reaching for the receiver. It might be Jessica cancelling their date. She probably had to wash her hair, or paint the walls in her flat, or get up early to run a marathon tomorrow, or…

Stop being an idiot and answer the phone!

"Storey," he mumbled, sounding as if his mouth had been stuffed with cotton wool.

"Hi, Dad. How's it going? What time are you off out?"

"If I can't work out what to wear, I won't be going anywhere."

Katy laughed. "Now that's not something I ever expected to hear from you."

"I know," Paolo said, "I sound like a teenager on a first date. I feel like one, too! Come on, Katy, help your old dad. What should I wear?"

"That depends. What did you have in mind for this evening?"

Paolo felt a hot flush rising up from his feet and travelling through his body. Surely Katy wasn't asking...

"Dinner," he said. "I thought we'd go out for dinner somewhere."

"Borrrr-ring!" Katy said. "I'd expected better from you, Dad. Does Jessica know about this exciting plan of yours?"

"I don't know," he said. "I didn't mention dinner or anything else. I just said I'd pick her up at eight."

"Which restaurant?"

"I thought we'd stroll around until we find a place we both like the look of."

He heard Katy sigh. "So the poor woman doesn't even know where you're going or what you might be doing? You think you've got problems deciding what to wear? That's nothing to what she'll be going through. You should ring her and tell her you're going out to eat and which restaurant. At least that way she'll know the dress code. Honestly, Dad, you've got a lot to learn."

Paolo laughed. "Yes, Katy, I know that. What did you mean by dinner being a boring idea?"

"Why not do something different? You could go bowling, or ice-skating. That would be more fun than sitting down over a plate of food trying to make conversation."

Paolo pictured the scene – long silences punctuated by small talk that meant nothing. Jessica would be so bored she'd never want to repeat the experience. Maybe not ice-skating but bowling wasn't a bad idea. They could always go on for dinner afterwards if the evening went well.

"Katy, you are a star. Did I tell you I love you to bits?"

"Cupboard love, Dad. You only love me because I'm brilliant. Anyway, you need to decide what you're going to do, give Jessica a ring so that she knows what to wear and then get yourself ready."

"Will do. Did you ring for any particular reason, or just to harass me?"

"Not just to harass you, although it's fun and I do get a buzz out of doing it. I wanted to know if it's okay to come over tomorrow. I've had a few thoughts about my future and wanted to run them by you."

"Of course you can come over. If you get here in time for lunch I'll treat you to a plate of food in a boring restaurant and we can make boring conversation. How does that sound?"

"Perfect! See you tomorrow. And, Dad…"

"Yes?"

"Relax and enjoy yourself."

He replaced the receiver and looked up Jessica's number. Feeling more at ease than he had all day, he dialled.

"Hi," he said when Jessica answered. "Have you ever been ten pin bowling?"

"Not for years, but I used to be pretty good. Why are you asking?"

"I just wondered if you'd like to do that tonight."

"You mean instead of going out to eat?" Jessica asked.

Paolo tried to detect how she felt about the idea from her tone of voice, but couldn't pick up any clues. Some detective you are, he thought.

"I was thinking more along the lines of bowling and then going to eat afterwards. But we don't have to do—"

"That sounds like a great idea. You still picking me up at eight?"

"If that's okay with you, yes."

"I'll be ready," she said, ending the call, but this time Paolo heard definite enthusiasm in her voice. He owed Katy a special desert to go with her lunch. In fact, he'd even allow her to choose a restaurant with Mc in its name.

***

The pretender stood in the shadow of the railway arch closest to the river. Honeysuckle growing wild over scrubland scented the air with a sweet cloying perfume. The silence was broken only by the gurgling of water swirling over rocks on the river bed. He'd arrived early to get into place before Mr Fulbright arrived. He wanted to make sure there were no witnesses to their meeting. Not that there were likely to be many people around at two in the morning, but he couldn't take a chance on getting caught just yet. Later, when he'd worked through his list, it wouldn't matter, but for now he needed to stay out of the clutches of the police.

He wondered when they would make the connection – join up all the dots that would lead them to him. He shrugged. It didn't matter. By then he would have the satisfaction he craved and would go willingly to face whatever punishment they meted out.

Gravel skittering from under the wheels of a car alerted him to the surgeon's arrival seconds before car lights signalled the man had driven into the railway siding. The car's engine seemed deafening after the earlier peace and the pretender breathed a sigh of relief when the driver switched it off. From where he stood, he could see there was only one person in the vehicle. He hadn't truly expected anyone to come with Fulbright, but that had always been a possibility.

He wouldn't go to the car yet – let the man sweat a bit. While waiting for the minutes to pass, he went over his plan one more time. This time would be trickier, the timing had to be just right, but the result would be worth it if he could carry it off.

Reaching down to pick up his laptop case, he walked silently over to the parked car and opened the passenger door. As he slid inside, the surgeon's reaction gave him confidence. He'd been expecting someone full of bluster, but the man cowering against the driver's door didn't look as if he'd be able to put up as much of a fight as the pretender had feared.

"God, you gave me a fright. Where did you spring from?"

The pretender ignored the question. "Good morning, Mr Fulbright," he said, setting the laptop case at his feet. "I'm so glad you decided to come after all."

The surgeon looked away. "You didn't leave me much choice. Have you brought the proof?"

"Ah, I see, no pleasantries, just straight down to business."

"Business?" The man had been staring ahead into the dark, but his head whipped round as he said the word. "So this *is* blackmail, after all. I should have known. I'll go to the police, you know. I have no intention of giving you a brass farthing, so you might just as well get out of my car right now."

The pretender laughed. "Relax. I told you on the phone my only role in this is on behalf of my sister, who's trying to save her marriage. She wants your wife to stop her affair with Scott. She's tried to get her husband to end things with your wife and failed. Apparently your wife and Scott are besotted with each other. My sister is scared he intends to leave her and the children." He paused. In the dim light he could just about make out an expression of anguish on the surgeon's face. *Good! Let him suffer.* "My part is to give you the flash drive with the photos of the two of them together. My sister believes you can use the images to better effect than she could. She's convinced your *young* wife won't want to give up the privileged lifestyle you provide."

"My wife's age has nothing to do with this, so you can stop stressing the word young."

"No? Have it your own way, but I wonder what she would answer if asked what first attracted her to the *extremely* wealthy surgeon nearly thirty years her senior."

"We have a great deal in common and we're very happy together. Not that it's any of your damned business. Give me the flash drive. I'll put a stop to the affair. If there even is an affair. My wife hasn't given me any reason to doubt her."

"So why are you here at this ridiculous hour of the morning? If you don't believe she's screwing around with my brother-in-law, why come out to meet me?"

The surgeon fell silent, but the pretender hadn't expected an answer. Mr Fulbright had fallen for his lies, whatever he might say to the contrary. The pretender wished he could let someone in on how clever he'd been. Not only did he not even have a sister, but, as far as he knew, the young woman married to the surgeon was as faithful as her loving husband had protested she was. Planting the seed of doubt had been ridiculously easy. Fulbright was a much older wealthy man married to a beautiful woman; of course he would fear a younger rival.

A strangled sound snapped him out of his reverie. He glanced over and was astounded to see the man was sobbing. Remorse briefly rose and was ruthlessly quashed. *So what if the man was suffering with a broken heart? What about the pain Mr Fulbright had put him through all those years ago?*

He waited. Eventually the surgeon managed to stem the flow of his tears and blew his nose with a sound that vibrated around the inside of the car.

"Here's the proof," the pretender said, holding out the flash drive.

"And the printed images you mentioned? I want to be able to confront my wife with photos, not wave a flash drive around."

"I have them right here."

This was where it got tricky. It would be easier if he was in the driving seat and the surgeon the passenger, or if he was left handed instead of right. But he'd gone over this scenario in his mind time and time again. He could do it.

He reached down and picked up the laptop case, sliding it onto his knees. Unzipping it, he reached inside. He'd positioned the syringe in one of the pockets, so that it was easy to locate, but his shaking hands made it difficult to grasp. *Calm down! You can do this.* Taking care to avoid the needle tip, he eased the syringe from its compartment. *Now! Do it now!*

Before he could lose his nerve completely, he pulled the syringe from the laptop case and stabbed it into the surgeon's leg, depressing the plunger as he did so.

"What the…"

The surgeon grabbed his hand, pulling the syringe out, but the pretender had already injected the full dose. He reached across and snatched the car's keys, dropping them into the laptop case.

"I don't want you to die believing your wife was having an affair," he said. "I made it all up to get you here. As far as I know, she might have married you for love, but console yourself with the thought that she'll make a beautiful widow."

"What…wha…inject…wha…wassit?"

The pretender opened the passenger door. "I'm not going to tell you; you might know a way of neutralising the effect."

He climbed out of the car and walked around to the driver's side and opened the door. Searching through each of the surgeon's pockets, he located the man's mobile phone and removed it. He turned towards the river and threw it in an arc. Smiling with satisfaction as it landed in the water with a resounding splash. He put the laptop case on the ground and opened it, taking out the surgeon's car keys. These followed the mobile phone into the river. There was now no way for the surgeon to reach help before morning came.

He leaned back into the car and picked up the flash drive Fulbright had dropped.

"I'm going to leave you now. I expect you'll be dead by the time it gets light. I hope so; I don't want you to suffer for too long. Not like the pain you put me through. You should thank your stars I have a kinder heart than you."

Mr Fulbright's eyes widened in shock as his body began to spasm.

"Plisss," he whispered. "I...I...wha..."

The pretender reached into his pocket and removed a white envelope, which he placed on the dashboard behind the steering wheel.

"That's for the police," he said.

He looked at the man now slumped unconscious in the driver's seat. Is this really what he wanted? Yes! Now wasn't the time for pity. The bastard hadn't shown him any. By his actions all those years ago, the surgeon was simply reaping what he'd sown. There was no point getting soft and wishing things could be different. He had to remember he wasn't doing this just for himself. He'd made a vow and had no choice but to keep it.

"Goodbye," he said, shutting the door and turning towards the road.

Another one down, four still to go. Maybe the next one would be easier, but somehow he doubted it. He'd thought exacting justice would make him feel good, but it hadn't so far. He shrugged. Too bad. He'd just have to accept the guilt as a price worth paying and see this journey through to the end.

CHAPTER NINE

Paolo opened his eyes and stretched. Peering at the bedside clock, he was astounded to see it was well after nine. This was amazing. He never slept in so late, not even on a Saturday. He got up and padded through to the bathroom, pausing briefly to grin at himself in the mirror. God, he felt good this morning.

Coming out of the bathroom, he stopped: should he go back to bed, or make some coffee? He settled for the wake-up brew. He wouldn't be able to fall asleep again now, and nor did he want to. What he wanted to do, and had every intention of doing, was think about how much fun last night had been.

Jessica had been every bit as bad as him when it came to bowling – each of them achieving only one strike and in both cases more by luck than judgement – but he couldn't remember the last time he'd laughed so much. One particularly memorable throw by him had so much spin on it, the ball came back towards him, instead of travelling towards the pins.

Dinner afterwards had been the perfect end to a magical evening. They'd drifted through the town and ended up at the Italian restaurant where they'd first got to know each other. By unspoken agreement, it seemed the right place to eat. The only blight on the evening had come at the end. When he'd dropped her at home, instead of moving towards her as he'd wanted, he'd found himself shaking her hand and saying thanks for a great evening.

He cringed at the memory as he depressed the plunger on the cafetière. Inhaling the aroma of fresh coffee, he consoled himself with the thought that she'd agreed to see him again.

Flopping down on the sofa, coffee and newspaper at hand, he made himself comfortable. Saturday mornings were to be savoured and he had every intention of...

His thoughts were interrupted by the tune playing on his phone. Damn it, that was Dave's ringtone. Sighing, he picked up the phone.

"Dave, please don't give me bad news. I'm in far too good a mood to hear it."

"Sorry, sir, but it looks as though our insulin killer has struck again. We've had a call from an early morning angler. Dead body in an expensive car down by the railway arches."

Paolo glanced at the cafetière. A burning mouthful while he threw some clothes on would be the only enjoyment he'd get from that.

"I'll see you there in about twenty minutes, Dave, but I may never forgive you for calling me."

As Paolo showed his card to the constable keeping the press and public away from the crime scene, he spotted Barbara standing next to Dave outside the tent erected to make sure prying eyes didn't get to see or photograph anything they needed to keep hidden.

He walked over and joined his detective sergeant and was just in time to hear Barbara ripping up.

"Oh, great, here comes your boss. I have no doubt he will also be asking impossible questions and demanding answers before I've had chance to do my job properly."

She stalked back into the tent, leaving Paolo wondering what on earth Dave had said to cause that sort of response, but he was none the wiser when Dave answered his questions.

"Sir, I swear to you, I have no idea what I did or said wrong. All I asked was did she think there was a connection to the professor's murder last week."

Paolo glanced towards the tent. "Yes, I heard her reply. She wasn't happy with you, that's for sure."

"Believe me, sir, what you heard was nothing. You should have got here five minutes earlier. According to Dr Royston I have less intelligence than a flea and far less value to the community."

Paolo frowned. That wasn't like Barbara. She might get ratty, and frequently did, but she never levelled personal insults at anyone.

"That's out of order," he said. "You want me to take it up with her?"

Dave shook his head. "Nah, she most probably had a relaxing day lined up and this ruined it for her."

"Even so..."

"It's fine, sir. Let it go. I didn't take it to heart."

Paolo nodded. "Okay. Right, what do we know so far?"

Dave flipped open his notebook. "Deceased is Edwin Fulbright, surgeon at Bradchester Central. Married, fairly recently judging by the wedding photo in his wallet."

"Has his wife been notified?"

"Yes, sir. Uniform have already called on her and a family liaison officer is still at the house with the widow."

"Good. What else?"

Dave referred to his notes. "Fingerprints all over the car. We'll run a check against those in Professor Edwards's home, but I'm already fairly certain there will be some matching prints because of this," he said, putting the notebook in his pocket and pulling out a plastic evidence bag. "Another envelope with a card inside. Printed using the same font as the other one. This time it says two down, four to go."

"Before she bit your head off, did Barbara give you an estimated time of death?"

"She felt it would have been the early hours of this morning. Certainly at some point during the night, anyway. It was trying to pin her down on a more exact time that precipitated the outburst you caught the tail end of."

Paolo laughed. "I think I'd better brave the lion's den and see what I can find out. In the meantime, who found the body?"

Dave pointed to a man sitting on a fisherman's folding seat. "He's a Mr Graham Jensen. He says he arrived at about nine, expecting to have the place to himself because most fishermen go further upriver. When he spotted the car, he wondered if someone was going to disturb his spot, so went over to find out where the driver intended to pitch. He saw the body, tried the handle and found the car unlocked. He intended to try some form of resuscitation, as he's a first aider, but as soon as he touched the body he realised the man had been dead a while. So he called us."

"And he didn't see anyone coming or going?" Paolo asked.

"According to the PC who questioned him, Mr Jensen had neither sight nor sound of another person, sir. I was just about to go over and question him myself when you arrived."

"You mean, you were going to do that once Barbara Royston had finished wiping the floor with you," Paolo said. "Friday night murders ruin weekends. Maybe that's why Barbara is so uptight." He took a step towards the tent, stopped and turned back to Dave with a grin. "If I'm not out in ten minutes, send in the medics to pick up the pieces."

He opened the tent flap and looked around. Barbara Royston was kneeling next to the car. Had she lost even more weight since Wednesday? Surely not. It must be the coverall, Paolo decided. He went to stand next to the driver's door and coughed.

"Don't bite my head off," he said when Barbara looked up.

She smiled. "I'll try not to, but if you ask me idiotic questions like your detective sergeant, I can make no promises."

He crouched down next to her. "Okay, how about if I don't ask anything and you just tell me what you've discovered so far?"

"Are you humouring me?"

Paolo laughed. "Which is more likely to get me in trouble, saying yes or saying no?"

"Both," Barbara said, standing up.

As she did so she seemed to lose her balance. Paolo stood quickly, catching her arm as she fell.

"What's wrong, Barbara? Are you not well?"

She shook off his hand. "I'm fine. Just tired, that's all. I had a late night and was hoping for a lie in this morning, but got called out on this instead."

"Are you sure. You don't look well to me. I…"

"For God's sake, Paolo, will you give it a rest! I am fine. Do you want to talk about our victim or not?"

Startled by the venom in her tone, Paolo took a step back. "Of course. Sorry. What can you tell me?"

Paolo watched as Barbara made an effort to control her emotions, wanting to reach out to her, but knowing it would be the worst thing he could do.

"Time of death," she said after a few moments, "I would put at somewhere between midnight and three am. We are looking at the same killer without a doubt. I'm sure Dave has already filled you in on the envelope containing the note. Cause of death is almost certainly insulin overdose, but I need a tox screen to confirm that. At the moment, that's all I have for you."

She turned back to the car and knelt down again. Paolo crouched next to her.

"Barbara, you can push me away as often as you like and as hard as you like, but I'll keep coming back and I'll keep asking what's wrong because I care about you and can't bear to see you like this. If you don't want to tell me what's going on, that's fine, but please, please, for the sake of our friendship, don't try to convince me there's nothing wrong."

He waited until she gave a slight nod and then squeezed her arm.

"You've got my number. Call me. Anytime, day or night. Okay?"

She nodded again and he stood up.

"I nearly forgot. When will you be able to do the autopsy?"

"Tuesday, but not until late. It will probably be last on

63

my schedule. Will you be there?"

Paolo shrugged. "If I can, but it depends on what else is going on with this case. So far we're nowhere near knowing who or why."

Barbara grinned, looking more like her old self. "So what else is new? You'll get there in the end."

Paolo left the tent wishing he had as much faith in his abilities as Barbara, but so far he couldn't even spot a connection between the two victims. He went to find Dave, trying not to feel as if this was a jigsaw puzzle with the edge pieces missing.

"Dave, I'm heading back to the station. I'll call CC and get her to come in as well. Did you get anything more from the witness?"

"Not a thing, sir. I'll see you at the station. I was supposed to be spending today with Rebecca, so I need to call round at her place on the way to explain why I can't."

"Tell her you'll be free this afternoon. I'm not sure how far we can get today anyway."

Paolo stood at the front of the main office, once again wishing George hadn't sold his soul to the press. They really needed someone with his skills at digging into the background and making connections often overlooked by the rest of the team. Still, there was no point in dwelling on that. George was out of the force and lucky not to be locked up. Paolo made a mental note to draft someone in with research skills.

"Right, what have we got so far?" he asked.

"I've looked at it every way from here to Friday and back again," CC said. "I can't see an association, sir. The only similarity is that they are both medical men, but there it stops. The professor was a psychiatrist and Mr Fulbright a surgeon. From what I can discover, they have no professional crossover and no social connections either."

"Maybe our killer doesn't like professional people, or disapproves of the medical profession," Paolo said. "No, it can't be that. There has to be something that links the two men. We just haven't found it yet."

Dave looked up. "What about schools, university courses, lectures, that sort of thing? Maybe they attended the same conference or stayed in the same hotel?"

Paolo sighed. "That's the problem. The link could be something so tenuous we might only see it when he's finished working through his list of six. I wish I knew who else was on the list. It might give us a clue as to where to start looking."

CHAPTER TEN

Paolo was still searching for a possible connection between the victims when Katy arrived at his flat to have lunch.

"Where would you like to go? After your brilliant suggestion yesterday, I'm happy to go wherever you choose."

Katy grinned and flopped down on the couch. "It went well then? Score one for me. Where did you go in the end? Ice-skating or bowling?"

"We went bowling and I officially suck at it, but it was good fun. You didn't answer my question about restaurants."

"Um, what do you think about getting some takeaways delivered? It will make it easier to talk if we stay here."

"Easier to talk? That sounds ominous. Is this going to be deeper than a discussion on your future career?"

"No! Yes. Sort of," Katy said. "I need to ask your advice on something."

Paolo felt uneasy, without being able to put his finger on exactly why. "Am I going to end up being blamed for any decision you might make?" he asked, trying to lighten an atmosphere that suddenly felt heavy. He'd expected Katy to reassure him, but the opposite happened.

"Not blamed exactly, no. But Mum might not be too happy with you. She's going to call you later to 'get you to talk some sense into me' as she put it," Katy said, making finger movements in the air as she repeated Lydia's words.

The uneasy feeling deepened. "You're right. Takeaways and a chat here is better than going out and not being able to say whatever is needed. So, what's it to be? Chinese, Indian, Pizza, burgers or Thai?" he asked, flipping a sheaf of takeaway menus onto the small table next to the couch.

By the time the pizzas arrived they'd already started on the topic of what Katy intended to do with her future.

"So you see, Dad, when I go back to school in September I've already worked out which subjects I need to take to make it easier to get into a good university."

"Are you sure you're not wanting to follow in Jessica's footsteps just because she helped you?"

Katy frowned at him as if he'd said something really stupid, then her frown cleared and she laughed.

"I've just realised. You must have misheard. I want to become a *psychologist*, not a *psychiatrist*, which is what Jessica is. You do know the difference between the two, don't you?"

"I'm not completely stupid, but clearly I'm not as bright as I'd thought. I assumed you wanted to go into psychiatry because that's what you'd experienced as a patient and it helped you recover after you were attacked."

She grinned and picked up a slice of pizza, shaking her head before taking a bite.

"Nope," she said when she'd swallowed the mouthful. "I don't want to go into the caring side of it. That's not where my interest lies."

Paolo felt more confused than ever.

"If you don't want to help people, then why take that path?"

"I want to get a BSc in Psychology and Criminal Behaviour. I'd like to go into criminal profiling. I want to help the police track criminals down."

"Is this what your mum is opposed to?"

Katy shrugged. "She's not thrilled about it, but I expect she thinks I'll change my mind in a year or so. That's the impression I got when I told her what I wanted to do." She stopped and smiled. "No, that's not what I need your help with."

"Go on then, tell me what it is your mum objects to and I'll see if I can help."

"It's my boyfriend."

Paolo's appetite deserted him and he pushed his plate away.

"I didn't know you had one. I only moved out a week ago and you didn't mention you had anyone in your life while I was living at home."

"That's because he's only become my boyfriend this week. We've been chatting online for, like, forever and ever, but now we've met up and…"

Paolo felt the hairs rising on the back of his neck. "You met up with someone you only knew online? Katy, you know better than that!"

"Well of course I do! I should, you and Mum hammered it into me often enough. I didn't meet up with some unknown man. The brother of one of my friends plays in the same Sunday football team, so I knew he was a real person and not some pervert out to kidnap me. I went to watch them play last week and…well, I like him, Dad."

He should have been reassured, but something still wasn't quite right.

"What aren't you telling me? If your mum's not happy there must be more to it."

"She's being unfair. Just because Danny's brother got into trouble once, that doesn't make Danny a bad person. You need to tell her for me, Dad."

"Tell her what?"

"That it's okay for me to go on seeing Danny," she said, throwing her hands up as if the point she was making was obvious.

"But I don't know if it's okay. I've only just found out this boy exists. I don't know the first thing about him. What did his brother get into trouble for?"

Paolo sighed. "Katy, look at me. If you keep staring at your plate I'm going to think you've got something to hide."

She looked up and Paolo caught his breath. Suddenly she looked so much older. No longer a child, but not quite a woman.

"His brother was supposedly dealing drugs, but Danny

says he was innocent. Mark was set up."

"Are you telling me your boyfriend was...his brother was...Katy, no wonder your mum isn't happy."

"Dad! You're not listening to me. You're as bad as Mum. Danny didn't do anything. Mark got caught and is in prison. Danny isn't guilty of anything other than caring about his brother, but because he's in a home people just assume the worst."

"In a home? Why?"

"Are you going to hold that against him as well?"

"As well as what? Katy, stop coming across all defensive. I haven't said anything yet to make you take that attitude."

"Yet! You haven't said anything *yet*."

Paolo felt as if his world had tilted so far out of balance he hadn't a clue which way was up.

"Let's start this again, shall we? You like a boy who is in care. His brother is in prison for drug dealing, but your friend wasn't involved. Did he know what his brother was doing?"

Katy stood up. "I expected more from you, Dad. Mum was always going to be prejudiced because that's the way she is, but you? I thought you'd at least understand he shouldn't be blamed for what his brother did and try to make Mum see things my way."

Paolo also stood and reached out for her. "Katy, his brother was dealing drugs!"

She pulled back and put her hands on her hips. "And so? Granny's brothers were all involved in crime in London. Did that make her a bad person?"

"What the...how...when did you find out about my uncles?"

"Granddad used to talk about her all the time before he died. He told Sarah and me loads of stories about Granny and why you moved to Bradchester after she was killed. So you see, just because Mark has a record, it doesn't mean Danny is bad. Granddad said Granny was..."

Katy's voice faded into the background. Paolo's mind

went back to a memory he'd suppressed and never wanted to revisit. No way was he going to allow Katy to follow that path. He snapped back to the present.

"I'm sorry, Katy. You know I'd back you if I could, but I think your mum is right. This isn't the right boy for you."

She stared at him without speaking, then turned on her heels and headed for the hallway.

"Katy!"

"What?" she said, turning back at the door.

"Don't leave like this. You haven't finished your pizza."

She shrugged. "I'm not hungry."

When she'd gone, Paolo stood in the lounge listening to the sound of silence and feeling a hundred years old.

An hour later, Paolo picked up the phone for the tenth time and then put it down again. He couldn't put it off any longer, though. He had to talk to Lydia.

Her phone rang only once before he heard her voice.

"Paolo! What happened with you and Katy? She came home in a foul mood and went straight upstairs. She's been in her room for the last hour and won't answer when I talk to her through the door. What did you say that upset her so much?"

"I told her I agreed with you about this boy, Danny."

"Oh! That's not what I expected to hear. I thought you'd taken her side and she was mad at me."

"Nope. She's mad at both of us."

The black humour in the situation made Paolo laugh.

"Great isn't it? The only time we agree on something to do with Katy and it turns her against us. What's the score with this Danny kid? I handled the situation so badly Katy walked out before I could even ask what his surname was. If you know any details I can check out the boy and, more importantly, the brother who's inside."

Lydia sighed. "I didn't do much better. She came back last Sunday full of what a great time she'd had and how nice the boy was. I asked a few questions, found out about the brother and freaked out. Since then Katy hasn't so much as mentioned the boy's name."

"Leave it with me. I'll see what I can uncover. It might be okay. Did Katy tell you she threw my uncles' criminal activities in my face?"

"No, she didn't say a word, just stormed upstairs like I said. That must have been hard for you."

"Well, it left me without any real strength in my argument."

Lydia sighed again. "That wasn't what I meant, Paolo."

"I know what you meant, but I don't want to talk about my mother. Not at the moment. Okay?"

They said their goodbyes and Paolo put the receiver down in its cradle. He didn't want to talk about his mother's death now or at any time. He couldn't.

***

The pretender lay back, reliving the emotions he'd gone through that morning as he'd stabbed Fulbright with the needle. He'd expected to feel overjoyed, or at least justified, but his overriding emotion was one of guilt. There were still four more to go if he was going to keep his vow. Could he do it? Four more to kill. He shuddered. This wasn't giving him the sense of satisfaction he wanted. Maybe he should stop. But then he thought about exactly why he was doing this. He remembered everything he'd lost. Everything they had taken from him. Why should they get away with it?

He glanced down at the piece of paper he held. Professor Edwards was crossed through and so was Mr Fulbright. Peter Bishop was next, which would take him halfway. Then would come the upper-class bastard who'd let him down so badly, followed by the one he'd struggled to track down. He remembered the sense of satisfaction he'd had when he'd finally traced him. In fact, tracking them all and planning how he would deal with them had given him more joy than carrying out the deeds. But that was okay; it just meant he was a decent human being – unlike the six on his list.

Only when he'd wiped out all of them would he be able to find the peace he craved. Yes, he'd be in prison, but that didn't matter. He had nothing to live for, no one to care about in the outside world, so what difference would it make if he was locked up? He'd been in a place worse than prison for over a decade.

They all deserved what was coming to them, but they would never know why they'd been chosen. Maybe he'd tell the police when they came for him, but everyone on his list would die wondering what it was they'd done to deserve their fate. But then dying was kinder than what they had put him through. He'd had to *live* wondering why fate had chosen to destroy him.

CHAPTER ELEVEN

Jon opened his locker door Monday morning, almost glad to be back at work. Andy's moaning had reached fever pitch over the weekend and even visits to the pub hadn't stopped the tide of complaints. He took down his porter's coat and hung his jacket on the peg. As he closed the door he heard a burst of laughter coming from the other side of the row of lockers dividing the room into two. He was about to stroll round to join in the banter when he heard his name.

"You should hear what Jon has to say about you guys," Iain said, "but don't worry, I've told him I won't put up with him slagging you off."

Jon stopped mid-stride. What the fuck?

"Thanks for telling us, Iain," one of Jon's co-workers said.

Recovering his wits, Jon stormed round the lockers to find Iain holding court with half a dozen porters.

"What's going on?" he said. "I haven't slagged anyone off."

Most of the men looked embarrassed and sloped off, but a couple stood their ground next to Iain.

"I told them what you said about your locker," Iain said.

"What did I say? I mean, I didn't say anything. About anybody."

Sean, one of the oldest there shook his head. "Really? So how come each of us has to go in to see Mr Montague?"

"I don't know! How would I know?" Jon said.

Iain smiled. "That's right, brazen it out. Like you didn't complain to Mr Montague that someone, *one of us*, had opened your locker and gone through your stuff."

Jon felt as if the ground under his feet was no longer

solid. "But I didn't. Sean, you've got to believe me, I really didn't."

Sean shrugged. "I would have, but I've already been asked by Montague if I did it. As if I'd want to rummage through anyone else's locker. You can deny it all you want, but we've all been called in to account for ourselves and it's you who lodged the complaint. Now, I don't know about anyone else, but I'm going to get some work done."

He pushed past Jon and left the room along with the other porters, leaving Jon alone with Iain. Black rage built inside him until he could almost feel the other person inside taking control. He forced himself to calm down. He mustn't lose control. Not here.

"You did this," Jon said. "You've turned them all against me."

Iain said nothing, just grinned until Jon wanted to smack his head against the locker doors.

"What have I ever done to you?"

Jon watched as the smile left Iain's face.

"Not to me, arsehole. You've never done anything to me. I'm paying you back for someone else. Someone whose life *you* destroyed."

"What...who?"

"You don't even remember her, do you?"

"Iain, I haven't a fucking clue what you're on about. Tell me," Jon pleaded. "You obviously think I've done something, but I don't know what. Just tell me."

Iain looked him up and down. "You're even more of a bastard than I'd realised. Think back over a decade. Try and remember what you did back then. I bet she'd remember you, if she was capable of remembering anything. You make me sick," he said, shoving past and leaving the room.

Jon staggered and clutched the nearest locker. Over a decade? Did Iain mean the woman who'd died in the accident? But what connection could Iain have with her? He didn't even know him back then. God, if only he could turn the clock back. Before everything changed, his life had been pretty good. Any girl he'd wanted had been his for the asking. He'd had friends and a social life. Not like now where the only person he could talk to was the new barman at the pub. Okay, so he'd needed the medication to keep his mind in order, but he'd been as good about taking it then as he was now.

***

"Good morning, everyone," Paolo said as he faced his team. "I would like to introduce Detective Sergeant Andrea Styles, who has come to join the team. Andrea has been working in Leicester and has now moved to Bradchester."

He waited until the chorus of welcome died down.

"You'll be delighted to hear that Andrea specialises in research. I know we all miss George for his skills in that regard." Loud groans greeted George's name. "Yes, I know few of you will forgive him, but we have to agree he was the best when it came to ferreting out information."

"You don't have any connection to the press do you? A secret bank account for them to pay into?" someone shouted from the back of the room, to hoots of laughter.

Paolo was about to issue a rebuke, but Andrea laughed.

"If I do, I promise to share my ill-gotten gains with you all. Deal?"

"Deal," the heckler said.

"Right, Andrea, that's the welcome out of the way. Your desk is over there," Paolo said, pointing to the empty space next to CC. "Come on, team. Let's get down to work."

"CC, you start."

She waited until Andrea had dumped her bag and got herself settled.

"As far as I can see there is no social or professional connection between our two victims. Professor Edwards was universally unpopular; Mr Fulbright had an active social life. They were never involved in patient cases together; at least, I haven't been able to uncover any. They are, or were, in different age brackets. Professor Edwards was retired, Mr Fulbright was practicing and probably still had many years ahead of him. Professor Edwards was single and had never married. Mr Fulbright was on wife number three. Married only a short time ago to a much younger woman who used to be his secretary. The two men lived in different parts of town. The professor in a penthouse right here in the centre and Mr Fulbright has, or rather had, a mansion out in the country."

"Thank you, CC. So, do we think our killer might be targeting professional people? Is that the connection? Is he looking for educated men?"

"I don't think so, sir," Dave said. "The notes he leaves behind are very precise. He's got six victims in his sights. He's dealt with two of them, leaving four more. That sounds more like he has actual people in mind, rather than what they do."

Paolo nodded. "I tend to agree with you, Dave, but let's not rule the professional connection out just yet – especially as we don't have anything else to go on."

He picked up a piece of paper from the desk next to him.

"Andrea, this will be your first job. There are three men who trained under Professor Edwards that we haven't been able to track down and eliminate from our list of possible suspects. Michael Sergeant, Conrad Stormont and Patrick Kirkbride all need to be found and interviewed. It could be that one of them also knew and/or had reason to dislike Mr Fulbright."

He passed the paper to Andrea and turned to CC. "Would you show Andrea where everything is and help her to get settled in?"

CC nodded. "Of course."

"Dave, you and I will take a drive into the countryside to interview Mr Fulbright's widow. Let's see if she knows of any link between her late husband and the professor."

Paolo ran his argument with Katy through his mind once again as Dave drove out to the Fulbright property. Would she ever forgive him if he delved into her young man's background? Probably not. Maybe it was just as well;

finding out who he was would be an almost impossible task without a bit more information. After all, he could hardly turn up at Social Services and ask about a boy called Danny whose surname he didn't know, whose age he didn't know and whose length of time in care he didn't know.

"You're quiet, sir," Dave said.

Paolo shrugged. "I had a strange weekend," he said. "A bit like the curate's egg. Good in parts and bad in others. What about you? How was your weekend, apart from Saturday being messed up?"

"Good."

Paolo watched the smile spread across Dave's face. The weekend had clearly been better than good. It was great to see him looking so happy.

"We're here, sir," Dave said, turning off the road onto a short drive leading to a redbrick Georgian house. "Nice place," he said, pulling up outside and turning off the engine.

Paolo climbed out and looked around. Yes, it was nice, but miles from anywhere. He wouldn't like to be so isolated, but knew it suited some people to put distance between themselves and their closest neighbours.

The woman who opened the door when they rang the old-fashioned brass bell didn't look as if she belonged in the country. Immaculately made up and dressed in a designer outfit that probably cost the equivalent of a few months' police salary, she would have been at home on the cover of a fashion magazine.

"Please, come in," she said in a voice trying hard to be cultured, but failing to achieve it. Paolo could hear undertones of a London accent. Not quite cockney, but nudging in that direction.

They followed her through a large panelled hallway, past the central staircase, to a door half hidden behind a full-sized statue of a classical god. Paolo had no idea whether it was Greek or Roman, but wouldn't have given it house room. It looked a bit too much like it was about to throw a thunderbolt for his taste. Again, he was struck by how out of place Mrs Fulbright looked in her own home.

"Take a seat," she said, sitting on a fragile ornately carved chair.

Paolo glanced around. The place was full of antiques and gilt furniture that would have graced any French country home, but didn't fit as well in the English countryside.

Mrs Fulbright looked even younger than he'd expected. He knew she was in her mid-thirties, but could have passed for late twenties at the most.

"I'm sorry to have to ask questions at this difficult time," he said, "but we need to establish whether your husband knew Professor Edwards."

"The man who was murdered last week? Are you saying Edwin was killed by the same person?"

"We're keeping an open mind. Do you know if Mr Fulbright had any dealings with Professor Edwards? Were they, perhaps, on the same charity committees?"

She shook her head. "No, I'd have known if that was the case. I used to be Edwin's secretary, so I knew all his social and professional contacts. He definitely didn't know Professor Edwards in either capacity."

Paolo glanced across at Dave, waiting for him to finish writing before moving on with his questions.

"Did you notice anything significant in the days before your husband was murdered? Did he say or do anything out of the ordinary?"

She nodded as tears formed in her eyes and she brushed them away.

"He got several phone calls and acted funny with me afterwards, but when I asked him he wouldn't tell me what they were about. He said they were nothing to do with me, but I am pretty sure they were."

"What makes you say that?" Paolo asked.

"Because of the way he was with me when he'd received one of those calls. He wanted to know where I'd been and who I'd been with. It was almost as if he thought I was having an affair."

"I'm sorry," Paolo said, "but I have to ask. Were you?"

78

"No! I loved my husband. I know everyone thinks I married him for his money, but I didn't! I married him because he was a lovely man who made me happy."

She shuddered. "I don't know how I'm going to manage without him. His kids from his first marriage hate me and his two ex-wives have already told me they're going to contest his will and he hasn't even been buried yet!"

She sobbed and Paolo found it easy to believe she had genuinely loved her husband. He waited until she'd got her emotions under control again.

"When did the phone calls occur? Can you remember?"

She nodded. "They started about a week ago."

"Were they made to the house phone, or his mobile?"

"Here, as far as I know. He might have had some on his mobile, but I only knew about the ones here. He'd answer the phone, go all quiet and walk out. When he came back in the room afterwards he was different – a bit distant."

Back in the car, Paolo ran a mental checklist of things they needed to look into.

"Those phone calls could be significant," he said. "We'll need to get a printout of his home and mobile phone records. We should also look into his family background. It sounds as if there is some bad blood with his ex-wife and children from his first marriage. No children from the second marriage, but the ex-wife could be vengeful enough and seems to have joined forces with the first ex. Maybe one of Mr Fulbright's family members knew the professor. There has to be a link between them somewhere. We just need to find it."

He broke off as his mobile rang.

"Storey."

"Paolo, it's me. What have you been able to find out?"

For a moment Paolo couldn't think why Lydia was calling, but he dragged his mind back from the case and onto his own family issues.

"Nothing yet," he said.

"Nothing? Paolo, have you even tried?"

"Lydia, I don't even know his last name. All I know is that he's in care and called Danny. I can't start asking questions about all the kids in care called Danny!"

"So what are you going to do?"

"I'm going to try talking to Katy again. I handled it badly. She might open up if I take it easy on her."

"Yeah, well, good luck with that! She didn't even say goodbye to me when she stormed out this morning. I asked her where she was going and when she'd be back and she said she didn't know. This isn't like her, Paolo. It must be that boy's influence."

"Look, I'll talk to Katy. I promise."

He heard Lydia sigh before she said goodbye and ended the call.

"Problem, sir?"

"You could say that," Paolo said and filled Dave in on his weekend chat with Katy.

"It's none of my business, I know," Dave said, "but your Katy is pretty switched on. I think in your place I'd…"

Paolo looked across at Dave as he drove back into town. "Go on; finish what you were going to say."

"I think in your place I'd trust her judgement. She's brighter than most and is about the most balanced teenager I've ever known."

Paolo smiled. Dave had a point. Maybe he should ease back and give Katy a bit of room. He sighed. Who was he kidding? He'd give her room, but keep a watchful eye on her all the same. She was too precious to take any chances with her safety or happiness.

**

Jon trudged home after the worst day he'd ever spent at work. None of the other porters would speak to him, leaving him in a silent bubble for hours at a time. When he went in to speak to Mr Montague about it, he was told that he shouldn't have lodged a complaint with Iain if there was no foundation to it. He'd tried to protest his innocence, but Mr

Montague had rounded on him for accusing Iain of underhand behaviour.

"Why would he do such a thing?" the manager had demanded.

Jon couldn't give a reason because he didn't know himself why Iain hated him. He'd racked his brains, but couldn't connect Iain with anything or anyone in his past.

The manager had called Iain in and that had been the worst part of all. Iain had put on an outraged act at being accused of making up Jon's complaint. He'd offered to resign if Mr Montague doubted his sincerity and the manager had fallen for it. Jon had received a written warning and Iain had walked out with a shining halo.

He pushed open the metal gate and walked up to his front door. As he was rummaging for his key, the door opened and Gordon came out.

"Oh, hello, shame you've arrived too late for the action. We've been watching some hot babes," Gordon said with a wink that turned Jon's stomach. "If you'd got here a bit sooner you could have sat with us. Still, I expect you'll watch some of the stuff later. Andy's downloaded quite a lot."

"Has he?" Jon said, pushing past Gordon to get inside. "I hope to God it's all legal. Bye, Gordon. Sorry, gotta rush. Lots to do."

Gordon laughed. "When you've watched some of Andy's stuff you'll definitely have lots to do."

Jon shut the door feeling sick. Gordon always had that air of sleaze, but knowing he'd been sitting on his couch getting horny made Jon want to puke right there in the hall. He reached down and picked up the mail that Gordon had walked over. It wouldn't hurt Andy to come out and put it on the hall table out of the way, he fumed.

He flicked through the envelopes. Nearly all of them had windows, meaning yet more bills. The last one was a plain white envelope with his name and address printed on it, but no stamp. It must have been hand delivered. He was about to open it when Andy's whining voice reached him.

"Are you going to stand out there all night? I've been on my own all day and you can't even be bothered to come in and say hello."

Jon's temperature shot skywards and he couldn't breathe for the rage that consumed him. Slinging the unopened letters onto the small table against the wall, he stormed into the lounge.

"You lying little shit! You haven't been on your own. You've been watching porn with that slimy git upstairs."

Andy didn't even flinch. "So what if I have? I'm not going to sit here day after day with no one to talk to. Why should I?"

What was the point? Jon thought. Turning away, he went back into the hall and picked up the scattered mail. He opened the top one. Water bill. The next was the electricity. Andy paid bugger all towards his keep. The third one looked like his credit card statement and under that was the white envelope without a stamp. He was tempted to ignore the credit card bill, but knew he should look. With all the trips to the pub and other restaurants designed to keep Andy's moans to a minimum, Jon knew he'd overspent. With his job looking a bit precarious, he'd have to watch his step where money was concerned.

He ripped open the envelope and stared at the total. That couldn't be right! No way had he spent so much. Scanning the itemised bill, Jon could feel the rage burning inside like a volcano about to erupt.

"Andy, you little shit!" he yelled, going back into the lounge. "Have you been using my card to buy stuff online?"

Andy glanced up. "Have I? I suppose I might have mixed our card details up and given yours by mistake."

"Over two hundred pounds is a bloody big mistake. Especially as it took ten entries to rack up that much. What the fuck have you been spending my money on?"

Andy grinned. "Quality doesn't come cheap. I've got to do something with my time and watching—"

"Porn! You've spent *my* money on porn?"

Andy grinned. "You can watch it as well if you like."

Jon turned and went into the kitchen before he could explode. He slammed the door behind him and leant against it. He had to get away from Andy. If they continued to live together Jon didn't think he'd be able to control himself. Right now he wanted to lash out and do his brother a greater injury than any he'd suffered in the car crash.

The rage grew until he blacked out. When he came to again there was broken china scattered over the floor. He could hear Andy laughing at him in the lounge.

"You arsehole, you lost it again, didn't you?" Andy called. "What a wanker!"

Jon shuddered. That hadn't happened to him for a long time. Or had it? There were times when he'd felt as if there was something he should remember. Something he'd done when the other one took over his mind.

Eventually, he stopped shaking. As he turned to get the dustpan and broom, he spotted the two envelopes on the worktop. He must have put them there before chucking the mugs around. One of them had the logo of the hospital in Leicester where he'd gone for an interview. The way today had gone, this could only be a 'sorry, but we don't want you' letter.

He ripped it open and scanned it, ready to screw it up the moment his eyes hit the word sorry, but instead 'happy' jumped out at him. Hardly crediting the evidence of his own eyes, he read the letter in full. They wanted him to go for a second interview. There was still a chance he could get away from this place. Get away from Andy. Start out on his own somewhere.

Feeling better than he had for days, he opened the unstamped envelope and took out a single sheet of paper folded into a neat square. He unfolded it and his stomach heaved. There was only one word printed in large type in the middle of the page.
Murderer.

CHAPTER TWELVE

Paolo arrived early for the autopsy of Edwin Fulbright in the hope of catching a moment alone with Barbara, but she was already gowned up and talking to her assistant, Chris, when he got there. She looked up and smiled, but continued her low-voiced conversation with her colleague. Paolo stood against the wall and tried not to eavesdrop, but the acoustics carried the softly spoken words clearly, giving him no option but to overhear.

"So I'll be out all afternoon and may not be in tomorrow," Barbara said.

"But we've got a full programme for tomorrow," Chris answered. "I'm not sure I can deal with them all on my own."

"If I can't get in, you'll simply have to cope. It's about time you took on more responsibility instead of doing the bare minimum. If you're looking for promotion, this attitude of 'I can't do it' isn't going to get you very far."

Barbara's back was to him, but Paolo had a clear view of Chris's face. He looked every bit as shocked as Paolo felt. Never had he heard Barbara speak in that tone of voice to Chris. If anything, she'd always gone out of her way to be more supportive than Paolo sometimes believed her assistant deserved. Maybe she'd decided on a tough love approach, but it seemed out of character. He'd never been so glad to see Dave as when he walked through the door a few seconds later.

Barbara turned as he shut the door behind him.

"Nice of you to show up, Detective Sergeant. Should we apologise for dragging you away from something more interesting?"

Dave looked at his watch and opened his mouth as if he was going to argue, but Paolo stepped between him and Barbara.

"Okay, we're all here. Let's make sure this victim mirrors the first one, shall we?"

By the time Barbara declared the autopsy complete and ordered Chris to finish up, she had sniped at all three men, becoming steadily more aggressive as time wore on. Dave and Chris both looked shell-shocked, which was pretty much how Paolo felt.

"I'll get back to the station, Paolo. See you there."

Paolo nodded and followed Barbara down the corridor to her office. As she slid into the seat behind her desk she glared at him.

"I hope you haven't come in here to pry again."

"No, I haven't done that. I've come to tell you that if you ever speak to Dave like that again without reason or provocation, I won't stand by and keep quiet as I did today. Dave did nothing to deserve your tongue lashing and neither, for that matter, did Chris, but that's for him to bring up with you. I've known you a number of years, Barbara, and I know there is something very wrong in your life right now. I'm here if you want to talk. I've already told you that. But I am not going to let you speak to a member of my team as if he equates to something you'd scrape off the soles of your shoes."

He waited to see if she would answer, but she picked up the phone and began dialling.

"Sorry, I have calls to make. Close the door as you leave."

* * *

When Paolo got back to the station his team were already in place, waiting to hear the autopsy findings.

"From what Dr Royston has been able to establish, the same person killed both the professor and Mr Fulbright."

"I think we already knew that, sir," CC said.

Paolo smiled. "We believed it to be the case, but we didn't know absolutely. What news on the fingerprints lifted from the car?"

CC handed Paolo a sheet of paper. "Only one set matches both crime scenes, sir. Sadly, they are not in our database, so no help to us at the moment."

"No, but they will be when we find the killer. Andrea, what have you been able to find out for us? Any joy with the phone records of both men?"

"Not yet, sir. I've checked the professor's and there was only one call received on the morning of his death and that was from a pay as you go phone which we haven't been able to trace so far."

"And the three missing men?"

Andrea shook her head. "Nothing on any of them so far."

Paolo was disappointed. He'd had such good reports of Andrea that he'd expected results. Turning back to the group, he was about to assign research duties to other officers when Andrea's voice interrupted him.

"Sorry, sir, I have made some progress."

"But you said you hadn't," Paolo said.

"No, what I said was that I hadn't yet been able to track down the missing men, but I have had one breakthrough. I've found the ex-wife of Conrad Stormont. She might know where he's hiding out."

"Well done, Andrea. Fill us in on what you know."

"It wasn't easy tracking her down because she's remarried and goes under her new married name. She's now known as Beatrice Hunt, last known address 44, the Glades, Hambley Estate."

"Blimey," Dave said, "that's a comedown for a doctor's wife. From an address in the best part of town to a grotty flat on one of the roughest estates in Bradchester."

"How do you know it's grotty?" Andrea asked.

"It's a haven for drug users, pushers and pimps," Dave said. "I can't imagine there being a non-grotty flat on the estate."

"Let's find out, shall we?" Paolo said. "Andrea, good

work. Dave, you and I are going to visit Mrs Hunt and discover if she's managed to turn her place on the Hambley Estate into a piece of paradise."

Half an hour later they were trudging up four flights of stairs.

"Do you think they ever fix the lift here? I've never yet been into any block on this estate and been able to reach the upper floors without climbing the stairs," Paolo said, trying not to inhale the stench of rotting garbage, cats' piss and stale urine.

Dave shook his head, but didn't answer. Sensible man, Paolo thought, wishing he hadn't spoken. Keep your mouth shut and maybe the germs won't get in.

When they reached the fourth floor, they edged along the corridor running alongside a row of identical front doors. Empty cigarette boxes, plastic supermarket bags and used condoms made walking an obstacle course.

"How can anyone bear to live here?" Dave asked.

"Little or no choice," Paolo said. "Just thank your stars you don't have to."

Number 44 certainly didn't look like a portal to paradise, so Paolo wasn't surprised when it was opened by a woman who didn't look as if she'd taken a bath in recent memory. Her mouse-coloured hair was greasy and her face had the look of someone who has been kicked too many times, figuratively and literally. Paolo could see resignation in her eyes. She knew they weren't there for anything that was going to make her life better.

"What's he said now? The little shit doesn't even live here, so why he has to stir people up is beyond me."

The voice took Paolo by surprise. The words were coarse, but the way she spoke belonged in a country club environment, not here. Mrs Hunt sounded as if she'd been raised by the aristocracy and took tea with the Queen.

"I'm Detective Inspector Paolo Storey and this is Detective Sergeant Dave Johnson," Paolo said. "Sorry to disturb you without calling ahead first, but would it be possible to come in and talk to you about your ex-husband, Conrad Stormont?"

She looked surprised, as if that was the last thing she expected to hear, but stood back and let them pass.

"Go in the sitting room," she said. "It's not too bad in there."

There it was again, a note off-key, Paolo thought. How many residents on this estate would call the tiny room they entered a sitting room? A smell of stale food and spilt beer lingered in the air and Paolo spotted several takeaway cartons on the floor. They must have been there a while as quite a few of the local fast food outlets were represented.

Beatrice Hunt stood just inside the doorway, looking as if she was prepared to run at a moment's notice. Paolo wondered if she always took up that stance or if it was because they were the police.

"You said you were here about Conrad. Have you found him?"

"No," Paolo said. "We were hoping you might be able to help us in that regard."

"I haven't seen him for at least seven years, maybe more. I divorced him after he'd been missing for three years."

"Do you still have his last known address?"

Beatrice laughed and then launched into a violent coughing fit. "Third bench from the oak tree, Bradchester Park," she said when she was finally able to breathe. "He turned to drink when he lost his licence. Felt so sorry for himself he didn't have any emotion to spare for the effect losing his position had on me or our children."

Paolo looked around for photographs, but there weren't any. "Your children didn't keep in touch with their father?"

"How could they?" Beatrice said. "He fell into a gutter and crawled away. We lost touch with him years ago."

"How many children do you have?"

"Three. Two boys and a girl."

"Would it be possible to speak to them?"

"Why? I've already told you they were not able to keep contact with their father. They know even less than I do about Conrad. I tried to shield them from the worst of his excesses when he was still living with us, but unfortunately, it soon became impossible to hide. They decided they didn't want to know him and who can blame them?"

Clearly she knew nothing that would help them locate the missing doctor. Paolo was about to thank her for her time when the front door opened and then slammed.

"Bea," a man's voice called. "Where the fuck are you?"

Paolo saw Beatrice shiver, but she answered without a tremor.

"In here, Carl. These two men are from the police," she said as the man came in. "This is Carl Hunt, my husband."

"What the fuck do you two want? What have you been telling them, Bea?"

Paolo looked at the shaven-headed man looming over his wife and understood why she looked permanently on the verge of fleeing.

"We are looking for her ex-husband," Paolo said before Beatrice could answer. "We were just about to leave, but perhaps you knew Conrad Stormont and might have some idea of his current whereabouts?"

"Like fuck, I do. That poncy prick couldn't handle life and left Bea in the gutter. If it weren't for me she'd still be down there, wouldn't you?" he finished, rounding on his wife.

She nodded. "Yes, Carl's been very good to me," she said, but Paolo noticed the body tremors had increased and her eyes glistened with unshed tears. "I'm sorry I couldn't help you."

"If you think of anything, please call me," Paolo said, pressing his card into her hand and trying to get across to her by telepathy that he was there to call on for help if she ever needed it. He'd seen too many domestic violence situations not to know this was a powder keg waiting to explode. He'd make sure to put the word out that if a call came in from a Beatrice Hunt, the response should be immediate. The man had bully written all over him and Paolo's hands itched to dish out a bit of what he was sure

Beatrice received on a regular basis.

Carl came with Paolo and Dave to the door without saying a word. He slammed it shut as they stepped through, barely giving them time to clear the entrance.

"He's a real charmer, isn't he?" Paolo said picking his way through the debris in the corridor.

Dave nodded. "I wouldn't like to be on the receiving end of his temper."

"Me neither," Paolo said as they went down the foul-smelling stairs. "But I have a feeling that his wife is far too often for her safety. I didn't see any sign of children there, did you?"

Dave shook his head. "Let's hope her parents took them in when she married the caveman."

"Parents!" Paolo said. "I wonder if Andrea would be able to track down the parents of any of our potential suspects."

He glanced at his watch when they reached the bottom of the stairwell. "Let's get back to the station, Dave. I want to ask Andrea what avenues she's covered and suggest the parents if she hasn't already been in contact with them."

But when he put the question to Andrea he found she was ahead of him.

"Patrick Kirkbride's mother died when he was quite young. His father didn't remarry and Patrick had no siblings. His father is in a home for the elderly in Scotland suffering with advanced Alzheimer's. He is unable to recall that he even has a son, far less tell us where he might be living."

She looked down at her notes. "Michael Sergeant's parents live in Switzerland, but they are on a world cruise until the end of August. I have contacted the ship and requested their assistance, but no information has yet come back to us. He has one sister who is a Carmelite nun. If you're Catholic you'll know the Carmelites aren't allowed to speak to anyone. I had no idea such barbarous practices still existed, but you live and learn."

She drew breath, pushed her fringe out of her eyes and

looked down. Paolo watched, fascinated, as the stream of information continued to flow.

"I have requested special permission to speak to her via her Mother Superior, who is going to pray for guidance and get back to me tomorrow. I am hoping that God might be on our side, but if he isn't, I intend to ask the Mother Superior to ask Sister Benedicta if she could write down any information she might have."

Pausing briefly, Andrea rummaged among the numerous pieces of paper littering her desk. "Conrad Stormont's parents divorced when he was at university. His mother is trekking in the Himalayas with a Buddhist group and it is unknown when she will return, or even if she intends to come back. According to her cousin, she is seeking enlightenment. The mother's cousin knows nothing about any other family members because she fell out with them years ago over his great-grandfather's will. The father, that is, Conrad's father, not his mother's father, has moved to France. He wasn't home when I called, but I have left a message on his answering machine – in English. I failed French at school."

Paolo was relieved when the stream of information came to an end. He was exhausted just listening to her.

"Andrea, I promise never to question your research ever again. Let me know when any of your leads turns up something positive we can chase down."

"Will do, sir."

"In the meantime, could you look into the background of Conrad's three children? They obviously aren't living with their grandparents. I can't bear to think of them in that dreadful flat with Carl Hunt for a stepfather."

***

Paolo stood in the restaurant doorway savouring the aromas of garlic, herbs and tomatoes that always reminded him of his early life, when his mother had still been alive. He scanned the restaurant, but Jessica wasn't yet seated at their table.

Moving towards the back of the room, he greeted the waiter and ordered a bottle of water. Jessica had said she might be held up on a case review, so he settled down to wait, allowing his mind to run free. Often it was only when he stopped trying to join the dots in a case that a spark of inspiration would strike. Tonight wasn't one of those times. All he could think about was the woman he was waiting for. When the door opened and he looked up, his breath caught in his throat. She'd come straight from work, but still managed to look as fresh as a mountain stream.

"Sorry," she said as she pulled out the seat opposite. "Have you been waiting long?"

"No," Paolo said, shaking his head in amusement as the owner, Giuseppe, appeared from nowhere to tenderly assist Jessica to sit down.

"How come you don't rush out of the kitchen to help me with my chair and jacket?"

"Because, Signor Storey, *you* are not an intelligent woman in the full bloom of her beauty. Signora," he said, kissing Jessica's fingers, "as always, it is my pleasure to serve you."

Having put Paolo in his place, he went back into the kitchen, leaving Jessica laughing and Paolo trying hard not to smile. The waiter placed a bottle of water and their menus on the table and asked if they wanted wine.

"No, thank you. Just water for me, too," Jessica said. "Are you going to break with tradition, Paolo, or have what you always do?"

Paolo glanced at the menu. "I know I should try something new, but this is one of the few restaurants where you can get Osso Bucco almost as good as my mother made. I'm going to be boring and have that as usual. What about you?"

Jessica looked over the top of the menu. "I'm going to have the Saltimbocca."

By the end of the meal, after they'd shared zabaglione as dessert, Paolo felt there had been a shift in their relationship, but didn't want to push it. He paid the bill as they drank coffee, refusing Jessica's offer of going halves each. He wanted this to be his treat.

They walked outside and Paolo suddenly felt like a fourteen-year-old without a clue what to say to the gorgeous woman standing close enough to kiss.

He opened his mouth to speak, but Jessica put her finger on his lips.

"Ssh," she said. "Don't speak, just nod or shake your head. Would you like to come back to my place?"
Paolo nodded.

CHAPTER THIRTEEN

Paolo woke up wondering where he was. The bed felt different; the room was wrong. Then he remembered and turned to look for Jessica, but her side of the bed was empty. He lay there trying to work out what he should do. Get up and shower? He couldn't stay here, even though the memories of the night before made him want to do exactly that.

He was about to climb out of the bed when the door opened and Jessica came in, fully dressed and holding a tray with coffee and toast for two. She sat on the edge of the bed and smiled. His stomach did a triple somersault that would have won a gold medal in any Olympic gymnastics event.

"I didn't want to wake you, but I have to be at the hospital early today. I've just got time for a few mouthfuls of coffee and a slice of toast."

He reached across and caught her hand. "Jessica, about last night—"

She grinned and picked up her cup. "If you say anything other than wow, you'll be showering in very hot coffee."

"You read my mind. Wow was exactly the word I was about to use."

Jessica sipped from the cup and replaced it on the tray. Picking up a slice of toast, she stood and leaned forward to drop a kiss on Paolo's lips.

"I'll munch on this in the car," she said, waving the toast at him. "Sorry, I have to go."

"Can I see you tonight?" Paolo asked.

"For more wow?"

Paolo laughed. "Definitely more wow and maybe a bit of oh my God thrown in for good measure."

"That's a date," she said. "Sorry, I would stay if I could."

"Go," he said. "You're taking my mind off my breakfast anyway. I'll be wanting wow instead of toast if you stand there much longer."

She blew him another kiss and disappeared through the doorway in a blur of motion. Paolo heard her skipping down the hallway and then the front door opening and closing. He looked at the clock on the bedside table – seven-fifteen. He had enough time to finish his toast and coffee, then go home to shower and change before heading to the station. He leaned back against the headboard and thought about how little sleep they'd had, but he felt wide awake. In fact, he felt wow.

***

Paolo wondered if his vision was coloured by the events of the night before, but he was convinced everyone looked happier this morning. CC and Andrea had their heads close together, poring over whatever it was Andrea had collated on her desk. They both looked up when he called out good morning.

CC grinned at him. "That's the cheeriest good morning I've heard from you since I've been stationed here. Did you have a good evening, sir?"

Paolo felt his cheeks redden and thanked his genetic background. Maybe no one would notice the blush under his olive complexion. He could see from the look of understanding on CC's face that he had no such luck! His face felt as if you could fry breakfast on it.

"Yes, thank you. Very pleasant. Where's Dave?"

"Holding hands with Rebecca in the canteen. Working in this place is like being in a chick flick these days," she said, eyes alight with laughter. "I keep expecting an orchestra to start playing. And here, walking on air through the doorway is our romantic hero, floating on a glow of love."

Dave laughed. "You're just jealous," he said, throwing a paperclip at her.

CC caught it. "Not me. I'm enjoying my freedom, thank you very much."

Paolo glanced at Andrea. He wondered if CC was aware of how the younger woman looked at her. Now there was an interesting development. A happy one, as long as it didn't affect the team dynamics.

"Okay, enough banter. Let's get down to work. Andrea, we'll start with you. Any new information in overnight?"

Before she could speak, Paolo's phone rang. He glanced at the LCD screen and groaned. Chief Constable Willows. That's all he needed to bring his mood crashing down.

"I have to take this," he said. "Hold fire a moment."

"Paolo, could you come up to my office, please?"

"Yes, Chief Constable, I'll be right there."

He put the phone back in his pocket and grimaced. "I think I'm in for a bollocking. Does anyone have any good news I can take upstairs with me? No? Okay. With a bit of luck my trip will be a short one. I'll be right back."

Paolo left the office to a chorus of good luck wishes and knew he needed them. He wouldn't be called upstairs unless the chief was taking serious flak from the press. Climbing the stairs two at a time, part of the exercise regime he'd got into when he turned forty, he was pleased to find he was barely out of breath when he reached the Chief Constable's door and tapped on it.

"Come in."

Paolo opened the door and studied Willows, trying to gauge his mood. The man certainly didn't look as though he wanted to throw a party in Paolo's honour any time soon.

"Take a seat, Paolo, and for Christ's sake tell me you've got a lead you're following in this insulin case. The press are all over me, screaming incompetence again. It's the same hacks every bloody time, looking for reasons to trash our efforts, instead of reporting the facts."

Paolo let Willows rant. He knew it would be better for him if the chief was able to let off steam before they got down to discussing where the case was going. Although, at the moment, *not going* would be a more honest description.

"Needless to say, the press are having a field day over this. Two of Bradchester's most distinguished residents have been murdered in the same manner and we can't come up with anything to connect them. What am I supposed to say to the reporters who ask if you're competent to lead the case when you don't give me a bone to throw to them?"

"Sir, if I had something, I'd give it to you, but we have nothing other than some fingerprints tying the killer to both crime scenes. The prints aren't a match with anyone on our database. We can't find a social or professional connection between the two men. They moved in totally different areas in all aspects of their lives. I can't give you what I haven't got, sir. Sorry."

Willows glared. "That's not what I wanted to hear, Paolo."

"I know, but I can't magic clues or evidence out of thin air. I've had photographs taken of the crowds hanging around both crime scenes, but we haven't found anyone who was present at both. I've got my team looking into the backgrounds of those who stand to gain from the two deaths, but so far, once again, there's no connection. We're digging into the Fulbright extended family, but although there is plenty of ill-feeling over his latest marriage, none of them had anything to do with Professor Edwards. If it's the same killer, and it certainly looks that way, there has to be a link between the two men. We're searching for it, sir, but..." Paolo paused and shrugged knowing he wasn't going to win a popularity award, "whatever it is isn't obvious."

"You'd better hope your team come up with something. I've arranged a press conference for you for tomorrow afternoon."

"But, sir, we've got nothing!"

"Then you'll have to tell them that. Maybe the thought of appearing in front of the cameras will galvanise you into finding something."

Paolo walked back down the stairs a lot slower than he'd gone up. He hated holding press conferences even when he had information to give, or when he needed to ask the public for assistance, but what the hell Willows thought he could achieve this time was beyond him. His earlier euphoric mood evaporated. Damn Willows. He was throwing Paolo to the wolves to get them off his own back.

Going back into the main office, it was almost as if his team picked up on his frustration as a collective groan greeted him.

"What did he have to say, sir?" Dave asked.

"Press conference tomorrow afternoon, so I'm going to need something to tell them. Let's get back to where we were before I was summoned. Andrea, anything new?"

"Yes, sir. Starting with the Fulbright phone records. He received several calls from a pay as you go phone, but not the same one as Professor Edwards. Each call seemed to last fractionally longer than the one before, which makes me think whoever called was reeling Mr Fulbright in. You know, giving just a little more information each time. Mrs Fulbright thought the calls might have been to do with her, but there's no way of knowing."

Andrea shuffled papers. "I've found Patrick Kirkbride, sir, and spoke to him this morning. He's in South Africa and has been there for nearly five years. He comes home twice a year to visit his father, but the last time was four months ago. I've made a note to check with airlines and other forms of transport, but I think he's telling the truth about that, sir. He remembers Professor Edwards as a good psychiatrist, but a poor human being."

"You'd think you needed to be both," CC said. "I'm not sure I'd want to tell my troubles to someone who was as nasty as the professor seems to have been."

"Psychiatry is more to do with medical faults affecting the brain. If you were looking for someone to talk to about your emotional troubles you'd go to a psychologist," Paolo said, feeling the flush rising again. This was ridiculous; he couldn't even discuss Jessica's profession without blushing. "Anyway, that's a side issue. Do you have anything else, Andrea?"

She nodded. "Michael Sergeant's mother left a message

overnight. Her son died in a hang gliding accident over the Alps last year. I'm afraid I still cannot find any trace of Conrad Stormont. He simply dropped out of sight and hasn't reappeared."

"Thank you, Andrea. CC, how are you getting on with the Medical Council findings which led to Stormont losing his licence?"

"It all seems pretty straightforward, at least on the surface. Stormont admitted prescribing the drug that led to the patient's psychotic episode. He insisted that he was following the written instructions of his superior, Professor Edwards. The patient, Jon Miller, and his brother, Andrew, both claimed compensation from Conrad Stormont and received healthy sums through a medical malpractice insurance pay-out."

Paolo sighed. "But no mention of Edwin Fulbright in that case?"

CC shook her head. "No, sir. His name doesn't appear anywhere."

"You know, even though on the surface there doesn't seem to be a connection, I can't help feeling the events leading up to Stormont losing his licence to practice are the key to solving this. Dig deeper, everyone. The connection is there, we've just got to find it."

"By the way, Andrea, did you have any joy with finding out about the Stormont children?"

"Yes, sir. The children were officially passed into their maternal grandmother's custody six years ago. The grandmother lives on the other side of Bradchester to their mother, so I don't know how much contact she has with them. It's possible they might know more about their father's whereabouts than she does. I called the grandmother's home while you were upstairs, but there was no reply. I'll keep trying."

"Good work, all of you."

He glanced at his watch. Now would be a good time to call Katy. Over dinner last night he'd explained his dilemma and Jessica had given him some good advice. He wanted to put it into action before the rift between him and Katy deepened. He went into his office, but left the door open. He liked to hear the buzz of conversation in the background.

Settling himself at his desk, he forced himself to feel calm, just as Jessica had advised, then hit speed dial for Katy's number. It rang for longer than usual and he wondered if Katy had seen who was calling and decided not to speak to him.

"Hello, Dad."

She sounded wary and he couldn't blame her. As Jessica had pointed out, and Dave, too, for that matter, Katy was a very together person and yet he'd jumped in as if she was five years old and incapable of making sensible decisions.

"Hi, Katy. I wondered if you wanted to have lunch with me today."

Normally she'd have said yes before he'd finished the question. The fact she didn't answer immediately told Paolo how far he'd damaged their easy going relationship.

"Are you going to nag me?"

"On my word as a boy scout, no. Dib dibs and all that."

Paolo was relieved to hear her laugh.

"So what's the special occasion? You don't usually offer me lunch during the week. Shouldn't you be doing your superhero stuff and get out there chasing crooks?"

"Yes, but even superheroes have to eat or they lose their powers. Want to meet me in town?"

"And you're not going to get on my case about me and Danny?"

"Katy, no nagging, no prying and no questions. If you want to tell me about Danny, I'm interested, but I am not going to get on your case about it. I promise – word of a super hero."

"Okay, then, but you have to pay a penance."

"Not McD, please, not that."

"'Fraid so," she said, laughing. "At least that will taste better than humble pie."

***

100

Jon couldn't face going straight home after another shitty day at work, so headed into the White Horse when he got off the bus.

As he approached the bar, he saw Bradley chatting to one of the regulars. It hit Jon that the barman was the only person he could call a friend at the moment and he'd only known him a few weeks. Still, he was a good listener and Jon desperately needed someone to talk to before he lost it completely. Andy was too much part of the problem, so there was no point trying to talk to him.

He sat on a bar stool and waited for Bradley to come over.

"What'll you have?" the barman asked. "You look as if you need a lot of it, whatever it is."

Jon tried to smile, but couldn't quite get his lips to move without quivering.

"A pint of lager, please."

He watched as Bradley moved away to pull the pint, wishing his life could be as uncomplicated. Surely pulling pints and chatting to people all day must be better than what he was going through. He'd barely had any sleep since getting the murderer letter and had made all sorts of errors at work through lack of concentration, giving Iain even more ammunition to use against him with Mr Montague.

"Here you go," Bradley said, putting the pint on a mat. "I don't want to stick my nose in where it's not wanted, but you're looking a bit rough. Your brother giving you stick again?"

Jon laughed. "When doesn't he? I've got to get away from him, Bradley. I'll go nuts if I hang around here much longer."

"Any news on that job you went after in Leicester?"

"Yep, I've got a second interview tomorrow afternoon. I've not told Andy I've even got the interview. I'm going to book into a B and B and stay overnight. Let him see what it's like fending for himself for a change."

"I expect your charming neighbour will keep him company."

Jon looked up from his pint. "That sounds like you don't like Gordon either."

Bradley shook his head. "I don't know him very well. He doesn't come in that often, but let's put it this way, if I had a daughter, I wouldn't want him anywhere near her."

"Have you got any kids?"

"Nope, sometimes I wish I had, but it didn't work out for me and my wife."

"I didn't know you were married."

Again, Bradley shook his head. "I'm not anymore. Which is just as well doing this job. Long unsociable hours don't exactly make for easy relationships. But, as I said, if I did have a daughter, I'd make sure your neighbour never set eyes on her. There's something very dark about him."

Bradley moved back down the bar to serve some new customers, but his mention of Gordon brought the murderer letter to Jon's mind again. Gordon had been leaving the apartment the day it arrived. Could he have left it? Or was it Andy? Was Andy playing silly buggers, trying to get him wound up?

The more he thought about it, the more he believed his brother was behind the letter. The bastard was always digging at him. When they were younger it had been Jon who'd played practical jokes on Andy. Maybe Andy saw this as payback time. There was no point asking him, he'd deny it even if it was true.

"You with us, Jon?" Bradley said. "That's the third time I've asked if you want a refill."

Jon nodded. "Yes, please. Sorry, I was miles away."

"I could see that," Bradley said. "Wherever you were, it didn't look like you were enjoying it."

"You're wrong," Jon said. "I was thinking how much pleasure I'd get from choking my brother to death. If I thought I'd get away with it, I'd do him in without a second thought."

***

Paolo lay back against the pillows with Jessica's head resting on his chest. Her hair was tickling, but he'd put up with any discomfort just to keep her there. Eventually, she moved away and gently touched the scar on his face.

"How did you get this?"

"A thug threw a full beer can at me when he was trying to get away. The edge of the can caught my skin at just the right angle to split it. I've had the scar for so long now I'm always surprised when anyone notices it."

She sat up, drawing the duvet over both of them.

"How did it go with Katy?"

"I think we're back on track. I didn't ask any questions, but I now know more about her friend Danny than I would have done if I had. She's quite taken with him, but..."

"But?"

"She's only sixteen, Jessica. She's so young. What if this boy hurts her?"

"She'll learn from it and move on. Besides, how old were you and Lydia when you fell in love? Didn't you tell me you were still at school?"

Paolo laughed. "That's unfair, using my own past against me. Considering Lydia and I are no longer together, that's hardly an advertisement for young love."

"I think you two might have still been together if it hadn't been for the tragedy of losing your other daughter."

Paolo sighed. "You could be right. When Sarah died our lives went into free-fall. By the time we found ourselves again we'd changed too much to reconnect."

"So it wasn't age but circumstances that got between you and Lydia. I'm not saying Katy and her young man are serious about each other, but they are far more likely to become so if they meet with opposition."

Paolo pulled her close and kissed the top of her head. "How did you get to be so wise?"

"I was born that way."

"Hmm, modesty becomes you," Paolo said. "By the way, do you have any advice to give on how to conduct a press conference when you have nothing to say?"

103

Jessica shook her head. "Nope, you're on your own with that one tomorrow."

"Not so wise then," Paolo said. "I'm going to need lots of moral support and tender handling tomorrow evening to help me over the trauma."

He felt Jessica's fingers running over his chest.

"I'll see what I can do," she said, "but don't forget I'll need to have a fairly early night tomorrow. I leave at six on Saturday morning."

"Damn, I'd forgotten about the conference. It's going to be a long fortnight without you."

CHAPTER FOURTEEN

Week Three – Friday 8th August to Thursday 14th August

The pretender watched the news showing yet another rerun of the press conference and nearly choked with rage. What the fuck did that stupid policeman know about anything? He was making out the murders had been committed by some mindless idiot without right and justice on his side. He wanted to scream, but he had to hold himself in check. He'd come this far, he wasn't going to mess it up now. The policeman was mouthing off about avenues of enquiry and following different leads, but that had to be a pack a lies. No way would they have worked it out yet. Only with the death of the final name on his list would it all become clear. Until then, they hadn't a hope in hell of catching him. He'd planned so carefully. What could they know of his reasons? What did anyone care about his suffering over the last decade? Nothing! Let the police spout about how close they are to catching him. After tonight they'll be scratching their heads again looking even more stupid than they do already.

He looked at the clock. It was nearly seven. Time to chat. He turned off the television and reached for his laptop. Powering it up, he slipped into the persona needed to snare the next on the list.

Searching under favourites, he clicked on ukgaychat.com and keyed in his username, StormyC, and password.

He looked to see who was online and quickly located Peter Bishop's username: the clergyman. They'd been chatting for over a month. Tonight it was time for them to meet.

The clergyman: Helloooooooo, I thought you'd deserted me. Where have you been?

StormyC: Busy, busy, busy. You know how it is.

The clergyman: I thought we were finally going to meet, but you disappeared. You haven't been on here for days. I missed you. I tried your mobile, but you didn't answer.

StormyC: I know. I've been away and forgot to take my charger. When the battery died I couldn't do anything about it. Only got back an hour ago and couldn't wait to chat. You're not sulking are you?

The clergyman: No way. I never sulk, darling. Happy little sparrow, that's me. I'm going to that new club tonight. The one that's been so heavily advertised. Sparklers. It would be a good place for a little rendezvous, n'est-ce pas?

StormyC: I was thinking of it, but parking is going to be a pain.

The clergyman: No, there's a multi-storey opposite.

StormyC: I hadn't thought of that. Is it safe at night?

The clergyman: It's where I'm planning to park. I can't see it being a problem.

StormyC: In that case I'll see you there. What time are you going?

The clergyman: I thought I'd get there about ten. No point in going early.

StormyC: I can't believe we're going to meet at last. Butterflies here.

The clergyman: Me too. Tell me, do you look as gorgeous in real life as you do in your avatar? I mean, that is you, isn't it? I will be able to recognise you?

StormyC: You'll know it's me. Don't worry about that. What about you? Is that a recent image, or are you really ten years older?

The clergyman: It's me, sweetie. I look exactly like my photo. Shall we meet somewhere first and go together, or meet up in the club.

StormyC: Let's meet in the club. I'm not sure what time I'll be able to get there.

The clergyman: You will come, won't you?

StormyC: Now that's a double entendre if ever I saw one. Let's hope we both do.

The clergyman: Naughty! I'll see you later.

StormyC: Definitely. Put your phone on vibrate. I'll call you when I'm inside.

The clergyman: No comment on that! lol

The pretender shut down his laptop and pondered what to wear. This was going to be his trickiest disguise yet. He'd been watching the gay bars to see what the standard dress code was, but it seemed to vary from place to place. He'd just have to hope his smartest outfit would be good enough to pass if anyone saw him hanging around outside. There was no fear of being recognised by Peter or anyone else from the chat room site. The avatar he'd been using he'd copied from one of the members of a chat room devoted to gays in Aberdeen. The only possible flaw in his plan would be if Peter didn't take the bait. If that happened he'd have to resort to plan B, which would mean a long wait hiding out in the car park.

Standing in the shadow of a shop window next to the club's entrance, the pretender watched as Peter Bishop crossed the road from the car park and entered the club. He had no intention of going in himself. Apart from the fact that years had passed since he'd been anywhere near a club of any kind, he'd never been inside a gay club. He'd most probably be picked out as heterosexual before he'd even ordered a drink.

Now that he knew Peter was inside, it was time to move across to the car park and find out which level he'd parked on. The pretender had taken the bus. Less chance of being caught on CCTV. It didn't matter too much if the cameras did catch a glimpse of him. Under the hoodie, he was wearing a dark wig, glasses and false teeth. He looked completely unlike his normal persona, but putting a car registration on film was a risk too far.

He strolled along the ground level, but couldn't see Peter's car. That was a relief. There was less chance of

107

being spotted on the upper floors. Down here, anyone passing could glance in. He took the stairs to level one, but the car wasn't there either. Better and better. He finally located it on level four, which was almost deserted, but luckily had a few other cars parked. Scanning the cars, he picked a black BMW furthest from the lifts and stairs as his decoy. It was parked mainly in shadow, which would make his story seem plausible. He needed to act quickly, just in case more clubbers decided to use the car park.

Pulling out his mobile phone, he called Peter's number. It rang for quite a while and he worried Peter might not have switched it to vibrate as he'd asked. A ring tone probably wouldn't be heard above the music. He sagged with relief when he heard Peter's voice.

"Where are you, sweet cheeks? I'm looking all around and can't spot you."

"I'm not in the club. I'm in the car park opposite."

"What are you doing there? Come over. It's buzzing in here."

"I can't. You'll never believe what I've done. I drove here wearing my glasses and went to put my contacts in just now and I've dropped one. I can't find it."

"You want me to come and help you look?"

"There's no need for that," he said, injecting as much pathos into his voice as he could. "I'll carry on searching. I just wanted you to know I hadn't stood you up. There'll be another time."

"Can't you put your glasses on and come over?"

"I would, but the contacts are brand new. Top of the range. Cost me a freaking fortune. I can't afford to replace them."

The pretender could hear the music throbbing in the background. This wasn't going to work. Peter wasn't going to fall for it.

"What level are you on?"

"What?"

"In the car park, what level are you on?"

"Level four."

"How's that for coincidence. I'm also parked on four. We're obviously meant to be together tonight. I'll be over in a few minutes."

"You are such a honey. I knew there was something special about you the moment we started chatting."

"See you in a bit," Peter said.

The pretender ended the call and pulled the syringe from his pocket. Filling the well with liquid, he knelt down and put it under the BMW. As long as he stayed on his knees Peter wouldn't be able to see him when he came up. He hoped the man wouldn't be long. Kneeling on the cold concrete was agony. Eventually, he heard the sound of the lift mechanism. The lift stopped and he listened as the doors opened.

Footsteps clattered loudly in the silence. Was it Peter, or someone come to claim a car?

"Where are you?"

"Over here," the pretender called back. "Black BMW. I'm looking underneath using my phone as a torch, but can't see the contact."

As the footsteps approached, the pretender reached for the syringe.

"Let's see if my eyes are better than yours," Peter said.

As a man's shadow fell on the car, the pretender turned and stabbed the syringe into Peter's thigh, depressing the plunger.

"What the fuck?"

Peter fell, his body shaking as it went into shock. Within seconds, he'd stopped moving. The pretender searched Peter's pockets until he found the car keys. Lifting himself up, he held onto the BMW for a few moments. Nausea made his stomach heave. Why wasn't this getting easier? Why wasn't he getting the rush of satisfaction he craved? Pulling himself together, he forced his feet to move in the direction of Peter's car. He needed to move quickly in case someone came up. Unlocking the car, he opened the driver's door as wide as possible, pushed the seat back to give him lots of room to manoeuvre and then went back to fetch

Peter's body.

Putting his hands under Peter's armpits, he heaved upwards. Fuck, for such a scrawny little man, he was really heavy. The pretender managed to drag Peter across the floor to his car and manhandled him into the driver's seat.

He felt all the pockets until he located Peter's phone, which he placed in his own pocket. As he did so, Peter's keys fell to the floor. This time he knew he didn't need to worry about picking them up. Peter Bishop certainly wouldn't be driving anywhere. Taking an envelope from his back pocket, he placed it on the dashboard and shut the door.

He'd reached the halfway mark.

***

Paolo glanced at the bedside clock. It was nearly eleven.

"What time have you set your alarm for tomorrow?"

Jessica snuggled deeper into his embrace. "Five. I need to leave here no later than six."

"I'd better go," Paolo said, but made no move to leave. This was as close to heaven as it was possible to be while still breathing. He didn't want to move.

"Mmm, in a minute," Jessica said.

"You'll be tired tomorrow if you don't go to sleep soon."

"I know, but I can nap on the train. I'll be fine. Can I ask you something? You don't have to tell me if you would rather not."

"Sure, what do you want to know?"

"Why do you never talk about your mother? You've told me lots about your dad and how much you missed him after he had his heart attack, but you never mention your mother. Were you not close to her?"

Paolo's body stiffened. "Are you asking as a shrink?"

Jessica sat up and looked at him. "No, I'm asking because I care about you. If you'd rather not talk about her, that's okay."

Paolo lay there thinking about his mother and how much

he'd loved her. He'd never yet put into words what happened the day she died and wasn't sure he could now. But he'd lost Lydia by not sharing his feelings, was he prepared to take the chance on losing Jessica the same way?

"I'm sorry, I shouldn't have asked," Jessica said, snuggling back down against his chest. "Let's talk about what we're going to do in two weeks' time when I get back."

"My mother was the only girl. She had four brothers and they were bad news."

Paolo felt Jessica's body go still. He was amazed the words had come out. He hadn't meant them to, but now he'd started he didn't want to stop.

"The family lived in Southeast London, all very close to each other, and I now know, but didn't at the time, the brothers were up to their necks in petty crime. My dad told me afterwards that he'd known they were into all sorts of minor stuff, but as long as they didn't drag my mother into it, he tolerated them for her sake."

He felt his pulse racing and tried to calm his breathing.

"Did she know what her brothers were doing?" Jessica asked.

"I don't know. Dad said she didn't, but she might have done and turned a blind eye to it. I'd like to think she believed they were innocent. She was a devout Catholic, but apparently the brothers were all regulars at mass and confession, so what did being devout prove?"

"What happened? Did she find out about them?"

Paolo shuddered. "She certainly knew before she died."

His mind went back to the day of her death, the events appearing in his mind on a loop, like a YouTube video set to continuous replay.

"I don't know what they did, but somehow they trespassed onto the territory of some really bad people. My uncles went into hiding, taking some property with them that belonged to the people they'd crossed. My mother didn't know where they were. If she had maybe…if she… she…"

111

He was surprised to find his face wet because he hadn't been aware he was crying. There were no sobs, no shuddering, just a constant flow of water from his eyes. Jessica's voice soothed him, telling him he didn't need to go on, but he did. If he didn't get it out now, the story would remain locked inside him forever.

"One morning she looked out of the window and stopped what she was doing. She stood like a statue, the butter knife in her hand and toast on the plate, but no longer bringing the two together. Then she dropped the knife and swore. My mother never swore and laid into anyone who did, but that morning was different. She turned and grabbed my shoulders, told me to go upstairs and hide in my wardrobe. Said I mustn't come down until she called me. No matter what. I should only come out for her voice, no one else's. I'll never forget the look on her face. She was terrified."

Still the silent tears flowed and Paolo wondered why he couldn't cry properly. Let the emotion out, but he'd never been able to.

"Whoever she'd seen started hammering on the front door. She shoved me towards the stairs, put her finger to her lips to tell me to keep quiet and then pointed up. I was so scared I scrambled up as fast as I could and climbed into the wardrobe, pulling the door behind me. I couldn't get it to close properly and kept expecting it to fly open and someone to reach in and drag me out. And all the time I was in there, I could see that look of terror on my mother's face. That was the last time I saw her alive."

"They killed her?"

Paolo nodded. "The police found me in the wardrobe hours later. They thought the killers had come looking for the whereabouts of whatever it was my uncles had stolen, but they couldn't prove anything. No one was prepared to stand up in court and say who they'd seen breaking down our front door. When my uncles came out of hiding I think they went after the killers. They certainly got involved in some gang warfare. After the funeral, my dad moved us here so that I wouldn't grow up close enough to be corrupted by that side of my family." He wiped his face with a tissue taken from the box on the bedside table. "It's because of them that I joined the police force. I wanted to be the complete opposite of the people who'd killed my mother and that included my uncles. They were every bit as responsible for her murder as the bastards who did it."

"Paolo?"

"Yes?"

"What did you hear while you were in the wardrobe? Have you ever told anyone?"

He shook his head.

"Do you want to tell me? It will get the pictures out of your mind and into the open."

Paolo's body trembled. He wanted to tell Jessica, but couldn't bear it if she turned away from him. Better that she knew the truth about him from the outset. He was a coward who'd saved himself and left his mother to face her killers.

"I can still hear her voice begging for them to stop. Screaming that she knew nothing – that she wasn't involved with her brothers' business. And even though I could hear how much pain she was in, I didn't do anything to save her. I hid in the wardrobe while she screamed and begged for mercy and I did nothing. I loved her so much but I left her alone to face them."

Waves of anger and guilt flooded his body. And then the dam burst. Huge raking sobs made him gasp for breath. He couldn't speak, couldn't move, just lay there feeling as he had so many years earlier. Helpless, terrified and a weakling for saving himself and letting his mother die.

He felt Jessica sit up and pull him roughly into her arms.

"It's okay," she said. "I'm here. I've got you."

"I did nothing, Jessica. Nothing."

"Paolo, look at me. *Now!* Look at me."

Scared he would see only contempt in her eyes, he forced himself to face her.

"What happened wasn't your fault."

The look of understanding on her face brought a fresh wave of emotion to the surface. Maybe he wasn't such a bad person. If someone like Jessica believed in him, knowing what she now did, maybe there was some hope for him after all.

"You were a child and if they'd known you were there they probably would have tortured you to try to make your mother talk. You did what she told you to do. There was nothing else you could have done. Not a thing. You've held this in for too long. It's time to forgive yourself."

As he sobbed in her arms, the six-year-old child that Paolo had once been, finally found peace.

CHAPTER FIFTEEN

Paolo woke up wondering what the noise was thundering through his brain. It stopped as suddenly as it started and he realised Jessica had reached out and switched off her alarm. Memories of his confession brought a hot flush surging through him. What must she think of him? His last waking thought was being held by her as he sobbed like a baby.

Would she make some excuse not to see him again when she got back from her conference? If she did, he wouldn't blame her. But then he remembered her words and the way she'd held him. He didn't want to lose her. Why oh why had he told her about his mother? Nobody else knew what he'd heard that day, not even Lydia and he'd been head over heels in love with her since he was a teenager. He'd lied to the police and his dad and said he hadn't heard a sound because he'd covered his ears with clothes, which was true, but his mother's screams had penetrated the padding he'd put round his head. Her pleas were a memory he'd kept hidden, never to come into the open, and now he'd told the one person he really wanted to see him in a good light.

Jessica turned back from the clock and laid her head on his chest.

"Good morning, sleepyhead. You'll have to get your own breakfast this morning. I'll eat on the train."

"Okay," he said.

"Hey, what's wrong?"

"Nothing, why?"

Jessica pushed herself up on one arm and looked straight into his eyes.

"Is it about what you told me last night? Scared I might judge you and find you wanting?"

Paolo nodded. He couldn't find the words to express how he felt. Vulnerable, scared and uncertain all came close.

"Paolo, this might be too soon. I don't know if this is going to scare you off, but I love you. I've loved you since last year and I didn't think I'd recover from the hurt when Lydia asked you to give your marriage another try. No, don't say anything," she said, putting her finger to his lips. "What happened to you as a child helped shape who you are today. I love the man you are now and I'd like to help the child you were to come to terms with your past."

He tried again to speak, but she leant forward and kissed him, stopping his words. "Don't say anything," she said when they came up for air. "We need to take things slowly. I just wanted you to know how I felt." She grinned. "You still have to make your own breakfast, though, because I have to get up, get showered, get dressed and get going."

He held her, sensing that he didn't need to say anything, and then let her go.

"I'm not staying here again if I'm condemned to do it yourself catering. Last time I was served breakfast in bed."

Jessica laughed. "In that case, you owe me. Next time will be at your place and you can return the favour."

He threw the covers off. "I'll put some clothes on while you get ready, then I'll drop you off at the station on my way home."

As the train pulled away, Paolo shivered in the early morning air. It was only the beginning of the second week in August. The weather should still be good. Then he reminded himself it was only six o'clock, so it wasn't surprising it was crisp. He headed back to his car. He'd be home in fifteen minutes. What to do first? Shower or sleep. The way he felt, sleep was definitely ahead in that race.

For the second time that morning, Paolo shook himself awake wondering what the hell the noise was that had disturbed him. His clock wasn't set, so what was it? It took a few moments to work out it was his phone vibrating against a glass. He'd switched off the ring tone, but left the vibrate setting on.

His head felt like someone had filled it with porridge. His brain was in there, but surrounded by so much sludge the thoughts couldn't get in or out. Suddenly the phone became still and the room held only a blessed silence, but then the vibrations started up again, even worse this time because the phone had buzzed itself across the bedside table and was cosying up to his keys. Maybe it was Jessica. He reached out a hand and snatched it up.

"Hello," he said.

"Paolo, that you?" Dave's voice demanded.

"Uh, huh, what d'you want, Dave? I was sleeping."

It was amazing how lack of sleep mirrored the way a hangover felt. Dry mouth, groggy head, shaking body.

"Sorry, but you've got to wake up. We've got another one. The car park opposite the new gay club. Cleaners found the body in a car this morning."

Paolo was suddenly wide awake. "What is it with this killer and making sure the bodies are discovered Saturday morning? Where are you?"

"I'm at home, but I'm about to head out to the crime scene. Want me to pick you up on the way?"

"Yes, please," said Paolo, climbing out of bed with the phone held to his ear. "By the time you get here I'll have had time to wake myself up under a steaming hot shower."

He switched the phone off, his mind buzzing with questions, but there was no point in speculating. He needed to get over to the crime scene. Maybe this one would point them towards something that linked the first two victims.

By the time Dave knocked at his door, Paolo had showered, dressed, swallowed a cup of instant coffee and had just finished working his way through a bowl of cornflakes.

"Come in for a moment, Dave. I intend to call CC, but didn't want to wake her too early. I think it would be a good idea to get as many views of the crime scene and surrounding area as possible. Maybe one of us will pick up on something the others miss."

Dave nodded. "We certainly haven't got very far on the first two murders, have we?"

Paolo shook his head and picked up his phone, hitting speed dial for CC's number.

"Mpft?" CC said.

"Good morning to you, too."

"Sir?" she said, and Paolo could hear she was instantly awake. "What's up?"

He gave her the bare details he knew. "I want you to meet us at the car park. Can you call Andrea and get her to come over as well. We need all hands on this one."

"Er, yes, sir. I'll, er, call Andrea. Yes."

"Do you have a problem with that?" Paolo asked.

"Oh, no, sir. No problem at all."

Paolo could hear reticence in CC's voice and was about to comment when he heard a woman's voice in the background asking what the call was about. He couldn't swear to it, because he didn't yet know her very well, but he was fairly sure it was Andrea speaking.

Well, well, he thought. We live and learn. As long as relationships didn't cause problems in the office, he had no issues with work colleagues getting involved outside the station. Sadly, all too often when the relationship broke down, so too did the ability to work together.

"Come on, Dave. Let's see if there's anything useful to find on this one."

The car park was already taped off when they got there, but that didn't stop onlookers from straining their necks trying to see round corners into the car park. One man was remonstrating with the uniformed officer manning the tape.

"I'm telling you to let me in. You can't do this. I need my car. I'll go to the press and tell them how you treat members of the public."

The officer shook his head. "I'm sorry, sir, it's more than my job is worth to let you in. This is a crime scene."

"What the fuck has that got to do with me? There's my

car. Right there," he said, pointing to a dark blue Saab. "It's nowhere near your poxy crime scene."

Paolo stepped forward. "What seems to be the problem, sir?"

The man whirled round. "You're the copper who was on television yesterday. Can you please tell this idiot that I need my car? He seems to think he's got the right to keep me from going in there."

Paolo shrugged. "Sorry, but that's exactly what he does have, the right to keep everyone out. We'll be through here in about an hour. Perhaps you could come back then?"

"I don't want to come back in an hour. I want my fucking car now. I only left it there because I'd had too much to drink to drive it home. See what happens when you obey the law? You get treated like a criminal."

"Were you in the club across the road last night?" Paolo asked.

"What's it to you if I was? Typical copper, picking on anyone who's a bit different."

Paolo sighed. "Shall we start this conversation again? Would you like to step inside the tape so that we can have a chat about whom you saw in the club last night? You might be able to help us."

"Are you saying it was a clubber who got done in? It doesn't surprise me. They're a right anti-gay bunch of shits in this town and your lot don't do anything to protect our rights."

Paolo was beginning to feel as if he was pushing a boulder uphill. "Sir, were you or were you not in the club last night?"

"Yes. There's no need to get narky with me."

"Dave, nip upstairs and see if the deceased was carrying any identification with a photograph."

"If he was in the club, he'd have an ID card with his photo on," the man said.

"Thank you, Mr?"

"Williams. Cornwall Williams."

Paolo's face must have betrayed his surprise because the

man laughed.

"I know, stupid, isn't it? Apparently it's where I was conceived. Like anyone wants to advertise where their parents did it."

"Mr Williams, please come through. When my colleague comes down, I'd like you to have a look at the ID card, if there is one, and tell me if you remember the man from last night. Then, as long as you leave your contact details, I can't see any reason why you can't retrieve your car and enjoy the rest of the weekend."

Dave reappeared with a club card ID in a plastic evidence envelope. He passed it to Paolo.

"Why's he dressed like a spaceman? It's not contagious up there, is it?"

"No, Mr Williams, that's standard wear so that we don't contaminate the crime scene. Now, did you see this man?" he asked, holding out the ID card.

"Yeah, I remember him. He was only in the club a short time, but instead of dancing or drinking, he wandered around as if he was searching for someone. I don't mean like he was looking to get picked up. It was more as if he was searching for a particular person."

"What made you notice him?" Paolo asked.

"Well, you can see he's an oldie. Older than me and my mates, anyway. He stood out a bit. The club caters for my age group mainly. Early twenties. Anyway, as I say, he didn't stay long."

"Did he leave with anyone?"

"I don't think so. I wasn't really watching him and if he hadn't been creeping around looking in all the corners of the room, I probably wouldn't have noticed him at all. Oh, hang on. I've just remembered. He must have got a phone call because he stood in the middle of the dance floor like a prize pillock and people had to dance round him, but I don't know if he left straight after that. I don't *think* I saw him again."

"Thank you, Mr Williams. You've been most helpful. Give your name, address, phone numbers and email to the constable and then you can go. With your car," Paolo added when he saw the belligerent look return to the man's face.

"Let's go upstairs, Dave. CC and Andrea can find us when they arrive. Who's on duty? Dr Royston?"

"No, sir. It's Chris. Apparently Dr Royston wasn't answering her phone. Chris isn't too charmed. He's not supposed to be on call this weekend."

Paolo shrugged and slipped the ID card into his pocket. "Barbara covers for him far more often than she should. So what if he's had to give up a Saturday to come in. He'll live, which is more than we can say about our victim. Let's see what Chris can tell us."

They walked up to level four and Paolo donned protective coveralls, to match those Dave was wearing, before stepping out into the car parking area. There were already evidence markers in place on the concrete floor and the forensic photographer was busy taking image after image.

Paolo waited until he was sure the man didn't want to cross their path and then went to a parked car, where the pathologist was studying the body.

"Hi, Chris, what can you tell us?"

"Not very much at the moment, except that he wasn't in the car when he was injected."

"How can you tell?" Paolo asked.

"Point of entry of the needle," Chris said. "The serum —"

"Insulin?"

Chris frowned. "Too soon to tell. The serum was injected here, on the outer right thigh, where the thigh is almost touching the seat. The angle is impossible if he was sitting here. He would need to be standing up for anyone to inject at that precise point."

"Okay, so we need to find where the attack took place."

For the first time, Chris smiled. "I can show you where I think it happened," he said. "Come with me."

Paolo and Dave followed him to the far side of the floor where a black BMW was parked.

"I think this might be the spot. We found a syringe under the car. I'd be amazed if it wasn't the murder weapon. Also, I'd be willing to bet my house that those fingerprints on the car's door belong to the killer."

Paolo thought he was probably right, but until they had someone to test the prints against, they weren't as helpful as they could have been.

"I take the syringe is already bagged for evidence?"

Chris nodded. "And the envelope from the dashboard. Same as the first two, only this one says three out of six. Anyway, I'm finished here. We'll be taking the body away now."

"Any idea when the autopsy will be? Will you be doing it?"

"To be honest with you, I have no idea on either count. Dr Royston needs to get her act together. I don't know when she's coming in half the time these days. I shouldn't have been on call this weekend. I had plans for today."

Paolo watched as he stomped back to the victim's body.

"Not a happy camper, that one," Dave said.

"No," Paolo agreed, but he couldn't stop thinking about how out of character it was of Barbara to leave her assistant to cover for her. She might rip his head off, but he decided to call in at her apartment later. Something was definitely out of kilter with her and he had a strong feeling she needed help to get through it, whatever 'it' might be.

At that moment CC and Andrea came through the level entrance. Paolo shook off thoughts of helping his friend. Right now he had a crime scene to manage. He waited for the two women to walk over.

"CC, I want you and Andrea to track down the club's owner and get the names and addresses of his bouncers. The victim's name was Peter Bishop and we have a witness who saw him in the club last night. Call on the bouncers. See if you can establish time of arrival and departure. Did they see him with anyone? You know the questions. Here, take his club membership ID card with you," he said, handing over the evidence bag.

"Dave, you come with me."

Paolo led the way to where a young policeman was questioning an older man. Judging by the cart next to them, the older man was the cleaner who'd found the body.

"Dave, you talk to the constable to bring us up to speed on what he's found out so far. I'll have a chat with the witness."

Paolo tapped the uniformed officer on the shoulder and signalled for him to go with Dave, then turned to the older man.

"Good morning. I'm Detective Inspector Paolo Storey, in charge of this investigation. I know you've already told the constable everything, but would you mind going through it again with me?"

"Is good."

"Thank you," Paolo said. "Let's start with your name. I can hear from your accent you're not originally from around here, so you might need to spell it out for me."

"I Polish. Name is hard. You give paper. I put."

Paolo handed over his pad. AMBROZIJ MACIEJEWSKI the man wrote out in capital letters.

"Thank you, Mr Maciej...Maciej..."

"Is Maciejewski. Is hard for you."

"It is, sir. Thank you. Now, can you tell me what you found here this morning?"

"I come early always Saturday. I begin up," he said, pointing skywards, "and I end down." He swept his arm as if encompassing the world, ending by pointing at the floor.

"You start on the highest level and work your way down through the floors?"

"*Tak*," he said, nodding.

"What happened when you reached this floor?"

"I broom. See man in car. *Jak* to powiedzieć? Is not let."

"It's not allowed?"

"*Tak*! Is not allowed for sleep in car. I..." the man mimed tapping on the car window, "but he no wake. I do more loud. He no wake. I pomyśleć he dead. I call

123

policja."

"Thank you, sir."

Paolo continued to question the man, but it quickly became clear he hadn't seen anything or anyone before he found the body. Having got the man's address and phone numbers, he allowed him to go home.

"I no do rest?"

Paolo shook his head. "Not today."

"I no paid if no do rest. Boss he say no do, no pay."

"Don't worry about your boss. I'll explain to him why you weren't able to finish cleaning. You will get paid for today. I guarantee it."

The cleaner went to push his cart away, but Paolo stopped him.

"Sorry, sir. You'll have to leave that here for the time being. We'll make sure it gets put back wherever it needs to go."

He watched as the man made his way towards the stairs, thinking how hard life must be for anyone wanting to make a living in a country where they couldn't communicate in the official language. That's what it must have been like for his great-great-grandfather when he first came over from Naples in 1892. Funny, he'd never thought about it like that before. Did his Italian forebear arrive with any knowledge of English? Probably not. He forced thoughts of his ancestors out of his mind, but thinking of his Italian roots brought up memories of last night's conversation with Jessica.

Dave came back, effectively shutting off Paolo's uncomfortable thoughts. Paolo sighed with relief. That road was still too painful to travel easily.

"What have you got, Dave?"

"The vic's name we already know, but his car reg checks out with a Peter Bishop living here in Bradchester. I've got the address and phone number. I've tried it, but just get the answering machine."

"Okay, we'll leave forensics to finish up here and pay a visit to his home. Have you got his house keys?"

In answer, Dave held up a bunch of keys. "Found under the car. House, car and various others."

"We can work through the rest once we know more about him. You get another chance to play with your Sat Nav."

"I don't know why you don't like them. Beats not knowing where you are all the time."

They walked over to the stairwell. Just before putting his foot on the top step, Paolo turned and grinned. "I always know where I am, I just don't always know how to get to where I'm going. By the way, have you arranged for us to collect the CCTV footage?"

"Yes, sir. It's not held on the premises. It's covered by a security firm who have contracts with all the city car parks. I've spoken to their office and it's ready for collection."

"Great, we'll stop off there on the way to Peter Bishop's place."

Half an hour later they pulled up outside a well-cared for apartment block in Westside, one of the newer developments in Bradchester.

"Have you noticed, all three of our victims lived in nice areas?" Dave said as he locked the car.

Paolo nodded. "We don't know yet what Peter Bishop did for a living, but I'm willing to bet it was in a professional capacity and earned him a good living. I've got a feeling the missing link in this case is to do with what the victims did, rather than who they were."

"What makes you think that, sir?"

Paolo shrugged. "Could be intuition, could be desperation, just wanting to see a link where none exists. I'm baffled and I don't like it."

Dave touched the fob to the security sensor and the door latch sprang open. They walked into a spacious central lobby smelling faintly of lavender. Lush greenery grew from planters along one wall facing gleaming lift doors on the opposite side.

Paolo contrasted this entrance with that of the tower

block where he and Dave visited Conrad Stormont's ex-wife. It could have been used in a television documentary showing the true divisions in society. Coming home to a place like this would make anyone want to care for their environment. Living in the council block would have exactly the opposite effect.

"Which of the flats is his?" he asked.

"Number 23. Lift or stairs?"

"Lift," Paolo said. "We've climbed enough stairs recently. Let's give our legs a rest."

The lift opened onto a long corridor and Paolo couldn't help but make another comparison. There was no litter to step over. Instead, the parquet corridor flooring shone with cleanliness.

"Do you ever feel life isn't fair to those on the bottom rung of society?" Paolo asked as Dave tried various keys in the lock before the door swung open.

"Are you all right, sir?"

"Yes, why?"

"You seem a bit pensive."

"Do I? Mmm, I suppose I am. Don't worry about it," he said, grinning. "I don't think it's catching."

The apartment wasn't as big as Paolo had expected, but it was nicely laid out with two bedrooms, both with en suite bathrooms, a lounge and spacious kitchen/diner, all leading off from a square central hallway. The furnishings were clearly expensive, but not designer. Paolo got the impression Peter Bishop had been comfortable in his own skin. There was nothing that stood out as trying to make a statement. The overall feeling was one of a man who didn't feel the need to make out he was anything other than himself.

He noticed the red light winking on the answering machine and pressed the replay button, but none of the messages seemed to be personal. Paolo slipped the tiny tape into an evidence bag. You could never be certain that what sounded innocuous really was.

He moved to the laptop and switched it on, but it only

126

loaded as far as the password prompt.

"How good are you with computers, Dave?"

"Useless, sir. I can switch mine on, play games, answer emails and surf the web. That's about it. Why's that?"

"This one is password protected. Is there any way past that?"

Dave frowned. "There is, but I think we'll need the IT people to do it. Mind you, he might have his passwords written down somewhere. A lot of people do."

Paolo searched through the drawers of the computer desk, but didn't find anything that looked like a password. What he did find was some headed notepaper.

"I think I know what our victim did for a living. Look at this, Peter Bishop & Associates Solicitors. The address is in the law district. When we've finished up here we'll see if any of those keys fit his offices. Not that we can go in without permission. You know how touchy the legal bods can be about client confidentiality and keeping their secrets to themselves."

He dialled the number on the letterhead. After half a dozen rings, an answering machine kicked in outlining the hours of business. Paolo was about to put the phone down when the voice continued.

"...for matters of urgency, please call..."

Paolo scribbled down the number and then ended the call. Keying in the new number, he prayed it wouldn't ring through to this flat. He sighed with relief when a woman's voice answered.

"Yes, can I help you?"

"I hope so. This is Detective Inspector Paolo Storey. To whom am I speaking?"

"Constance Myers. What is this about, please? Is there a problem at the offices? Have we been broken into?"

"No, it's nothing like that. Are you the key holder for Mr Bishop?"

"Not exactly. I'm a paralegal. I work for Mr Bishop and handle out of hours calls if they are urgent."

"Would it be possible to meet us at the offices in, say, an

hour?"

"Not without Mr Bishop's permission. I'd have to call him first and come back to you on this."

No matter how many times he had to do it, Paolo hated this part of his job.

"I'm calling from his home. I'm sorry, Ms Myers, but Mr Bishop is dead. It's in connection with his death that we need access to his offices."

He heard the woman gasp as the news hit home.

"What? I mean, how? I...this can't be true."

"I wish that was the case, but I'm afraid Mr Bishop is dead."

"Okay," she said, sounding to Paolo as if she was in a state of shock. "I'll be there."

She put the phone down without saying goodbye. Another person's life affected by murder. It was never just the victims and their families. The ripples spread much further than that. On the subject of family, they didn't even know if Peter Bishop had any, but he was fairly sure Constance Myers would have the answers to those questions.

They methodically checked each room, but uncovered nothing more interesting than some gay porn and a few erotic paperbacks in the same genre.

"We can drop the laptop at the station on the way to Peter Bishop's offices," Paolo said. "Let's hope we uncover more in his office than we have here. Unless there is something on his laptop, we're no further forward in finding a link with the other victims."

In Paolo's experience, people rarely resembled the image he had of them from hearing voices on the phone. Constance Myers was the exception that proved the rule. From their brief conversation he'd built a picture of a thin, angular woman, with stern features and short grey hair. When they arrived at the offices of Peter Bishop & Associates the woman waiting for them in the reception area could have been created from Paolo's imagination.

"Hello, we spoke on the phone. I'm Detective Inspector Paolo Storey and this is Detective Sergeant Dave Johnson. I'm sorry to be the bearer of such bad news."

Constance blanched. A hand fluttered to her throat and then fell back to her side.

"I simply cannot believe it. It doesn't seem possible."

"We'll take as little of your time as we can, Ms Myers. Would you please tell us which of these keys belong to the office? We need to eliminate them from the bunch."

She held out her hand for the keys. "I can tell you what each of them is for," she said. "I have looked after Mr Bishop since he started out on his own six years ago." She held the keys in one hand and used the other to indicate. "These two are for his apartment, but you must already know that if you've been there. This one is for the front office door. This is for Mr Bishop's office. The small one is for his desk. This one is for his filing cabinet and the other is his car key."

Paolo took the keys back. "Thank you," he said. "Do you have duplicates?"

"Of his office keys, yes, but not his car and home. He kept the spares for those in his desk."

"Would you mind unlocking his office? We need to look through his desk and filing cabinet."

"No, I'm sorry; I cannot allow you to open the filing cabinet. There is client information in there that is confidential. If you want access to those files, you'll have to get a court order."

Paolo sighed. He'd expected that response, but it had been worth a try.

"We won't touch the filing cabinet, but do need to search his desk."

Constance nodded and unlocked the inner office door. The organised chaos that met his eyes was completely unexpected. After the neatness of Peter Bishop's home, the stacks of files around the floor, many of which looked in danger of toppling over, seemed to belong to a different person.

"You cannot touch any of the files," Constance said, hovering in the doorway. "I'm afraid I will have to watch to make sure client confidentiality is maintained."

"I understand," Paolo said, moving to the desk, which was covered in pieces of paper, yet more files, yellow post it notes, slips with telephone numbers and call messages, pens, pencils and legal pads.

"How did he work in this chaos?"

"Mr Bishop knew where every scrap of paper could be found. He was an amazing man. When I first started with him, I used to tidy up before I went home, but he asked me not to. He said if he put things down, he'd be able to find them again. If I moved papers, he wouldn't be able to keep their whereabouts in his head."

Paolo could hear the emotion in her voice. She was barely holding herself together.

"Do you know if Mr Bishop knew Professor Edwards or Mr Fulbright, either socially or professionally?"

"They're the two men who were murdered recently, aren't they? Was Mr Bishop killed by the same person?"

Paolo looked up from the clutter on the desk. "It is possible. We won't know for certain until after the autopsy, but it is looking that way."

"But why? Who would want to hurt Mr Bishop? Such a gentle, caring man, why would anyone harm him?"

"That's what we're here to find out. Does either name ring any bells with you?"

She shook her head. "No, I'm afraid not. Oh dear, I simply cannot believe this is happening."

Paolo handed the keys to Dave. "Open up the desk drawers, see if there's anything in there to help us. I'll continue going through the stuff on top here."

But a careful search of the desk and papers lying on top revealed nothing of obvious interest. Paolo straightened his back. It had been too much to hope that a piece of paper headed 'this is who killed me' might turn up, but even a tiny clue would have been better than nothing, which was what they had.

"We'll leave you to lock up, Ms Myers. If necessary, we will obtain a warrant to search the filing cabinet, but that doesn't seem probable at the moment. Are there any family members who need to be informed?"

"Only his sister living in America. I'd better let her know. She'll want to come back for the funeral."

"Could you give me her details? I'll make contact and break the news to her."

She scribbled the name and phone number on a pad, tore off the page and handed it to him.

"He was such a gentleman – in the old-fashioned sense of the word. He was gentle and kind and a wonderful human being."

She walked with them to the door and Paolo wondered if it was good manners on her part, or just making sure they didn't double back and peer into places she'd deemed inaccessible.

"Thank you for coming in and assisting us," he said. "I'm sorry for your loss. You obviously cared very much for Mr Bishop."

Paolo could see she was battling to keep her emotions in check. Despite her best efforts, a single tear fell as she gave a tremulous smile. "He was the son I never had."

In the car heading back to the station, Paolo couldn't get Constance Myers' last words from his head. The pain that humans caused to others never ceased to trouble him. He often wondered how killers were able to sleep at night. The irony of it was, the killer would probably sleep better tonight than Constance Myers.

"You know, Dave, I'm coming more and more to the idea that it's what these people did, rather than who they were. The only connection we can establish between them is an occupational one. All three were educated men working in the professions."

Dave indicated to make a turn and the tick, tick, tick played in Paolo's mind as why, why, why? But no answer came.

As they pulled up outside the station, CC and Andrea were getting out of CC's car a couple of parking bays further along.

"Good timing," Paolo called out as he got out of Dave's car. "I hope you've got more than we have. Our search turned up less than nothing."

"Don't forget the laptop, sir," Dave said.

"I haven't forgotten it, but I'm not expecting miracles from it. If his home and workplace are anything to go by, the laptop is also going to be a washout."

They walked into the station together. CC, Dave and Andrea each went to their desks. Paolo stood in front of the board where the investigation details were written up, but it seemed like they had precious little to help them on there.

"While we're waiting for the laptop results, let's get up to date with what we've found out today. Peter Bishop, solicitor, no obvious connection to either of the other two victims. Our killer seems to have a penchant for Friday murders. Is this significant? One a week for three weeks, all killed on Friday, but discovered on Saturday? I think, yes, that's his pattern."

He stopped writing and turned back. "What else?"

"He injects them in the leg, but not like a nurse or doctor would," CC called out. "The autopsy reports on the first two show the needle was stabbed in, rather than put in gently."

"Good point. From what Chris said this morning, the angle of this one also points to someone stabbing the victim with the syringe. So, not a medical professional. What else? How did you two get on with the club owner and bouncers?"

CC glanced at her notes before answering. "The owner was very helpful, but wasn't at the club last night. He gave us the names of the two bouncers who were on duty. One of them was inside for most of the night, looking for troublemakers, but doesn't remember seeing Peter Bishop. If the victim wasn't causing problems, there was no reason for the bouncer to notice him. We were luckier with the other bouncer, he gave us the approximate time of arrival and departure. The reason Peter Bishop stuck in his mind was because he looked considerably older than the average club goer. When our victim left after only being inside for less than an hour, the bouncer thought it might be because he'd felt out of place. Not that Peter Bishop said anything to that effect, that was simply the bouncer's take on it."

"He didn't see him talk to anyone before going in, or meeting anyone when he came out?"

CC shook her head. "No, he headed straight over to the car park."

"Okay, the witness this morning said he was on the phone before he left. We need his phone records. Andrea, can you get on to that, please?"

She nodded. "Will do."

"None of this seems to take us any further forward." He looked up as the office door opened and one of the IT team came in carrying the laptop and several sheaves of paper. "This looks interesting, James. Please tell me you were able to get into the laptop."

James laughed. "No offence, sir, but a child could have unlocked this. His password was PASSWORD. It was the first thing I tried."

Paolo realised he must be less computer savvy than the average child, because that would never have occurred to him.

"Anything interesting?"

"I've printed out some conversations Peter Bishop had on a gay chat site. He's been corresponding with a user called StormyC for several weeks. Getting to know each other. They arranged to meet up last night at the club. But this is the page that will interest you most. It's from an earlier conversation, shortly after they got chatting. Peter Bishop gives his real name and asked StormyC for his."

He handed Paolo a transcript of the conversation. Paolo smiled.

"At last! We've got a connection between two of our three victims – the professor and Peter Bishop. Listen to this: the person Peter Bishop arranged to meet up with last night called himself Conrad Stormont."

As his team cheered, Paolo waved his hands to bring them back down to earth.

"Yes, this is great. A breakthrough at last, but we need a connection now between Conrad Stormont and Mr Fulbright. Two out of three ain't bad, as the song goes, but we have to find that third connection. Either between Fulbright and Stormont, or Fulbright and one of the other two victims. Andrea, you're our research whiz kid, I want you to dig deep and see what you can come up with."

"Yes, sir."

"Any news yet on the Stormont children's grandmother?" Paolo asked, knowing Andrea would have told him if there had been, but needing the confirmation that nothing was being overlooked.

"Still no answer from her phone, but if she's been away on holiday, she might come back today, being Saturday."

"Okay," Paolo said. "Keep on it. I'm sorry for dragging you all in on the weekend, but you can blame our killer for that."

"As if we didn't already have reasons enough to hate him," CC called out.

"I've got a visit I need to make," Paolo said. "I'll be back in an hour or so. With a bit of luck you'll all astound me with masses of new information."

"Have you forgotten you haven't got your car here?" Dave said. "Want me to drive you?"

Paolo didn't want to draw attention to his concerns about Barbara and having Dave take him to her apartment would do exactly that.

"I'd rather borrow your keys, if that's all right with you."

"Of course," Dave said, throwing the keys over. "Take care of it. I'll need it tonight to take Rebecca out."

Paolo pulled up outside Barbara's house without any clear idea of what to say. All he knew was that she wasn't acting like herself. From a dedicated person who never took time off, she was suddenly not showing up when she was on call. Her personality had undergone such a radical change, he barely recognised her as the same person. Something was definitely wrong. He just hoped she'd open up enough to let him help her through whatever it was.

He walked up the short drive to her front door and rang the bell. After a few minutes, he rang it again. Then again. Her car was outside, so she was definitely in. There was no way he was leaving until he'd at least spoken to her.

Pulling out his phone, he hit speed dial for her mobile. He could hear the tune playing inside the house. It sounded like it was coming from upstairs. The call disconnected. She must have refused it.

He rang the bell again and held his finger on it until he felt his phone buzz for an incoming text.

Please go away. I am tired and need to sleep. I'll see you on Monday and tell you all. Okay? Barb x

Paolo looked up and could see the faint silhouette of a woman's body through the bedroom curtain. He nodded and the figure moved back.

He had no idea what the hell was going on, but at least Monday was only a couple of days away.

CHAPTER SIXTEEN

Paolo put the phone down and rested his arms on his desk. He and his team had worked flat out over the weekend, but they hadn't moved much closer to finding the connections they needed to put Conrad Stormont in the frame for Edwin Fulbright's murder. Maybe today would bring a change in their fortunes. Apart from anything else, it was easier to get answers on a Monday than it was over the weekend when other lucky buggers were off work and relaxing.

He picked up the phone again and dialled Barbara's office. The line rang on unanswered. Paolo sighed. It was now gone ten and she still wasn't in. She was usually the first in and last out. Beginning to feel like a stalker, he replaced the receiver and promised himself he wouldn't call again. She'd get in touch with him when she was ready to share whatever it was that was bringing her down. Standing up, he vowed to give her the space she needed.

A quick glance through the window separating his office from the open plan room housing his team showed them all with their heads down, hard at work. Andrea had slotted into the group as if she'd been there for years instead of just a week. And she was every bit as good at research as he'd been told she was. Just as well, he thought. There was an awful lot of digging into the past that needed to be done for this case. He looked at his watch. Almost time for the team meeting. He walked round his desk, picking up his notes on the way and had just reached the doorway when the phone on his desk rang. At last! Barbara must have decided to respond to one of the fifty million messages it felt like he'd left.

"Barbara, where have you…"

"Sorry to disappoint you, but it's one of the other women in your life."

"Jessica! Sorry, I thought it was...well, obviously, you've picked up on who I thought it was."

"Have you heard nothing from her?"

Paolo moved back to his desk and sat on the edge.

"No, nothing since a text on Saturday. I've been calling her this morning, but no answer from her office and I just get voicemail on her home phone and mobile. But never mind that, now. How's it going up there in the frozen north?"

She laughed. "Not so much frozen as fabulous. The sun is shining; it's a beautiful day and I would love nothing more than taking a walk around the loch. Instead of which, I'm about to meet up with a group of single-minded psychiatrists to discuss matters so deep Nessie might be lurking down there."

"I wish I could be there."

"Discussing matters of the brain?"

"No," he said, choking on the image that conjured up. "Taking a walk around the loch."

"Maybe we should do that one weekend," she suggested. "Anyway, I can't stop on. My conference is due to start in five minutes. I just wanted to say hi."

"I'm glad you did," Paolo said.

As he replaced the receiver and retrieved his papers, it occurred to Paolo that he couldn't remember the last time he'd taken a break. When this case is over, he vowed, a couple of weeks in Scotland with Jessica would be on the cards. It was time he looked up his Scottish relatives. He still had a few family members on his dad's side.

He moved out into the main office and walked to the board showing the case information. As he put down his papers on the desk next to it, Andrea called out.

"Sir, I've got some news for you."

"Good," he said, glancing at the board. "We certainly need information to fill in some of these gaps. Okay, listen up, everyone. Let's recap where we are."

He waited for the room to fall silent and then quickly ran through the few details they knew. Unfortunately, it didn't take him very long.

"Right, Andrea, what have you got for us?" he said when he'd finished.

"I'm not sure it's going to help the case, sir, but you wanted to find out what happened to the Stormont children?"

"Yes, did you finally get hold of their grandmother?"

"I did. As I suspected, she's been away on holiday and took her granddaughter with her."

"Not the two boys?"

"No, she only has the granddaughter living there. Apparently she found it too difficult to cope with three children at her age, so kept the girl and sent the boys back to live with their mother."

"Poor boys," Paolo said. "Have you arranged to speak to the daughter?"

She nodded. "Yes, sir, she said we can go over there any time today."

"Good," he said.

"Did the grandmother have anything to say about her ex-son-in-law?"

Andrea laughed. "Nothing it's worth repeating, sir. The devil himself isn't as evil as Conrad Stormont. According to her the mess her daughter is in today is a direct result of Conrad's actions."

Paolo picked up a note of disapproval in her voice. "You don't agree?"

"No, sir. From what we've uncovered, the ex-Mrs Stormont put herself and her unhappiness ahead of trying to do the best for her children. I feel sorry for her, but that doesn't stop me from thinking she brought a certain amount of misery on herself – and on her children, too."

"You could be right. Okay, moving on. Are we any closer to making a connection between Conrad Stormont and the surgeon, Edwin Fulbright?"

She shook her head. "I've searched through everything I

can find to do with Mr Fulbright's charity work, his marriages, his private practice and I've now got someone at the hospital going through his early cases covering the period when Conrad Stormont was there under the aegis of Professor Edwards."

"Good thinking. They might have crossed paths then, although I wouldn't have thought surgeons and psychiatrists dealt with the same cases."

"No, sir, but maybe one of the psychiatric patients needed surgery unrelated to their psychiatric condition and that brought Stormont and Fulbright into contact. Or maybe Mr Fulbright operated on someone and then referred that patient to Professor Edwards because he'd noticed the patient was unstable in some way. The hospital's administrator has allowed one of his staff to cross-check the patient lists of Professor Edwards and Mr Fulbright for that period. In fact, she is covering the time just before and just after Conrad Stormont was at the hospital, in case it was a patient who was already being treated, or one who had surgery just after Stormont left."

"I don't know how you've managed to get the hospital administrator in your pocket, but I'm impressed."

Andrea laughed. "Oh, that was easy, sir. I told him if he didn't get someone at the hospital to do it, you'd probably demand to see the records yourself and that would involve a court order and then a massive police presence. He saw the wisdom of keeping things quiet. As you know, he's very sensitive about the hospital attracting negative publicity. He has been ever since that young girl was murdered in her hospital bed last year and the papers were full of outrage over it."

Paolo knew better than anyone that the hospital hadn't been to blame over that. He'd placed a WPC outside the girl's room and yet the killer had waltzed in dressed as a nurse. If anyone had been to blame, it was him for not realising the danger the child had been in.

"Good work, Andrea."

"CC, I want you to continue searching through Peter

Bishop's laptop. There might be a link between Mr Fulbright and Peter Bishop we've overlooked. Get onto IT and see if they've been able to trace where Stormont was when he made contact with Bishop. Andrea, keep digging into Fulbright's extended family. One of them might know Stormont. Dave, you and I will go to call on Stormont's ex-mother-in-law and have a chat to his daughter."

The grandmother's home was on one of the housing estates that had sprung up in Bradchester during a property boom in the eighties. Detached houses surrounded by small, but generally well maintained, gardens seemed to indicate a cared-for neighbourhood. Dave pulled up outside number 53 Sunnybrook Terrace and switched off the engine.

"This is a bit nicer than where her daughter's living with her new husband. No wonder Granny took the kids in," Dave said.

"Yes, but from what Andrea said, she no longer has the two boys with her. Shall we go and find out why?"

As they walked towards the house, the front door opened and a teenager, maybe a year or so younger than Katy, stood on the step.

"Are you the police?" she called out.

Paolo pulled his warrant card out to show her. "Yes, is your grandmother at home?"

The girl nodded. "Granny said to let you in. We saw the car pull up and guessed it was you. She's so pleased you didn't come in a proper police car, but I think it would have been great to shake this place up a bit. It's like a morgue round here. I'm Celine, by the way."

She stood back and let them pass.

"Go in the front room. Granny's waiting. Should I come in, too?"

"Yes, please," said Paolo. "I'd like to ask you a few questions about your father."

She followed them into the room. "You were right, Granny. It was the police. They said they want to talk to me as well, so there's no point in trying to send me upstairs."

Paolo stepped forward and held out his card. "Mrs Hastings? I'm Detective Inspector Paolo Storey and this is Detective Sergeant Dave Johnson. We'd like to ask you a few questions about your former son-in-law."

"Take a seat, both of you," she said. "I don't know what you want me to say. I haven't seen him in years. Not since he ruined my daughter's life."

"Have you any idea where he might be now?"

"Not a clue," Mrs Hastings said. "And I don't want to know."

"What about you, Celine? Have you kept in touch with your dad?"

Paolo watched her face to see if she looked uncomfortable speaking in front of her grandmother, but she didn't appear to be fazed by the question.

"I don't even know what he looks like and I'm not interested in finding out. He buggered off..."

"Celine!" Mrs Hastings said. "I won't have that language in my house. I've told you that before."

"Sorry, Granny. My dad left us when I was only three. I've lived with Granny since I was four. I barely know my mother but at least I see her once a year. Granny takes us both out for a meal on my birthday, as long as Mum is sober and providing she can get away from that ape she married. But I wouldn't recognise my dad if I sat next to him on a bus."

"What about your brothers? Do you keep in touch with them? They might know more about where your dad is."

She shook her head. "They went back to live with my mum years ago and we sort of lost touch."

"You must miss them," Paolo said.

Celine laughed. "You have got to be joking. I hated it when they lived here. They were always fighting and yelling. Poor Granny couldn't bear it, could you?" she finished, turning to give her grandmother a smile. "It's much better since it's been just the two of us."

"Celine, go and put the kettle on and make some tea, there's a good girl."

She sighed theatrically, but stood up. "That means she wants to talk to you with me out of the way. I don't know why she does it. She knows I'll listen at the door."

"You'd better not, my girl," Mrs Hastings said, but the look she gave her granddaughter showed Paolo the girl probably got away with more than was good for her.

Mrs Hastings waited until the door was closed again before turning to Paolo.

"I didn't want to speak in front of Celine. I've tried to shield her from her mother and that dreadful man she's with. The two boys were completely wild. I couldn't control them. I tried for two years, but in the end I had to send them back to their mother. I've heard the older one's turned out to be a real bad lot. He fell under the influence of Beatrice's husband and got involved in some nasty doings, drugs and such like. I didn't want Celine in contact with her brothers, so whenever one of them phoned here I put the phone down. Please don't put ideas into her head about family ties and getting closer to her brothers. She's safe here with me and I intend to keep her that way."

She frowned, as if trying to put her thoughts into words.

"My daughter has lost her way. I tried to help her get her life straight, but she drinks and, I think, also takes drugs. I wouldn't trust her husband with any female, far less a pretty young girl like Celine. I don't know where Conrad is and I don't care. Please, don't come back again even if you find him. Celine knows she's got one parent to be ashamed of, don't introduce her to another."

In the car on the way back to the station, Mrs Hastings's words replayed in Paolo's head. Her thoughts and care for her granddaughter was laudable, and he could understand her wanting to keep Celine away from Carl Hunt, but she didn't seem to mind throwing her grandsons to the wolf. Were the two boys really bad news, or did Beatrice and Carl Hunt make them that way? A firm believer in nurture over nature, he only had to look at his own life compared to that of his uncles, Paolo decided to contact Social Services. The

Hunts definitely weren't ideal parent material and the thought of the two boys being raised in that environment made him shudder. Celine was the youngest at thirteen, which meant the other two would now be fifteen and seventeen. If the grandmother sent them back seven or eight years ago, what sort of home life had they endured?

Paolo was so deep in thought he hadn't even realised they'd reached the station until Dave's car came to a halt.

"Penny for them, sir? Although, you were so far away, your thoughts might be worth a bit more than that."

Paolo climbed out and smiled at Dave across the car's roof. "Just thinking about upbringing and how it shapes us."

Dave grinned. "See! I told you your thoughts looked expensive. That's a bit too deep for me on a Monday."

Making a mental note to find out about the Stormont boys, Paolo followed Dave into the station. As soon as they entered the main office, Paolo was aware of a buzz that hadn't been there when they'd left.

"We think we've got it, sir," Andrea called out.

Paolo grinned. "Okay, give me a clue. Got what exactly?"

CC handed him a piece of paper. "A connection between Stormont and our second victim, Edwin Fulbright."

Paolo looked down at a printed list of closely typed names and dates. Towards the end of the page he spotted Conrad Stormont's name.

"What is this?"

"It's a list of minor surgical cases Mr Fulbright worked on in 2004. He was the surgeon who saved Conrad Stormont's life by sewing up his slashed wrists. This connects Stormont with all three victims. He worked with one, had his life saved by another and hooked up with the third on the gay chat site."

It sounded good, so Paolo was surprised to find it didn't sit as well with him as he'd thought it would.

"Great work, you two."

"But?" CC asked.

"What makes you think there's a but?" Paolo said.

"Because, sir, I've worked with you long enough to hear it in your voice. What is it that's bugging you about this?"

Paolo sat on the nearest desk. "We know he had a definite connection to victims one and two, but how do we know that the man who chatted with Peter Bishop was, in fact, Conrad Stormont? We haven't found any trace of him for eight years, no phone records, no voting registration, no social security payments, no tax record, not a thing, and yet here he is on a chat site. Either he's been involved in some underground crime set up and managed to stay off the radar, or the man on that website used Conrad Stormont's name for a reason. We need to find out which is true. I'm going to try contacting Stormont's sons. Maybe one of them knows where he is."

He stood up and handed the surgery list back to Andrea.

"This is really good work. If nothing else, we now know for sure that the killer is connected to Stormont in some way. But why now? Apart from victim three, the contact goes back ten years. What's happened to make whoever it is act now and not a decade ago?"

He turned to CC. "I want you and Andrea to go to Peter Bishop's offices. Call ahead and get Constance Myers to meet you there. I know she's not going to let you loose with any files, but see if you can get her to go through his old cases and see if there's a connection with Conrad Stormont she can uncover. Maybe 2003 to 2005? That should cover the time period when the first two victims were known to Stormont."

"What about recent cases?" CC asked. "As you say, we don't know what's shaken whatever the motive is to the surface. Could it be something that's happened this year, or even last year?"

Paolo sighed. "Until we know the why, we probably won't know the when. Concentrate on the older cases. I've got a gut feeling that's where the answer lies."

He was about to go to his own office when CC called out.

"We've had a report back from our IT people. They've

looked into the records of the chat site hosts, who have been really helpful and cooperative."

"That makes a pleasant change," Paolo said. "What did IT find out?"

CC shrugged. "Not good news, I'm afraid. All contact from the StormyC persona came from internet cafes. He never used the same IP address twice. As if that wasn't bad enough, he closed his account on Friday, ten minutes after his last chat with Peter Bishop. So I don't think anyone will be hearing from StormyC again."

***

Paolo stood outside Barbara's office door, almost scared to knock and go in. Whatever it was that was affecting her he knew, deep down inside, was going to be bad news in capital letters on a flashing neon sign. He just hoped he'd be able to find the right words to help her with whatever it was she was going through.

He steeled himself and rapped on the door before his courage could fail. Without waiting for an answer he opened the door and stuck his head round it.

"Time to talk?" he asked.

Barbara was seated behind her desk and looked so unlike the Barbara of old Paolo felt as if he'd wandered into an alternative reality. She was completely bald and her beautiful long blonde hair lay in a heap in front of her.

"Come in," she said, "and shut the door before anyone else sees me. It's bad enough sharing this with you, without everyone in this department turning up to offer their sympathy."

Paolo closed the door behind him, but couldn't find the words to ask the questions burning in his brain. Barbara saved him the trouble.

"It's cancer, Paolo. I've been having chemo for the past six months."

"Oh, Barb," he said, "I don't know what to say. Shit, I thought it was something else. I wish now it was."

He came forward to hold her, but she put her hand up to stop him.

"I don't want to be hugged," she said. "Not at the moment, anyway."

Paolo sat down opposite her. "Where is it?"

"Bowel," she said. "Apparently I'm one of the lucky ones because they found it before it had started to spread to my other organs. The chemo has shrunk the tumour and I'm down for surgery in a couple of weeks."

"When exactly?"

Barbara smiled. "I was hoping you'd ask. Paolo, I know I've been a bitch the last few weeks, but I've got a favour to ask."

Paolo fought to control the feeling of seasickness that made him want to throw up.

"Of course," he said, "whatever you want. Just name it."

"My operation's scheduled for the afternoon of the 22nd of August. You know all my family are still in South Africa?" When he nodded, she continued, "I haven't told them. I don't want my parents or my sister worrying themselves silly when there's nothing they can do. I've kept it from my friends here as well."

She stopped and Paolo waited for her to get to the point of what it was she needed from him. Whatever it was, he would move mountains to give it to her.

"In fact, you're the only person I've told and I trust you not to tell anyone else. No one! Not even Chris. He thinks I'm going away on holiday for a couple of weeks."

Paolo smiled. "I hope you haven't told him you're going anywhere sunny. He'll expect to see a suntan when you go back to work."

She smiled. "I thought of that. I expect when I come back I'll tell him the truth, but I don't want to share this with anyone until after the op."

"Fair enough," Paolo said. "What is it you need me to do for you?"

Paolo watched in distress as Barbara's eyes filled with tears, spilling down her face and dripping onto her white coat. Ignoring her earlier words about not wanting a hug, he got up and went round to her side of the desk. As he held out his arms, she stood and walked into them. He pulled her to him and held her close until her sobs subsided.

Leaning back a little, so that he could look at her face, he smiled.

"Now, what was that favour you wanted?"

"When I come back from the operating theatre I don't want anyone to be there apart from you. Please, would you do that for me?"

CHAPTER SEVENTEEN

The pretender slipped outside to make his call. With a bit of luck no one would even notice he'd gone and if they did, he'd say he'd needed to go to the toilets. No way did he want anyone overhearing what he had to say. He'd memorised the hospital's switchboard number and ran it through in his mind before dialling. It would have been better if he'd been able to find out a direct number to the department he needed, but he hadn't been able to think of a way to do that without drawing attention to himself. He listened to the ringing tone and prayed he wouldn't get one of those automated menu set ups that took forever to put you through to the right place. He breathed a sigh of relief when he heard the operator's voice.

"Bradchester Central, how can I help you?"

"Could you put me through to psychiatry, please?"

"Ward or appointments?"

"Appointments."

He heard a click and then some annoying digital noise that was supposed to be music filled his ear. If he'd been a patient, he thought, listening to that crap would be enough to set off a psychotic episode. After a few moments he heard another click and the line went mercifully silent until a voice announced he was through to the psychiatry department.

"I'd like to make an appointment with Dr Carter, please."

"Are you an existing patient of hers?"

"No, I've just moved here from Bristol. Dr Sedgwick has given me a letter of referral."

The pretender smiled, thinking of all the phone calls

he'd had to make to various Bristol hospitals to discover a psychiatrist who was about to go on holiday. No one would be able to contact Dr Sedgwick for four weeks while he took his wife off on a world cruise.

"Do make sure you bring your letter with you when you come. I can give you an appointment for Monday 25th August at 2.30pm."

"Can she not see me this week?"

"No, I'm afraid Dr Carter is away until then. That's the first available appointment."

The pretender had to think quickly. It would mean rearranging his list, but he could put her at the end. It wouldn't make that much difference.

"I'm going to be away myself for most of that week. Is it possible to have an appointment on the Friday instead of Monday?"

He held his breath. It had to be a Friday. Had to be.

"She doesn't usually hold Friday appointments, but will occasionally do so if it's absolutely necessary, but not here at the hospital. Friday appointments have to be conducted in her private consulting rooms on the other side of town. The building is on a regular bus route, so isn't difficult to access. Would that be okay for you?"

"What's the address?"

As she read it out, he scribbled the details down on a scrap of paper. Getting her away from the hospital couldn't be better, he thought. Less chance of her body being found before the insulin had done its work.

"Yes, that suits me very well. It's more convenient for me, in fact."

"Good. In that case, I can book you in for the same time on Friday August 29th."

"That sounds fine by me."

"Your name, please?"

"Anthony Williams."

"Thank you, Mr Williams. That's 2.30pm on Friday August 29th."

He switched off his phone, ending the call, and grinned.

How many people would know that Tony Williams sang the lead vocals on The Platters original version of *The Great Pretender*? Even if they did, no one would connect Anthony Williams with the song until it was too late. Jessica Carter would be his final victim. No, not victim. She wasn't a victim. None of them were. She would be his final act of judgment. After that, he didn't care what happened to him. He would have avenged the terrible wrong they'd done to a truly innocent person. Someone only he remembered.

***

Paolo glanced up from the file he was reading and looked at Dave sitting across the desk from him. He'd never seen his young colleague look happier. What a contrast with the outwardly misogynistic idiot he'd pretended to be when he first arrived at the station. He and Rebecca must be getting on really well to give Dave that glow of contentment.

"Have I got ink on my face or something?" Dave asked.

"What?"

"You were staring at me."

Paolo laughed. "Sorry, Dave. I was miles away, thinking of the past." He looked back down at the Stormont file. "I think we should take a second visit to Stormont's ex-wife. She may not know where Conrad is, but it's possible one of her sons does."

Dave smiled. "Oh, good. Another trip to that beautiful housing estate. I can hardly wait. Please, sir, can we go now?"

"Don't be sarcastic, Dave, or I'll decide we need to conduct a door to door there and put you in charge of it."

Dave opened his mouth to answer, but a knock on the door distracted him.

"Come in," Paolo called out. "Ah, good, pull up a couple of chairs," he said as CC and Andrea came in. "Was Constance Myers helpful?"

CC flopped onto the chair she'd dragged across from the

wall.

"She was eventually, when we pointed out the only way her boss was going to get justice was by going back through the cases he was working on before, during or just after the time Conrad Stormont lost his licence to practice."

Andrea sat forward and took up the story. Paolo noticed the two officers were already working in synch, always a good sign in a partnership.

"We've asked her to pay particular attention to any cases where Conrad Stormont, Edwin Fulbright or Professor Edwards are connected, no matter how nebulous the connection."

CC nodded. "She says she's happy to do it, but warned it might take quite some time to get results. Nowadays, everything is on computer, so it's just a case of running a search for names, but in 2003 to 2005 they kept paper copies only."

"Is she doing the searching on her own?" Paolo asked. "That's going to take her months. We can't afford to wait that long."

"She's going to set a couple of office juniors on it," CC said, "but with her overseeing their work so that they don't take home any information that shouldn't leave the office."

"Are there any Fulbright family members we've overlooked?" Paolo asked. "I know we keep falling over Conrad Stormont, but I can't help thinking that's because we're supposed to. Someone wants us to make that link. Why else use that name in the chat room? If it really is Stormont behind the killings, why draw attention to himself? He must know we would search Peter Bishop's computer and find the evidence there." He shook his head. "Something isn't right with this, but it's all we've got to go on, so we need to see where it leads."

***

Paolo studied the three autopsy reports. Looking at them side by side, it was obvious the same killer was at work, but what else did the reports show? Paolo was convinced there must be something worth finding in them, if only he knew what to look for. But the more he looked, the less he understood.

He was saved from going over the same material for the hundredth time by his mobile playing the tune that told him Lydia was calling.

"Hi, Paolo here."

"Did you really tell Katy it was okay for her to see this boy with the criminal brother?"

"Good afternoon to you, too."

"Paolo, don't play the fool. This is too important. You of all people know what could happen if Katy gets in with the wrong crowd. Is that what you want for our daughter?"

"Don't be silly, Lydia, you know it isn't, but I trust Katy's judgment."

"That's a turn up for the books. Last time we spoke you were all in favour of finding out who the boy was and stopping Katy from seeing him."

Paolo sighed. "I was wrong. Katy is very clued up. If she feels he isn't a bad person then we have to believe in her ability to make that call."

"Where on earth did that rubbish come from? Katy is only sixteen, Paolo, or have you forgotten that?"

"Of course I haven't forgotten. Listen, Lydia, two people who know Katy made me look at her from a different angle. Not as a parent, but from the outside. We've got a lot to be proud of with our daughter – and we should trust her to make the right decisions."

"Are you mad? Who knows her better than us? Who are these two people who seem to have turned your brain to mush?"

"Dave Johnson and Jessica Carter, but neither of them —"

"I might have known it! Did you jump into bed with her the day you moved out of our home?"

"Lydia, my relationship with Jessica has nothing to do with this."

"It has everything to do with it. Jessica shouldn't even be discussing Katy with you. Katy was her patient, for Christ's sake. I've a good mind to report her to the medical council or whoever it is that deals with—"

"Just stop right there and calm down! Katy is no longer Jessica's patient and while she was there was nothing between Jessica and me. Not a thing."

He heard Lydia catch her breath. "But now there is?"

Paolo hesitated before answering. "Yes. I don't know how serious it is, but we are together as a couple."

"I see. Well, she may have enticed you into her bed, but that changes nothing as far as Katy is concerned. I'm her mother and I'll do what I think is best for her. When she gets back from wherever she's gone off to today, she won't be going out again without telling me exactly where she's going and who she's going to be with."

"Lydia, that's not the way to go with Katy and you know it."

"Is that what the sainted Jessica said?"

"Don't be childish."

"Tell your girlfriend to keep her advice to herself where *my* child is concerned."

Paolo heard a click and then silence. He threw the phone on his desk, angry with Lydia, but even angrier with himself for mentioning that he'd been advised by Jessica. Should he warn Katy what to expect when she went home? He reached for his phone. No, that might make matters worse. Katy was quite likely to go in with all guns blazing and that would solve nothing. He'd have to wait until Katy came to him for advice. But what advice could he give without setting himself up against Lydia.

Sighing, he stood up and put the phone in his pocket. It was time to visit another dysfunctional family and put his own out of mind for the time being.

He walked into the main office and called out to Dave.

"The moment for that treat I promised you has now arrived."

Dave looked up. "You spoil me, sir. I feel bad at getting

153

all this preferential treatment. I bet CC would like to go with you in my place."

"Go where?" CC asked, turning away from the computer screen showing CCTV footage of the car park. "Anywhere would be better than straining my eyes on this."

"The Hambley Estate," Dave said. "A second visit to Conrad Stormont's ex-wife."

"On second thoughts," CC said, grinning at Dave, "I wouldn't want to deprive you of a couple of hours in our exalted boss's company. I'm just a lowly, feeble woman, so it's best if I stay here and stare at the screen."

Dave screwed up a sheet of paper and threw it across the room. It landed short of CC's desk and she laughed.

"When you two have quite finished," Paolo said, "perhaps we could get going? In your own time, of course, Dave."

"Yes, sir, sorry, sir, coming, sir," Dave said, standing up and grabbing his jacket from the back of his chair and then hobbling towards Paolo in semi-crouched position. "Don't beat me, sir."

"Beat him, sir," CC called out.

Paolo laughed. "You two are both mad. Come on."

As they left the office, Paolo couldn't help but wonder what Katy would be facing at home, but when they got outside, all thoughts of Katy and Lydia disappeared.

They walked into a barrage of questions and flashing lights.

"Are you close to finding the killer?"

"What leads do you have?"

"Any ideas on the next victim?"

"Is this a homophobic killing spree?"

"Why has no one been arrested?"

"Do you have anything to go on?"

"Should the general public be worried?"

"What can you tell us about the case?"

Paolo and Dave pushed their way through the reporters and photographers, avoiding the enormous microphones being shoved in front of them every step of the way.

"Our enquiries are on-going," he said over and over until they reached the haven of Dave's car.

For once, Dave had his key ready and they wrenched the doors open and climbed in, with the reporters still pushing and shoving against the car.

"It's going to be dangerous to drive away, sir," Dave said. "I don't want to be had up for running over someone's foot."

"Just start the engine. If the idiots don't move away, run them over."

"Blimey, you sound mad."

"I am," Paolo said. "What the hell do they think I'm going to tell them? Even if we did have leads, we couldn't share the information with that lot."

Dave started the car and inched forward. The photographers in front of the car jumped to the sides, flash bulbs still exploding. Gradually they were clear of bodies in front and Dave was able to pull away.

As they made their way through town, Paolo's mind flitted between his conversation with Lydia and the questions he wanted to ask Stormont's boys, the eldest of whom must be only a few years older than Katy. That thought sent him back to his own teenage years and the worry he must have caused his dad at times. Maybe that's what a teenager's mission in life was, to remind older people that they were young once. Remembering his own youthful exploits made Paolo smile. It's just as well Katy didn't know what her sensible policeman dad had got up to with his mates.

"It's nice to see a smile back in place, sir," Dave said. "You've been frowning since we left the station. They're all savages, aren't they? Prepared to do anything for a story."

Paolo had been trying to work out why Dave thought teenagers were like savages, but the last sentence made him realise he wasn't on the same wavelength.

"It's their job, I suppose. No doubt their editors will give them hell when they come back without any new information."

Dave pulled up in the parking lot outside the Hunt's tower block.

"We could do with some information ourselves," Paolo said. "Let's hope the Stormont boys can provide some."

By the time they'd climbed the stairs, holding their breath as much as possible, and negotiated the litter-strewn corridor, Paolo was hoping he never had to come back to the place again. He rapped on the door with his knuckles and waited. After a few seconds, Beatrice Hunt's voice reached them.

"Go away. Not home. Not...not here right now."

Paolo knocked again. "Come on, Mrs Hunt, open the door."

"Whoever you are, go away. I...I'm not in."

Paolo rapped again, louder this time. Wincing, he looked at his knuckles.

"That hurt," he said to Dave. "I must be getting soft. Open up, we just want to talk to you," he yelled.

He was about to knock again when the door opened. Beatrice Hunt was still in her nightwear. A dirty blue silk gown hung open, revealing an almost sheer negligee beneath. She made an attempt at modesty by pulling the gown's edges together. A bruise disfigured one side of her face and her throat had clear finger marks on either side.

"What do you want?" she slurred and Paolo took a step back as the stench of alcohol and vomit hit him full in the face. "Carl is out."

"Could we come in? Just for a chat?"

She staggered back and waved her arm vaguely in the direction of the lounge. As they entered the room Paolo guessed what had happened the night before. The only bits of furniture still standing were those too heavy to throw. Carl Hunt must have lost his temper and taken it out on the room and his wife in equal measure.

Beatrice staggered into the doorway and collapsed against it as if that was all that was keeping her upright. It probably was, Paolo thought.

"Mrs Hunt, Beatrice, why do you stay? There are places

you can go, you know."

She laughed, clinging to the doorframe as if welded to it. "Where? Home to my wonderful mummy? She's a stuck-up cow."

"No, there are other places. Safe houses where you can stay until you get back on your feet again. Where your husband can't hurt you."

She shook her head. "Carl loves me. You, you don't understand. 'Scuse me," she said, turning and staggering down the hallway.

Within moments they heard the sound of her being violently sick.

"Should I go to her, sir?" Dave asked.

Paolo almost laughed out loud at the look on Dave's face, pleading with him not to say yes. He shook his head.

"It'll be better to let her be for a while. We've got time. Let's sit and wait."

Ten minutes later Beatrice reappeared in the doorway. She looked marginally better, but was still clearly unsteady on her feet.

"What do you want this time?" she said, enunciating the words so carefully she sounded as if she was reading a script.

"We'd like to have a chat with your sons, Mrs Hunt."

Beatrice laughed. "You and me both. If you find…if you…'scuse me," she murmured, rushing back to the bathroom.

She was only gone a few minutes this time. Paolo guessed there was little left to bring up.

"As I was saying, if you find them, tell them I…tell them…say I…oh, what's the point! They don't want anything to do with me."

"When did you last see them?"

She sighed and stared at the ceiling, then shrugged her shoulders, almost losing her balance in the process. She put out a hand to steady herself.

"I don't know. A year, maybe two years ago. Daniel was always so full of himself. He thought he was too good for us

157

and took himself off to live with a friend. Carl set Mark up in business, but something went wrong. Both boys blamed Carl, but he explained it to me. He said Mark screwed up. Mark disappeared, I don't know where, Daniel went off in a temper and I haven't seen either of my sons since then."

Paolo wanted to shake her, she sounded so pathetic and concerned only with her own feelings. How must her sons have felt, knowing she would always take her husband's side over theirs?

She began to cry, but the tears were for her, not for her children.

"You don't understand. I did my best. I just did my best. I want you to go now before Carl gets back. He's a good man, but he doesn't like it if I have anyone in here while he's out. Please go."

CHAPTER EIGHTEEN

Week four – Friday 15th August to Thursday 21st August

The pretender looked down at the leaflet he'd torn from the notice board outside the railway station a few months earlier. It was time to set up the next stage, but this was going to be trickier than the others. He had to convince Wittington-Smythe or find another way of getting close to him. Taking a deep breath, he called the number on the leaflet.

"Marcus Wittington-Smythe."

The cultured tones of the barrister set the pretender's teeth on edge. His voice brought back all the pain and rage from the distant past. Waves of nausea flooded his body, but he forced himself to hold back his emotions. If he let his feelings come through in his voice the barrister might suspect something.

"Mr Wittington-Smythe, I saw him. Your boy. I spoke to him last night."

"Where? Tell me."

"Well this piece of paper I've got, it says you're offering a reward, like. How do I get it? I mean, if I tell you where he is, how do I know you'll pay me what it says on here?"

"I promise you, Mr...what is your name?"

"My name's not important."

"I have to call you something."

The pretender smiled. "You can call me Freddie, if you like. Freddie Mercury."

"Okay, Freddie. I promise if you lead me to my son the reward will be paid to you. But first you have to convince me you really do know where he is."

"I told you, I talked to him last night. He wants to come home, but he can't."

The pretender heard a sharp intake of breath and smiled again. Now he knew for sure he had the barrister hooked.

"What did he say? Did he tell you why he won't come home?"

"He said he was too ashamed to face his mother in the state he's in." The pretender was flying now, words falling into the phone that he didn't even know he was going to say until he said them. "He's heavily into drugs, but wants to get clean. He said he'd meet you tonight, but don't bring his mother. He wants you to take him to rehab somewhere and not tell your wife until he's clean again."

"I'll come without his mother, tell him that. He can stay in our town flat tonight and I'll take him to The Abbey Clinic tomorrow first thing. What time and where?"

"I'll have to call you. I don't know where he is right now, but he told me last night he was coming back this way to score."

"To score? I thought you said he wanted to go into rehab."

The pretender laughed. "You don't know much about junkies, do you? He wants to go into rehab, but that doesn't mean he'll stop using before he has to. As soon as he gets here, I'll call you."

"But where is here? You haven't told me where to meet you."

"No, and I'm not going to either. I want to make sure I get my money and if I tell you where to go, you might just turn up there without the cash. No, this is how it's going to work. I'll call you when he's in the area and tell you where to meet me. You bring five thousand pounds in cash. I check it's all there and show you your boy in the distance. I take the money. You go and pick up your son."

"How do I know I can trust you?"

The pretender laughed out loud. He couldn't help himself. "You don't, but look at it this way, if you can't see your son standing a little way off, don't give me the money.

What it comes down to is how much you want to get your son home again. It's as simple as that. I'll call you tonight," he said and ended the call before Wittington-Smythe could ask any more questions.

The pretender waited until it was nearly two in the morning. He liked that time. Everywhere was quiet and there were few people about. The ones who were roaming the streets were generally too drunk or stoned to notice anything out of the ordinary, but he made sure no one was around before he called the barrister.

"Marcus Wittington-Smythe here. Where have you been? I've been waiting for your call."

"Calm down, he's only just arrived. I can see him from where I'm standing. It looks like he's settled in for the night. Have you got the reward money?"

"Yes, but it's staying in my car until I'm certain it's my boy."

"Fine by me. I'm at the south gate of the Bradchester Memorial Gardens. There's an area in front of the gates you can park. If you look through the gates, you'll be able to see your son on one of the benches. If you're happy it's him, you can get the money from your car. If you're not, you can get back in and drive off. Don't take too long getting here, though. He might take off again."

Twenty minutes later the pretender watched as a sleek Mercedes pulled into the parking area. Wittington-Smythe got out and pressed the fob, setting the automatic locking. He dropped the keys into his pocket and looked around. The pretender strolled out from the shadows, making the barrister jump when he spoke.

"Come over here and look through the railings. You can see him clearly on that bench."

Wittington-Smythe rushed over and peered through the bars.

"Where? I can't see him!"

The pretender took half a step forward and stabbed the

syringe into the barrister's leg.

"You can't see him because he's not there."

He waited for the insulin to take effect and then searched through the barrister's pockets. When he found his mobile phone and car keys, he hurled both over the railings into the park. Another one who wouldn't be able to drive to the hospital begging for an antidote. Not that Wittington-Smythe looked as if he was going anywhere. He'd already stopped moving.

The pretender took an envelope from his pocket and walked over to the Mercedes. Lifting the windscreen wiper on the passenger side, he slipped the envelope underneath. Another one down, now there were only two left.

CHAPTER NINETEEN

Paolo arrived at the crime scene to find a mass of reporters already encamped. How the hell do these vultures know when to turn up? Then he realised they probably have someone listening in to the police frequency. He nodded to the constable manning the tape and showed his warrant card.

"Forensics already in there?"

"Yes, sir. Dr Royston said for you to find her as soon as you arrived."

"Who discovered the body?"

"The park keeper when he came to unlock the gates, sir. He's pretty shaken up. WPC Barker is sitting with him in the keeper's hut. It's that building over there, sir, just inside the gates."

"Do we have an identity yet?"

"Not on the body, sir, but the car is registered to Marcus Wittington-Smythe."

"Thank you. When Detective Sergeant Johnson gets here, tell him I've said he's to interview the park keeper."

"Will do, sir."

Paolo smiled his thanks and made his way to the tent shielding the body from the outside world. He stood for a few minutes watching Barbara at work. To his eyes she was getting thinner by the day. Considering she had never carried enough flesh in the first place, he thought she looked like a wraith. Her face was gaunt and the skin seemed stretched across her cheekbones. Surely those she worked with must have realised how ill she was. It seemed inconceivable to Paolo that her loss of weight and terrible pallor hadn't been noticed. The whiteness of her face made the birthmark on her neck stand out like a neon sign.

As if becoming aware of being under scrutiny, she looked up and smiled at Paolo. It was the kind of smile she used to flash at him before they were stupid enough to have their brief affair that had almost destroyed their friendship. He smiled back, glad to see her looking more relaxed than the last time he'd seen her.

"If I ask for your thoughts, are you going to bite my head off?" he asked, grinning and holding his hands up in mock defence.

"Not this time, no. Even without the tox tests, it's fairly obvious our man has struck again. What makes it certain is leaving his calling card on the windscreen."

"Another white envelope?"

Barbara nodded. "Four down, two to go. How the hell have you managed to keep that snippet of information out of the press?"

"I threatened to set fire to anyone who blabbed," he said.

Barbara raised her eyebrows in question. "And the sensible answer is?"

"I begged them not to let it out. The last thing we need is a copycat leaving similar notes around the town – not to mention more dead bodies to go with duplicated notes. But I don't think I needed to worry. We've not really recovered from George's antics last year. No one wants to go down the same road and end up out of the force."

"I take it you're no closer to finding the connection that links all the victims?" Barbara asked.

"We are," Paolo said, "but it feels like we're being led in that direction. I'm not convinced Conrad Stormont is really who we're looking for, but as his name is the only one that links the first three, we have to follow that wherever it leads us. I'll leave you to it. Are you conducting the autopsy, or passing it over to Chris?"

"All being well, I'll be doing it," she said. "Probably on Tuesday."

Paolo made a note on his pad. "Let me know the time and I'll be there."

He went back outside and walked over to the car which was being readied to load onto a transporter.

"Any sign of the keys?" he asked the man preparing the vehicle for winching.

"Not as far as I could see, guv."

"Pity," Paolo said. "It would make it easier for us to check inside."

"Good morning, sir."

He turned to see Dave coming towards him from the direction of the keeper's hut.

"Did you find out anything of use?" Paolo asked.

"Yes and no," Dave answered. "The keeper wasn't able to tell us much about the crime scene, but he has sharp eyes." He held up a bunch of keys and a mobile phone. "He found these on the path."

Paolo turned back to the transporter. "Hold on a moment. I'd like to check something before you take the car away."

He clicked the fob and the Mercedes's lights flashed at him.

"Let's take a look before it goes to forensics."

Paolo slipped on some latex gloves and opened the car door. On the passenger seat was a leather briefcase. He reached in and pulled it towards him. Flicking at the two catches, more in hope than expectation, he was amazed when they flipped up. He opened the case and whistled.

"Bloody hell, Dave, come and look at this."

He stood to one side so that Dave could see in.

"Wow, there must be a few thousand in there. Do you think he was being blackmailed?"

"I don't know," Paolo said. "It's a possibility, I suppose. Maybe all four victims were. There could be nothing more to this case than a desire for money. But if that's so, why didn't the killer take it when he left?"

"Maybe Wittington-Smythe, if that's who this is, was the one who chucked the keys into the park so that the killer couldn't get the cash."

Paolo sighed. "Seems a bit far-fetched, though, doesn't it? I think we need to find out more about Marcus

Wittington-Smythe before we jump to any conclusions."

"Another working Saturday for us?"

"'Fraid so, Dave. I've already called CC and Andrea and told them to meet us at the station. There must be some significance in the fact that all the bodies have been found on Saturday mornings. I wish I knew what it was!"

"I wish he'd chosen a weekday. Maybe then Rebecca and I could enjoy a lie in for a change."

***

Paolo sat on the desk at the front of the room and ran over what they knew about Marcus Wittington-Smythe.

"Firstly, we have discovered Wittington-Smythe is a barrister. In view of the fact that Peter Bishop is a solicitor, that could be significant. Unfortunately, it could also be a coincidence. Every time we think we're getting to grips with events in this case, something happens to take us in a different direction."

He stood up and walked across to the board, filling in information as he spoke. "He was staying in his Bradchester flat for the weekend because he was due to speak at a Bar Council dinner this evening. Obviously, we will have to notify the organisers, but not until we've spoken to his wife. She is at their home on Rutland Water. Dave and I will be going to break the bad news to her as soon as we've finished here."

He turned back to face the room. "He had five thousand pounds in his briefcase, locked inside the car. If it wasn't for the method of killing, I'd be thinking this was a case of blackmail gone wrong, but everything points to the same perpetrator. So, what's the connection between Wittington-Smythe and the others? Did Peter Bishop instruct Wittington-Smythe to act for him? That's something to ask Constance Myers to look into. It might help to narrow down the search. On the other hand, it might complicate matters unnecessarily. I feel as if we're sinking into quicksand with this case and I don't like it."

Paolo noticed CC staring into space. It wasn't like her not to pay attention.

"Are you with us, CC?"

She looked at him and frowned. "There's something running around in my head to do with that name, but I can't quite grasp it. I'm going to run an online search on it to see what I can come up with."

Paolo nodded. "You do that. Dave, let's pay a visit to Rutland Water."

Dave stood up, but made no move to grab his jacket. "Um, before we go, there's something I'd like to say."

CC and Andrea were side by side looking at the computer screen. Dave raised his voice.

"Um, it's something I want to say to you two as well."

"Sounds ominous," CC said. "Dave, are you blushing? Dear God, I do believe the man has turned into a lobster."

Dave grinned. "Last night, I asked Rebecca to marry me and she said yes. We're having an engagement party and you're all invited."

Paolo waited until CC and Andrea had hugged Dave before stepping over and holding out his hand.

"I'm delighted for you. When's the party?"

"And where?" CC called out.

"We're holding it at the ice rink. They've got a great function room upstairs and there's plenty of parking. It's on Saturday 23rd of August."

Paolo smiled. "That's great. Rebecca is back the night before, so I won't be turning up on my own."

"That makes a change, sir," CC said. "We'll have to get used to you being part of a couple. You usually arrive pretending you want to be there, stay for an hour and then disappear." She smiled. "It's nice to see you looking happy."

Paolo suddenly felt like an unwelcome spotlight had been shone on him. "Yes, well, let's not forget it's Dave's good news we're celebrating, not mine. As for looking happy, I'm only going to be able to do that once we've caught this madman."

***

Dave drove along Rutland Water to a tiny hamlet nestling on the edge of the shoreline. It seemed to consist almost entirely of large detached properties, many with gardens running down to the water's edge where private moorings had been erected. He pulled the car into the drive of Marcus Wittington-Smythe's house.

"One thing about the victims in this case, sir, none of them was short of money. Even though Peter Bishop was a pauper compared to the professor, Mr Fulbright and today's victim, he was better off than the average person. Do you think it could be simple class or money envy?"

Paolo unlocked his seatbelt and slipped out of the car. "It's a possibility, but I don't think so. My gut is screaming that there is an obvious connection, if only we knew where to look. Come on; let's break the bad news to Mrs Wittington-Smythe."

The intercom was answered by a young-sounding voice, but when Paolo said who he was and asked if he was speaking to Mrs Wittington-Smythe, the girl giggled.

"Oh, no, sir. She's still asleep. Shall I wake her up?"

"Yes, please, but could you let us in before you do so?"

There was a click and the gate swung open. They walked along a wide path bordered with vibrant and sweet-smelling shrubs until they reached a small wooden bridge spanning a pond with giant fish swimming contently in the reflected sunlight.

As he stepped onto the bridge, Paolo wondered if it was meant to symbolise a moat, then shook off the thought. If he was reduced to searching for symbolism where none probably existed, he really had lost touch with his own common sense.

"They're supposed to be lucky, sir."

Halfway across the bridge Paolo turned back. "What are?"

"Carp. I'm fairly sure they're carp. Koi's the proper name. The Japanese hold them in very high regard in the luck department."

"Really?" Paolo said. "Maybe we should get a couple and carry them around in the car with us. We need all the luck we can get with this case."

As they came off the wooden bridge, the front door opened and a young woman of about twenty stood smiling at them.

"Come in. I've woken Mrs Wittington-Smythe and she'll be down shortly. She said for you to go in and wait for her in the conservatory. I've already put the coffee on."

She gestured down the hall towards the back of the property, so Paolo and Dave followed her pointing finger. The conservatory when they reached it was nothing like the structure Paolo had pictured. This was a glass fronted room, almost as big as his flat, overlooking Rutland Water. The view was spectacular.

Dave whistled. "Wow, this place must have cost a fortune. Some people have all the luck. Those fish must have worked."

Paolo spun back and glared. "I know you're in a good mood and I'm happy for you. Really I am, but for Christ's sake, Dave, just come back down to earth will you! How lucky is the woman we're about to see? How lucky would you feel if I turned up to tell you we'd found Rebecca's body in a car park and had no idea who'd killed her or why?"

Dave looked down at his feet. "Sorry, sir. You're right. I've allowed my—"

He never got to finish his sentence. A middle-aged woman in a flowing black and gold kimono rushed into the conservatory.

"Have you found him? Where is he? Can I see him?"

"I'm sorry, Mrs Wittington-Smythe. Yes, we have. We will need you to make a formal identification later."

She sank into one of the overstuffed cane chairs facing the water.

"Oh God. When Sally told me you were here, I thought…that is, I hoped…but I should have known. Where did you find his body?"

Paolo sat down opposite. "You expected this?"

She raised a ragged, tear-drenched face. "Not expected it, no, but I'm not surprised either. Where did you find him?"

"In the car park outside the Bradchester Memorial Gardens."

"That makes sense. Was it drugs that killed him?"

Feeling completely at sea, Paolo wondered how on earth she knew.

"Mrs Wittington-Smythe, are you saying you expected your husband to die as a result of taking drugs?"

She shook her head. "My husband? No, why on earth would I think that?" Her face changed as the realisation hit home. "It's my husband that's dead?"

"Yes, I'm sorry. We found his body this morning."

"My husband? Not my son? You haven't found Gareth?" Then the enormity of what Paolo had said seemed to overwhelm her. "Marcus is dead? Why? How? It's not possible."

"Mrs Wittington-Smythe, your husband had a large amount of cash in his briefcase. Do you have any idea why he would be carrying so much around with him?"

She didn't answer, but sat staring out onto the water as if hypnotised.

"Dave, go and find out what's taking so long with the coffee. I think Mrs Wittington-Smythe is in shock."

Paolo waited until Dave came back with a tray laden with coffee and biscuits.

"She said she was waiting for Mrs Wittington-Smythe to call her to bring the tray in," Dave said.

Paolo poured a cup of coffee and then leaned forward to put it on a side table next to the stricken woman's chair.

"Mrs Wittington-Smythe, would you like to talk to me about your son?"

She shook her head. "No point. He's gone and not coming back. Now Marcus is gone, too."

"Did your husband mention meeting someone? Do you

know if he was planning to pay for something?"

"I expect it was the reward money. I told him it was a waste of time, but he never listened to me."

"Reward money?" Paolo prompted.

"Yes, five thousand pounds he offered to anyone who found Gareth alive. I don't think Gareth wants to be found. Or he didn't. He might want to, now that Marcus is dead."

"Your husband and son didn't get on?"

"Gareth is gay. When he...what's the expression? When he came out, my husband couldn't handle it. They had a massive argument and Gareth left. I think he went to London, but I don't know for certain. Over time Marcus convinced himself that Gareth had a drug problem and that was why he acted as he did. Isn't that funny?" she said, tears streaming down her face. "My husband thought it was more acceptable socially for our son to be a drug addict than to be gay."

She took a crumpled tissue from the pocket of her kimono and wiped away the tears.

"Marcus put up posters all over town some months ago offering a reward of five thousand pounds. You see, Inspector, he loved Gareth and wanted him to come home. He could deal with him being an addict, because that is curable. He couldn't deal with him being a homosexual because there isn't a cure for it. And now Marcus is dead. What happened to him?"

Paolo told her the little they knew, but his mind was running on a different track. Was there a connection between Peter Bishop, who had been gay and Gareth Wittington-Smythe? He made an arrangement for Mrs Wittington-Smythe to identify her husband's body and promised to keep her informed of any developments, but he had the impression she was mourning the loss of her son, rather than that of her husband.

As they crossed over the carp pond on the way back to the car, Dave touched his arm. He looked back.

"I just wanted to say sorry, sir. That was crass of me in there."

171

Paolo patted Dave's shoulder. "That's okay. Just don't let it happen again."

They finished the short walk outside in silence and Paolo was about to open the passenger door when his phone rang. Recognising the call tune as being from CC, he answered it before getting in the car.

"Two things, sir. Firstly, I know why the victim's name rang bells for me. His son is on the missing person's list."

"Well done," Paolo said. There was no point in taking away her pleasure in the discovery by spouting that they already knew. He'd fill her in on the reward angle later. "What's the second thing?"

"Not so positive, I'm afraid. Chief Constable Willows has come in."

"On a Saturday?"

"Yes, sir, and he's not happy at all. He wants you in his office as soon as you step foot in the station."

CHAPTER TWENTY

Paolo stood in front of the Chief Constable's desk and waited for the volley of words to dry up. While the tirade of blame for lack of progress swirled about him, his mind was listing all the possible connections to the victims. Conrad Stormont was connected to three of them, but that didn't necessarily make him the murderer. Peter Bishop and Gareth Wittington-Smythe were, or possibly still is in Gareth's case if he's alive, homosexuals. But that didn't sit right either. Why kill the father and not the son? Was the sexuality even relevant?

"Are you listening to me, Paolo?"

"Yes, sir, and I agree with everything you've said."

"You haven't heard a bloody word I've said, so don't give me that. What the hell is going on? We've got people dropping like flies and you don't have a clue who's doing it or why? What am I supposed to tell the press? Hey? Answer me that!"

Paolo toyed with the idea of giving an honest answer, but the Chief Constable already looked on the verge of a heart attack. Advising him to tell the press to stuff their notepads and microphones up each other's backsides probably wasn't a good idea.

"You can tell them we have several lines of enquiry and are following definite leads."

Willows glared. "And are you? Do you even have any leads?"

"In a word, sir, no. But we're doing the best we can. We will find the link between the victims, but unless the killer is going to do us a favour and send an email spelling it out, it's going to take time. This case only started on the 26th of

July. It's now the 16th of August. Not even a month. How many cases get solved in three weeks? Not many, you know that."

Willows thumped the desk with his fist. "Of course I know it, but how many cases turn up a dead body every Saturday over the same period? Very few. The press are calling him the Saturday Man. You know full well once they give the perpetrator a name they won't back off. It's news for them and sells papers."

"Let them sell their papers. I'm not interested," Paolo said, barely able to keep his voice level. "I'm doing the best I can, sir, and so is my team. I know it doesn't seem good enough, but I can assure you, none of us is slacking. We simply don't know where to look at the moment."

"Well, unless you come up with some answers fairly soon, I'm under pressure to bring in some outside help. I'd hate to do it to you, Paolo, but maybe this is a job for the Met."

When he was finally able to get away from Willows, Paolo went into the main office and rapped on the whiteboard to get everyone's attention.

"Okay, listen up, everyone. This is now a working weekend. I want volunteers for tomorrow. We are going to look into the backgrounds of all the victims, their families, their friends, work colleagues, children, previous partners, sexual preferences, alcohol and drug use, where they went to school, who they knew at university, where they've lived since birth and any other item of information I can think of between now and the time we solve this case. Right, who's in for the long haul?"

He was relieved to see Dave, CC and Andrea's hands shoot up. As long as he had those on side, Paolo knew if there was a connection to find, they'd find it. He walked over to the windows and looked down onto the street below. Photographers and reporters filled the road. He turned back and signalled for one of the uniformed officers to come over.

"Nip downstairs and get a couple of colleagues to go out with you and clear the street. Just because it's news to them doesn't mean they can turn my investigation into a circus."

Paolo left his team to man the phones and search through databases; he had a call to make that might just solve the riddle of how the deaths were connected. Or, if not solve it, at least it might rule out a few possibilities.

He walked into his office and swore he'd have a full weekend off at some point in the future if it killed him. As he settled behind his desk, he wondered how Jessica was getting on at the conference. They'd chatted a few times, but he missed her even more than he'd expected to. At least she'd be home in a week and back in time for Dave and Rebecca's engagement party. He smiled, thinking of the journey those two had made to be together. If he and Jessica could be as happy…he stopped himself from wandering down that road. Let's just see how things develop, he thought. Trying to find the link between the victims was his immediate priority.

Paolo picked up the piece of paper with Constance Myers' home number and hoped she wasn't out. He dialled and listened to the sound ringing on and on. Just as he was about to put the phone down, a breathless voice answered.

"Hello."

"Ms Myers, this is Detective Inspector Storey. I'm sorry to disturb you on a Saturday, but I need your assistance."

"Could it not wait until Monday? I was on my way to meet a friend for her birthday lunch. You're lucky to catch me. If I hadn't forgotten her card, I wouldn't have been here."

"I'd just like a few moments of your time. I'm afraid there's been another murder and we feel it might be connected to the death of Peter Bishop."

Paolo heard a sharp intake of breath.

"Good grief! Who? Not one of our office staff?"

"No, sorry, I should have realised you'd think that. No, not anyone from your office."

"Then I fail to see how I can help you. I'm sorry; I really

do have to go."

"It's a barrister," Paolo said before she could put the phone down. "I simply want to know if Peter Bishop ever instructed Marcus Wittington-Smythe."

There was another sharp intake of breath. "Yes," Constance said. "Mr Bishop and Mr Wittington-Smythe were professional colleagues and personal friends. They socialised quite a lot together, I believe. Please don't tell me that's who is dead."

"I'm sorry, I'm afraid it is."

"What do you need me to do?"

"Could you look closely at all the cases where Mr Bishop instructed Mr Wittington-Smythe to act for him?"

"But there will be so many. They frequently worked together on cases."

"Yes, but we are looking for a particular connection. I know you've been searching for any mention of Conrad Stormont, Edwin Fulbright and Professor Edwards, but we now need to add Mr Wittington-Smythe into the mix."

"I can't start today," she said, "but I'll go into the office tomorrow to see what I can uncover. On Monday, I'll set another girl to the task as well. That will be three of us going over the cases. We should be able to give you an answer in a couple of days, even if it's a negative one to say there isn't a case connecting them."

"Thank you, Ms Myers. Enjoy your lunch."

She laughed. "I will if my friend forgives me for keeping her waiting, which is not very likely as she is not the most patient of people and I obviously cannot tell her why I'm late."

"My apologies," Paolo said.

"Accepted, and now I really must go. Goodbye."

CHAPTER TWENTY-ONE

Jon sat in the hospital canteen on Wednesday and saw his life stretching ahead, unchanged for years to come. He'd be forever tied to Andy through chains of guilt and never able to live a life of his own. The letter from Leicester, saying regretfully he didn't get the job he needed so badly, lay on the table in front of him.

He'd picked it up as he'd arrived home the night before, convinced it was his passport to freedom. When he'd seen the words of rejection, he thought maybe he hadn't read the letter correctly. On second reading, with Andy's voice whinging from the front room, the truth had sunk in. He hadn't got the job. Fuck it, he hadn't got the job.

It wouldn't even have been a step up in pay scale, or anything close to a better job than he was doing here in Bradchester. But it would have meant moving to Leicester and getting away from Andy.

He looked at his colleagues, huddled together on a table as far from his as they could get. Every so often one of them would glance in his direction and the whispering would start up again. In the centre of it all sat Iain. Iain who'd turned everyone against him and wouldn't even tell him why.

Maybe he should go home and climb into bed. He could tell Mr Montague he was sick. It was almost true. He felt ill. He still hadn't figured out who put the 'murderer' note through his letterbox, although it seemed likely to be Gordon. It would be exactly the type of thing that moron would find funny. That's why Jon had kept it to himself. He was determined not to give Gordon the pleasure of seeing it had riled him.

Another burst of laughter from the table across the room

made up his mind for him. He'd never pulled a sickie since he'd started at the hospital, but he was going to today.

He stood up and carried his tray to the rack. Keeping his head averted, he left the canteen and went to find his boss. He'd say he had flu, get his things, and go home to bed.

As he got off the bus and walked towards his flat, Jon knew he'd made the right decision. Going to work each day was draining him of the will to live. No one spoke to him; no one even acknowledged his existence. Maybe he could find something different to do here in Bradchester. Even if he couldn't escape from Andy by moving out of town, he had to find somewhere new to work or he'd go insane. As it was, he'd had to get his shrink to increase his medication.

He wasn't used to being out in the afternoon sunshine during the week and thought about sloping off to the park, instead of going home, but he felt so weary, sleep was top of his list of things to do.

Jon eased open the front door as quietly as possible in the hope of sneaking through to his bedroom without Andy realising he was home. As he tiptoed across the hall, he heard footsteps in the lounge. Probably that bastard Gordon, he decided. Then he heard unmistakeable sounds from overhead, so it couldn't be their creepy neighbour. So who the hell did Andy have in today? Jon's anger, already simmering, rose to a furious boil. He stood and listened for conversation, but there wasn't any, just the sounds of someone going into the kitchen. Then he heard the kettle start to boil. Whoever it was clearly felt at home.

Should he go in and find out who the mystery visitor was, or go to bed? The slamming of a cupboard door convinced him. It sounded as though the person was preparing a feast in there with food Jon had had to work in that shithole hospital to pay for. Enough was enough. If Andy was inviting people round to eat, then he could bloody well pay towards the supermarket bill from now on.

Not bothering to keep quiet, he stormed across the hall and slung open the door, ready to let fly at Andy, but the couch was empty.

He looked towards the doorway to the kitchen and saw his brother standing with a fork in one hand and plate in the other. Standing! Not sitting, or crawling, but standing.

"Oh fuck," Andy said. "What are you doing home?"

"Never mind why I'm here, when did you learn to walk again?"

Andy grinned. "About a year ago. I thought I'd surprise you."

Jon felt the blackness rise. He had to stop himself from reaching out and strangling the little shit. "You bastard. You've nagged and moaned at me non-stop and you've been able to walk all this time? You fucking bastard."

"I'm the bastard?" Andy said. "Who put me in a wheelchair in the first place?"

"But you're not in a fucking wheelchair now, are you!"

"Would you prefer it if I was?" Andy said. "Is that what you want? A cripple for a brother?"

"No! Of course not, but...oh what's the point. Now that you can walk I'm off. You can get a job and take care of yourself. You'd better tell them down at the social that you're not entitled to benefits."

Andy shrugged and forked a portion of rice into his mouth. He swallowed and grinned. "I've no intention of telling them. Why should I?"

"Because if you don't, I will," Jon yelled.

Andy pushed past him and flopped onto the couch.

"No you won't."

Jon whipped round. "Yes, I bloody well will."

"And get done for fraud?" Andy said.

"Why would I get done? You're the one claiming benefits you're not entitled to."

"Really? What about the carer's allowance you've been claiming all these years?"

"But I didn't know you could walk," Jon said.

Andy swallowed another mouthful of food. "Prove it. I'll tell them it was all your idea. I'll say you made me pretend to be disabled so that you could claim for me. I'll have them

179

so much on my side I'll get a pat on the head and you'll get jail time."

Jon heard the front door open. Now what?

"Andy, you there, mate? I've got a parcel for Jon the postie delivered upstairs by mistake."

As Gordon came into the room Jon saw his eyes widen.

"Oh shit," he said. "What are you doing home during the day?"

"I fucking live here," Jon said. "Don't tell me you're in on this, too?"

Gordon grinned. "Course I am. It was me that got him walking again."

"Gordon set me a whole load of exercises. He used to be a physio," Andy said, "but he gave it up. Found out he could get an easier life without working."

Jon turned and thumped the wall until his rage passed. As he spun back, he saw the grins on both faces and the anger surged again.

"Get out," he said to Gordon. "Fuck off out and don't come back."

Gordon held out a small package. "Look, it's no good taking it out on me. I just came down to deliver this."

Jon snatched the package and slung it against the far wall, watching with satisfaction as it slid down and dropped behind the sideboard. He turned to Andy.

"Was that something else you've ordered using my fucking credit card? Well that's going to stop. You want stuff, pay for it yourself."

He whirled back to Gordon. "What the fuck are you still here for? I told you to get out. Go on, fuck off. Wait! Before you go, I want the key Andy gave you."

"What key?"

"Gordon, you've both been treating me like a moron, but no longer. I closed the door when I came home. The only way you could have got in here now was by using a key. So hand it over. And don't bother leaving any more stupid notes for me to find."

"What notes?"

"*What notes*?" Jon mimicked. "You know full well what I'm talking about. Now hand over that key."

Gordon grinned and held it out. "You need to lighten up a bit, mate."

"And you need to fuck off, *mate*."

Jon waited for the sound of the front door closing, then turned to Andy. "Are you going to stop claiming benefits and try to get a job?"

Andy shook his head. "Nope, don't see why I should."

"They'll look into it if I give up the carer's allowance, which I'm going to do. I'm not a thief and I'm not going to claim for something I'm not entitled to."

Andy stood up and sauntered through to the kitchen. "I told you, Jon, you do that and I'll tell them it was your idea all along. In fact, I might even tell them I was never disabled in the first place, that it was all part of a scheme you hatched so that I could claim compensation for the accident and you could claim carer's allowance."

"I could kill you right now," Jon hissed.

Andy laughed. "You couldn't lift a finger against me and you know it. You're a weakling, Jon, always have been and always will be. You let those idiots at work walk all over you and sit at home whimpering about it instead of smacking that fucker Iain in the head like he deserves. You've put up with me making your life hell for all these years and done fuck all about it. You won't kill me because you're too fucking useless."

"Don't be so sure, Andy. Right now I could stick a knife in you."

Andy picked up the breadknife and held the handle out. "Go on then. I won't even put up a fight."

Jon reached out, every fibre in his body willing him to take it and stab his brother, but his hand fell back to his side. He couldn't do it. Tremors wracked his body. He couldn't speak, couldn't function. He had to get away. Walk away and never come back. He turned and somehow made it to the front door.

"See," he heard Andy yell. "You haven't got the nerve."

Stumbling out through the gate he realised he hadn't shut the front door. Automatically, he turned to go back and close it. Then he realised Andy could do it. Andy could walk! Let him worry about keeping the place secure.

He had no idea where he was going, but when he found himself outside the pub, he went in. Desperate for a friendly face, he needed to be with other people. Now wasn't a time to be alone. Even a disinterested face would do. Just so long as he wasn't with anyone who hated him, used him, or wanted to make a fool of him.

There were only a few customers in. He'd expected more, but then remembered it was the middle of the afternoon. Walking up to the bar, he perched on a stool and slung his keys on the counter. They skidded off and landed on the other side of the bar. As had happened so often in the past, the flimsy catch on the binder sprang open and the keys scattered.

He might have known that would happen, Jon thought. It had been that kind of day.

Bradley came over and picked up the keys and holder. "How many times now have I collected your keys from the floor?" he asked with a smile.

"Too many. Did you ever find the one that went missing a few weeks back?"

Bradley nodded. "I gave it to your neighbour, Gordon, when he came in the next day. He said he'd pass it on to you. Didn't he?"

"He must have forgotten about it," Jon said, but that knowledge just added to his anger. Bloody Gordon. No wonder he'd handed over the key so readily. He'd had another one in reserve.

"Anyway," Bradley said, handing the keys over for Jon to reassemble, "you're in early. What can I get you?"

"A pint of cyanide would be magic."

Bradley smiled. "It can't be that bad surely. Who's been raining on your parade this time? That prick from work?"

Jon shrugged. "Nothing out of the ordinary from him, but he's the reason I came home early."

Bradley finished pouring a pint and placed it on the mat in front of Jon.

"Well, something's rattled your cage. If you want to talk, I'm all ears. If you don't, no problem, I'll push off to the other end of the bar and leave you to wallow."

"Sorry, I don't know whether I'm Arthur or fucking Martha today."

Bradley grinned. "If you're fucking Martha, don't do it in here; we'll lose our licence."

Jon laughed and choked on the mouthful of lager he'd been about to swallow.

"That's better," Bradley said. "Come on; tell Uncle Bradley all about it."

All the rage and frustration came to the surface and Jon blurted out all his woes, from not getting the job in Leicester he'd wanted so badly, to what he'd found when he'd arrived home.

Bradley's eyebrows shot skywards. "Bloody hell, you mean he can walk? Doesn't need the wheelchair at all?"

Jon shook his head. "Nope and what's more, when I told him to own up to the social and tell them to stop his benefits, the bastard turned on me and threatened to stitch me up."

Bradley shook his head and glanced down the bar where a customer was waiting. "I just need to serve that bloke. I'll be back," he said.

By the time he came back, Jon's anger had reached boiling point. He barely waited for Bradley to reach him.

"For fuck's sake, Bradley, Andy kept it from me for a whole year. A whole fucking year, the bastard played me like a fool. Every night when I got home from my shitty job I ended up spending an even shittier evening listening to Andy going on and on about how I'd ruined his life. Ruined his life? He's fucking lucky to be alive." He swigged back the last of his pint. "I'll tell you this much, if I got the chance and thought I could get away with it, I'd kill the fucker and not think twice about it."

He got off the bar stool and picked up his keys.

"Where are you off to now? I don't think you should go home in the mood you're in. Why not stay and calm down for a bit."

Jon laughed, but felt more like crying. "Home? I haven't got one. Don't worry, I'm not going to do anything to the little rat. I think I'll move into a B and B for a bit. I'll go back now and pick up some stuff and then leave Andy and his great buddy, Gordon, to laugh their arses off at making a fool of me."

CHAPTER TWENTY-TWO

Paolo pulled another report in front of him. Pages and pages of what had been done so far and not one single piece of evidence to help them get to grips with the case. What was he missing? The answers were in there somewhere, he just had to find a different way of looking at things.

His phone rang, giving him a welcome opportunity to push the paperwork to one side.

"Storey," he said, not recognising the number on his LED display.

"Detective Inspector? This is Constance Myers. I think I might have found something of interest for you. I'm afraid it doesn't include all the names you asked me to look for, but I have found a case where everyone apart from Edwin Fulbright is mentioned."

Paolo felt a shiver along his spine. At last!

"Could you fill in the details, please, Ms Myers?"

"Mr Bishop was acting on behalf of a young man by the name of Jon Miller who had been charged with dangerous driving and driving under the influence of narcotics. While he was driving, he caused the death of a woman, Grace Simmonds. Also, as a result of the accident, his younger brother, Andrew Miller, was left paralysed from the waist down. Mr Bishop instructed Mr Wittington-Smythe to act for Mr Miller in court. Mr Miller's defence was that the narcotic had been prescribed for him by Conrad Stormont. Mr Stormont had been standing in as his psychiatrist while Professor Edwards was on leave."

"Ms Myers, you are a star. This is exactly what we needed. Could you give me the dates and court docket numbers? I'll get one of my team to track down the court transcript."

She read out the details. "But that case doesn't cover everyone on your list. I'm sorry, I've searched and searched. There is no connection in our files to a Mr Edwin Fulbright. Not in this case or any other we have been able to uncover."

Paolo smiled. It didn't matter. They already had a connection to the surgeon. Edwin Fulbright had saved Conrad Stormont's life when he'd tried to commit suicide. As much as Paolo's gut instinct told him Stormont wasn't the killer, he had to follow the evidence trail and that was pointing firmly to the disgraced ex-psychiatrist. All they had to do now was find him.

"Thank you so much for your assistance, Ms Myers."

"You're welcome. If it helps to find the monster who killed one of the kindest men on the planet, that will be thanks enough."

Paolo said goodbye, saddened at the heartbreak in her voice. Too often in his life he heard that same tone and knew there was nothing he could do to ease the pain for those who'd lost a loved one, other than find the person responsible.

He got up and went out into the main office to let his team know what Constance Myers had uncovered. He rapped on the board to get everyone's attention.

"Listen up; we've finally had a bit of a breakthrough. Andrea, I want you to get a trial transcript from ten years ago." He handed over a piece of paper. "I've written down the details, including the court docket numbers. We need to know everything that happened in that trial. It was because of that case that Conrad Stormont lost his licence, but, even more interestingly, three of our victims were involved in the case. The fourth, as we know, was the surgeon who saved Conrad Stormont's life."

"Are you saying you think Stormont's our man?" asked Dave.

Paolo wanted to say yes, but something still niggled, holding him back.

"It looks that way, but I'm not convinced. It's almost as

if he's being set up. Everything points to him as the guilty party, but I just don't buy it. Why has he waited ten years? I can understand him having a grudge against Professor Edwards if he lied about his notes and Stormont lost his licence as a result. At a stretch, I can understand him wanting to kill the man who saved his life when all he wanted to do was end it. But if that's the case, why not kill them ten years ago? And why kill Bishop and Wittington-Smythe? Because they acted for the accused who'd been given the wrong drugs? We're missing a big piece of this puzzle. When we find it, maybe things will slot into place, but in the meantime, no, I'm not convinced."

A couple of hours later a tap on his office door made him look up to see Katy grinning at him.

"Hi, Dad," she said, coming into the room and almost dragging a young man with her.

"Danny, this is my dad. Dad, this is Danny. I've told him you might be able to help his brother."

Paolo was about to tell Katy he could do no such thing when the boy's obvious embarrassment stopped him. Damn Katy and her lame ducks. Now what had she let him in for. He gestured to her to close the door and pointed to the two chairs in front of his desk.

"I'll listen, Danny, but the chances of me being able to do anything at all for your brother are pretty remote."

"That's what I thought," Danny said, turning a brilliant shade of scarlet and standing up.

Paolo held up his hand. "Sorry, I didn't mean that to sound as dismissive as it came out. Let me hear your story. I might at least be able to point you in the right direction to find someone who can help."

Danny subsided onto the chair, looking as though he would rather have escaped while he had the chance. He gave Katy a pleading look, but she shook her head.

"Honestly, you've got nothing to fear from my dad. If he can help Mark, he will. If he can't, he'll tell you and no harm done."

Something stirred in Paolo's brain, but before he could pin it down, Danny sat forward.

"My brother's in juvenile detention, but he was stitched up. He didn't do anything. Well, he did, but he didn't know he was doing it. Oh, what's the point? I can see on your face what you're thinking."

Paolo smiled. "Really? And what's that?"

"You probably think my brother was involved with a gang and said he was carrying the drugs for someone else. Well, he wasn't part of any gang, but he was carrying drugs, only he didn't know that's what they were. He was just delivering a parcel for our stepdad. He's the one who should've been locked up, but instead Mark got picked up and no one believed him when he told them what had happened."

Before Paolo could react, Katy jumped in.

"So, you see, Dad, we need you to make the authorities listen to Mark. The real drug dealer is still on the streets and has a whole team of kids Danny's age and younger working for him."

Paolo already knew what the answer would be, but wanted to hear it from Danny.

"What's your stepfather's name?"

"Carl Hunt," Danny said as the name echoed in Paolo's head at the same moment.

Paolo smiled. "You're Daniel Stormont. I've been looking for you."

Danny jumped up again. "Why? You're not stitching me up like Mark. I'm out of here."

"No, wait," Paolo said, trying to avoid the look of suspicion in Katy's eyes. "I promise you I'm not planning anything. I've met your stepfather and I believe you. I'll try to help your brother, if I can."

Danny stood, clearly unconvinced. "Well, if it's not to stitch me up, what did you want with me?"

Paolo gestured to the chair. "Sit down, please. Would you like a drink of some kind?"

Danny sat, but shook his head. He looked as if he'd run

at the slightest provocation.

"What about you, Katy? Cool drink for you?"

"No, thanks, Dad. Let's just get to the point. I've brought Danny here to ask for your help and you spring that on us. No wonder Danny's suspicious. I'm feeling that way myself."

Paolo took a deep breath. "Right, I'll set things out from my side and then you can fill me in on what happened with your brother, okay?"

Danny stared at him, without moving, but then gave a nod so slight Paolo wasn't even sure he'd seen it. As the boy hadn't got up again, Paolo decided to take that as affirmation.

"Right, I cannot go into details, but we are investigating a series of killings that appear to be connected."

"The Saturday murders," Katy interrupted. "How is Danny connected to that?"

"I've just said, I can't go into the details, Katy, but you're on the right lines." He looked across to Danny. "One name crops up over and over, but I don't believe he is the killer. I want to repeat that. I *don't* believe he is the killer, but the name is that of your father. Your real dad."

Danny shrugged as if it meant nothing to him, but Paolo had spotted the tiny twitch of his mouth.

"Danny, we need to find your father."

"Join the club," he said. "If you run into him, tell him I said thanks for nothing."

"You have no idea where he is?"

Danny shook his head. "No, and I don't want to know either. If he'd stuck around, Mark and I wouldn't have ended up living with that psychopath my mother is so in love with. Did you know she lets him beat her senseless and still sticks up for him over us?"

Paolo waited to give Danny time to compose himself again. Only when he was sure the boy had his emotions under control did he move on to the next question.

"What about Mark? Has he had any contact with your father?"

Danny laughed and Paolo thought he'd never heard a sadder sound. "Mark's an idiot. He still thinks Dad's going to come back and save us. You know, even when he was in such deep trouble, all he could say was that Dad would turn up and put things right. I don't know how he thought that was going to work, but he believed it body and soul. If he'd known where to find Dad, he'd have told me to go and fetch him."

"Danny, do you mind if I just go over a few things with you. I'm trying to get the timeline straight in my head, but there are gaps."

Danny shrugged. "Sure, go for it."

Paolo looked at the notes he had on the Stormont children. "Okay, here's what I know so far. When your father disappeared, your mother became dependent on drugs and alcohol. As a result the court placed you, your brother and your sister in the care of your grandmother."

"She's still got Princess Celine," Danny said. "Granny didn't want us, but she loves her precious granddaughter."

The bitterness in his tone could have stripped paint from the walls, but Paolo didn't blame him. He'd have been feeling that way himself in Danny's position.

"When your grandmother decided she couldn't cope with the three of you, how come you ended up back with your mother and weren't placed in care? You'd been taken away from your mother, so I'm surprised they agreed to you going back to her."

"They didn't know about it. Granny didn't tell them. She salved her conscience by sending Mum money and taking us out to lunch every so often." He smiled. "It wasn't so bad at first. Mum tried hard to stay off the drugs and booze, but then she met the monster."

His eyes filled with tears and Paolo handed him a tissue. He brushed it across his eyes, almost as if he was angry for showing weakness.

"He moved in even before they got married and it changed everything. What he wanted came first and Mark and I stopped existing for Mum. I stuck it out as long as I could, but pushed off to live with a friend when he started knocking her about." He glared at Paolo. "You needn't think I abandoned her, because I didn't. I tried to stop him from hitting her, but then he'd lay into me and she did nothing. Afterwards, she'd blame me for upsetting him. Said it was my fault he lost his temper. I had to get away. Mark has, or had, a rosier view of life than me. He was convinced there must be good in Carl somewhere. He thought if he was pally with Carl, maybe he'd keep his fists to himself. And look what happened to him!"

Paolo saw Katy reach across and squeeze Danny's hand. He wondered just how involved she was and hoped she wasn't going to end up hurt. Danny was emotionally damaged.

"What happened to you after you left home? You're in care now, so at some point you moved out of your friend's house."

Danny nodded. "Yes, it was after Mark was arrested. Social Services remembered we existed. They found out where I was living and came for me. I've been in care for six months, but I won't be there for much longer. They can only keep me until I'm sixteen if I've got somewhere to go."

"And have you?" Paolo asked.

Danny nodded. "At the moment I help out at the homeless shelter on weekends. John, who runs the place, is a good guy. He said one of the lads is moving out from the flat upstairs. It'll just be a room, sharing the kitchen and bathroom with the other three living there, but I won't have to pay any rent as long as I give them a hand in the evenings when they're dishing out the food."

"What about your schooling?"

He smiled at Katy before turning back and answering. "I've got plans for the future, Mr Storey. I intend to finish school and see if I can get into a university."

Paolo had an idea the plans for the future included Katy and had to stop himself from saying something which would alienate her. She's a sensible girl, he told himself.

Trust her judgment. Easier said than done, but he was determined to try.

"Okay, tell me about Mark. Let me see if I can do anything to help his situation."

Danny kept quiet for a few moments, then seemed to come to the conclusion that Paolo might be on his side, because he nodded.

"I wasn't living at home, if you can call it that, but Mark was. He says Carl and Mum had cut back on their drinking and Carl had been less aggressive for a few days. He was on the phone a lot, talking about some business deal he was planning; a takeover."

He looked directly at Paolo. "Yeah, I know. Looking back now it's pretty obvious, but Mark always looks for the best in people, even now. He says Carl mentioned a garage in Leicester. He used to be a mechanic, and Mark thought maybe Carl was going to rent a place to work in. Mark is really good with his hands and thought Carl might take him on as an apprentice. Anyway, Carl told Mark he needed him to take a gift to Leicester for the garage owner. He called it a sweetener against future business. What Mark didn't realise was that the parcel he was carrying contained enough ecstasy tablets to keep a club full of ravers happy."

Paolo nodded. "I remember the story now. The police had received a tipoff from a rival gang that a delivery was going to be made. They watched your brother walk in with the goods and then raided the garage. He was caught red-handed. The garage owner went down, but I can't recall how long for."

"Not long enough," Danny said. "And Carl should have gone to prison as well, but he claimed he knew nothing about the drugs. Said he'd been worried about Mark and had been going to talk to him about his," he made quote marks with his fingers, "wayward behaviour."

Danny's eyes once again filled with tears. "It's not fair. He stays free and Mark gets put away in a remand home in Leicester. Can you do anything?"

"Please, Dad, say you can help," Katy begged, taking

Danny's hand again.

"Danny, I've met Carl and I believe every word you've told me, but whether or not I can get others to see things the same way, I just don't know."

"But you'll try, Dad, please say you'll try."

Paolo nodded. "I'll try, but don't get your hopes up. This has already gone through the courts, so it's highly unlikely I can get any conviction overturned without new evidence, but I might be able to do something about Mark's incarceration."

Katy jumped up, rushed round the desk and hugged him.

"I knew I could rely on you. You're the best."

When they'd left, Paolo reflected on Danny's story. He could imagine how a young man in Mark's position could get suckered into dealing drugs without even realising he was being used as a mule. It was a crying shame if Danny's version of events was true, but just because his brother believed in him, that didn't necessarily mean Mark was innocent.

On a positive note, at least Paolo now knew where to get hold of Conrad Stormont's other son. If nothing else, he'd find out whether or not Mark knew where his father was hiding out.

He got up and went to find Dave. It was time for a trip to Leicester.

Paolo shifted on the seat. It was one of the most uncomfortable he'd ever had the misfortune to sit on. He glanced across at Dave, also fidgeting in an effort to find a better position. Not only were the chairs hard, unyielding plastic, but they had to have been designed by a sadist. No one had a body shape which would fit into a seat that turned up at the sides and dipped at the front.

The door opened and he was able to force his mind off his numb posterior and take in the scared face of a youth who was undoubtedly Danny's brother. He was a year or two older, but his attitude was one of a kid much younger.

He had that desperate to please look that came with spending time with other offenders. Some of the youths in detention were hardened criminals, had been since they could hold a knife. Mark looked more like a victim than an offender. Maybe Danny's version of events was true after all.

"Take a seat, Mark," Paolo said. "I won't tell you to make yourself comfortable because that's impossible on these chairs."

Paolo had expected a smile at the very least, but Mark's face looked, if anything, even more haunted.

"Why am I here?" Mark said.

"Do you mean why are you in this room, or why are you in the detention centre?"

"Here, in this room. What have I done now?"

He lifted his left hand and chewed at his thumb nail as if he hadn't eaten in days.

"I wanted to ask you a few questions about your dad."

"Carl's not my dad, and I *did* take that parcel to Leicester for him without knowing what was in it, whatever he says."

"I believe you," Paolo said, surprised to realise it was true.

He made up his mind to see if he could at least get the boy moved to Bradchester under supervision. "It's not Carl I want to ask you about, it's your real dad. Have you seen him in the last year or so?"

Conrad Stormont had proven so elusive, Paolo had virtually given up hope of anything other than a negative answer. He was astounded when Mark said yes.

"It was about five months before…before I ended up in this mess. I thought I'd seen him earlier in the year. This man was staring at me. Or, maybe he wasn't, but it felt like he was. At first I didn't think of Dad, because he didn't look the way I'd remembered him."

"If he didn't look like your father, what made you think that's who it was?"

Mark shrugged. "I know this sounds mad, but it was the

way he was standing. Sort of leaning a bit to one side and his hands in his pockets. I can't explain it properly, but my brother stands in exactly the same way. That's what made me think it was Dad. He reminded me of the way Danny stands."

Paolo thought back to earlier that day when Danny had been waiting for him and Katy to say their goodbyes. He had a vivid image of Danny's stance and knew what Mark meant.

"Did you approach the man?"

Mark shook his head. "He was too far away. By the time it registered who he was, he'd gone."

"But then you saw him again?"

"Yes. I was going into the train station and there was an argument between one of the porters and this bloke in a dirty tracksuit. I didn't even realise at first it was the same man as before, but when he turned round I saw it was Dad. He was close enough this time that I could make out his face. He nodded as if he knew who I was, then turned and ran off towards town. I ran after him, but he dodged down a side street and when I got to the end of it, I couldn't see him anywhere."

Paolo stood up and held out his hand. "Mark, I am going to try to get you moved to Bradchester. No promises, but I'll do my best. Keep out of trouble in here in the meantime."

Mark's bottom lip trembled. He reached out and grabbed Paolo's hand. "Is there really a chance, sir?"

"There should be if I vouch for you, but that won't work unless you've got a clean record here. Okay? I'll keep in touch."

In the car Paolo's hands clenched and unclenched as he thought about Carl Hunt and the way he'd let the boy take the fall for his crime, but his real anger was at Mark's mother. What sort of woman would believe someone like Carl over her own son? Whatever happened, Paolo vowed two things. He would get Mark a transfer and he'd watch and wait. One day, Carl Hunt would put a foot wrong. On that day, he'd find Paolo Storey standing right behind him with a pair of handcuffs ready for use.

CHAPTER TWENTY-THREE

Week five – Friday 22nd August to Thursday 28th August

Paolo pulled into the railway station car park and turned off the ignition. He looked at the clock on the dashboard. Only nine-twenty. Jessica's train wasn't due for another twenty minutes, but he hadn't wanted to take a chance on being late.

He'd missed her more than he'd thought possible. From what she'd said on the phone, she felt the same way. He smiled. The thoughts in his head would be more at home in the mind of a teenager. Then again, why should teenagers have all the fun? He got out of the car and locked it. As he made his way to the main station entrance he remembered Mark's comment from two days earlier. Was it really his dad he saw?

Paolo had arranged for posters of Conrad Stormont to be put up all over town, but the only image they'd had of him to work on was ten years out of date. With Mark's help, they had been able to enhance the image, but Paolo wasn't certain it was close enough to do the job.

Where had Stormont been living? More to the point, what had he been living on? He hadn't drawn any benefits or paid taxes since he dropped out of sight, but if he was still alive and living in the area, he had to be getting money and food from somewhere. Paolo had checked with the shelter where Danny volunteered, but although a couple of drunks said the man in the picture owed them money, neither could say where they'd last seen him or when.

He'd had a similar reaction at the other shelters. People thought they knew him, but couldn't say where from or when they'd last seen him.

And he couldn't get the thought out of his mind that someone might be in danger tonight. The killer usually struck on a Friday for the body to be found on Saturday. But who would be the fifth victim? And why? Even if the killer was Stormont, they were no closer to getting inside the man's head.

Paolo's musings came to an abrupt stop when he heard the sound of an approaching train. He rushed forward, down the stairs and along the tunnel to the far platform, climbing the flight up just in time to see the train come to a halt.

He stood waiting, feeling for all the world like a kid at Christmas about to receive the present he'd been hoping for all year. As people alighted, his view of the platform was blocked by passengers eager to get home, or wherever they were headed for the night. Eventually he was able to get a clear sight along the platform and saw Jessica walking towards him, pulling her suitcase behind her.

His mouth dried out, his feet weighed him down like lead and his chest felt as if it would explode, but somehow he managed to close the gap between them.

When they finally broke apart, Jessica laughed.

"Wow, if I'd known I was coming back to that, I'd have caught an earlier train."

Paolo took the handle of her bag in one hand and slipped his arm round her on his other side.

"Have you eaten? We could go to the Italian place."

Jessica smiled and shook her head.

"I'm hungry," she said, "but not for food. You wanna come home with me?"

Paolo's heart fluttered so heavily it seemed to be full of moths dancing a tango.

He grinned. "I think I could force myself to do that."

***

The pretender looked down at the sleeping man. Another step on his quest for justice. The man looked almost graceful in repose. The pretender laughed. Graceful – full of grace, how apt and how ironic. This one hadn't required any planning. He'd simply had to follow the man and wait until he passed out.

He squatted on his haunches to make it easier to reach the man's leg. As he depressed the plunger to send the liquid into the man's system, his mind was already moving on to his final execution.

He pulled an envelope from his pocket and placed it on the man's chest. Five out of six dealt with. Only a week to go and then he would be face to face with the last name on his list.

But before then, he had another one to exterminate. One whose name had never occurred to him until recently. One he'd always seen as a victim, but not anymore. Instead of six, there would be seven to suffer. He laughed again. Maybe that was a sign. One for every day of the week. Pity the extra one couldn't go on a Friday like the rest, but he was determined to stick with his plan. Next Friday would be the last time he'd pretend to be someone he wasn't. After his final execution he'd stand proudly and tell everyone who he was and why he'd killed the six who'd hurt him so badly. Plus the extra one. He needed to be taught a lesson before he died.

In a way, he was now pleased Jessica Carter hadn't been available for the day he'd originally planned for her. Having a woman as the final act in his tragedy now seemed so incredibly right that he wondered why he hadn't thought of it before. A female's death to close the circle.
Perfect.

CHAPTER TWENTY-FOUR

Paolo opened his eyes and looked over at the bedside clock. Nine in the morning and no call from the station to say another victim had turned up. He gave a contented sigh and moved closer to Jessica, who was gently snoring next to him.

He knew he should get up, get dressed and go home, but just lying here in the comfort of Jessica's bed made him feel like a normal human being for once. He allowed himself the luxury of another hour in bed and promised he would then go into the station as he'd intended.

Jessica gave a small moan and stirred. As her eyes fluttered open, she smiled.

"Morning, sleepyhead," Paolo said. "Did I disturb you?"

"No, I was awake anyway, just wasn't ready to open my eyes."

Paolo traced a finger down her cheek.

"Do you always snore when you're awake?"

Jessica laughed. "I don't snore even when I'm asleep. Didn't your mother tell you that females don't...oh God, sorry, Paolo. I wasn't thinking."

He reached forward and kissed the top of her head. "It's okay. I'm quite sure if my mother had lived she would have told me lots of things that females don't do."

She grinned. "Like sweating. Did you know we don't sweat?"

"Really?" Paolo said, loving the early morning banter and wishing the moment could last forever. "What was that you did last night?"

Jessica wrinkled her nose. "Ah, that wasn't sweating. That, I'll have you know, was me glowing. Women don't sweat; women don't even perspire. We glow."

"I stand, or rather, lie, corrected, ma'am."

Jessica reached out for him. "On the other hand, we could do a little experiment. Shall we see if you can make me glow enough for it to be classed as perspiration?"

"I'm all in favour of experiments," Paolo said, as she snuggled into his arms.

***

Paolo looked across the room, proud to be part of a team like this one. It was one thing to come to work over the weekend when there was a dead body to investigate, but coming in when there wasn't one was over and above the call of duty. They were all here, even Dave who was supposed to be helping get things ready for his engagement party that evening.

"What time do you need to knock off, Dave?"

"I can stay until about half three, sir. Rebecca says if I'm not at the venue by four, helping to put out chairs and decorate the tables, there'll be no engagement because I'll be dead."

Paolo laughed. "Can't have that, we've already had a whip round for your present."

"We could always give it to Rebecca, sir," CC called out. "She could have it as a constant happy reminder of her near miss."

She ducked as a screw-up piece of paper flew towards her.

"I'll make the missile a bit heavier next time," Dave said, laughing.

Paolo sat back and watched the play fight. God knows, the team had worked so hard on this case with no reward, they deserved a few minutes of fun.

When the paper missiles stopped crossing the office, he stood up.

"Okay, listen up, everyone. Why do you think there hasn't been a suspicious death reported this morning? What do we think has happened to our man? Has he given up? Changed his tactics? Was he prevented from carrying out the next attack for some reason?"

"Maybe he's moved further afield, sir," Andrea called out.

Paolo nodded. "It's possible, but somehow I don't think so. His first four victims are all local to Bradchester in some way, either because they lived here, or because they worked here. I've checked with the Leicester force and their only reported murders all seem to be gang related. They had three stabbings and one shooting last night. No one was killed by injection either there or here, as far as we know."

"There is another possibility, sir," CC said. "Maybe we just haven't found the body yet."

Paolo nodded. "You could be right, but he made sure the four earlier victims were all found on a Saturday. I've been in touch with the morgue and the only deaths during the night or early this morning have all been from natural causes."

"Are we sure about that, sir?" Dave said. "Couldn't one of them have been death by insulin? Barbara Royston did say it could easily be overlooked unless there was reason to search for it."

Paolo nodded. "Yes, and I've asked that all natural causes be checked for insulin overdose. However, there was no note on any of them. Our man likes to let us know when he's killed."

He walked over to the board and looked at the photos.

"If the connection is Conrad Stormont, who would be the next logical victim?"

CC stood up and came to stand next to him. "If the killer is Conrad and he's looking for people who've hurt him in the past, what about his wife? Would she be on his list?"

Paolo nodded. "It's possible, but I still can't shake off this feeling that we're being deliberately led towards Stormont as the killer. What about if we look at things from another angle. What if Conrad Stormont is also a victim in this?"

"In what way, sir?" Dave called out.

Paolo shrugged. "I don't know really, I'm just thinking out loud. Every death seems to be linked to Stormont, so I'm probably way off base. Let's look at what we have so far. Andrea, any joy with the court transcript of the case that ultimately led to Stormont being struck off?"

She shook her head. "Not yet, sir. I've requested it as a matter of urgency, as you know, but I'm still waiting for it to arrive."

"Okay, first thing Monday morning, I want you to go to the records office and stay there until they put it into your hands. Remind them this is a murder investigation, not an enquiry into a speeding fine."

"CC, have you had chance to look through the photographs of the crowds at all the crime scenes?"

"Yes, sir. Unless he's heavily disguised, I haven't been able to spot the same person in any of the images."

"What about the CCTV footage from the multi-storey car park?"

"The killer's there, sir, but he knew where the cameras were placed. We've only got shots of him from the back and he was wearing a hoody, so we can't even guess at his hair colour."

"Damn," Paolo said. "This killing spree has been well planned. He didn't up and decide to get to it a few weeks ago. Something triggered his actions and made him plan each move. He knew how to worm his way into the lives of each of his victims."

He tapped on the first photograph. "For Professor Edwards it was his vanity. Posing as a *New York Times* reporter interested in the professor's life story opened that door with ease, but the killer could only have known that would work if he'd studied the man."

Paolo moved along to the next image. "The same goes for Mr Fulbright. He must have spent time observing the victim and finding out where his weakness might be. We don't know for sure, but it looks likely that he used Fulbright's marriage to a younger woman in some way. The phone calls Fulbright received, and his reaction to them, points to that supposition."

He pointed to the solicitor. "This, too, wasn't a spur of the moment attack. The killer found out Peter Bishop was a homosexual and got close to him that way. Not only that, but he discovered which chat site he used. How many gay chat sites are there? Andrea, could you look into that, please? My point being, it was highly unlikely he struck gold first time of trying. He must have spent a considerable amount of time on various sites before he found the right one – and even then, he had to build a relationship with Peter Bishop. We know they had phone contact. We also know from Mr Bishop's mobile phone records that he received a call while he was in the nightclub shortly before he left the building. Each crime has involved a different disposable mobile phone."

Paolo turned back to the board and tapped on the last photograph.

"For Marcus Wittington-Smythe it seems fairly obvious by the money left in the car that the killer used Wittington-Smythe's missing son as a lure. Once again, a carefully targeted approach that must have taken research and planning to pull off."

Paolo held up one hand and started ticking off items on his fingers.

"One, we know he's intelligent. He's bright enough to work out where each victim's Achilles' heel lies so that he can slip past their natural defences. Two, he's been working on his strategy for many months, possibly even years. Three, his notes have each pointed to six victims and the four he's killed so far have all turned up on Saturday mornings. If there isn't one this week it's because we haven't yet found it. I'm convinced he wouldn't have missed a week with the level of preparation he's used so far. Four, Conrad Stormont's name comes up so often, he appears to be the pivot around which everything else spins. He's possibly the killer, although you know my reservations on that."

He sighed. "Five, and this is the saddest point of all, if it *isn't* Conrad then we haven't a bloody clue who the killer might be."

Paolo made sure he had eye contact with each of them. "But six, and this is the one I want to stress, we *will* get to the bottom of this and we *will* catch him." He paused. "But I think, in the absence of a body, we can give ourselves a few hours off. Dave, go and do your stuff with Rebecca. I don't want to be an obstacle in the path of true love. For the rest of you, go home and enjoy what's left of today and I'll see you all this evening when I'm sure we'll all have a great time at Dave's party."

***

The pretender glared at the late night news. He'd been waiting all day for a report on the latest victim in what the press had dubbed the Saturday murders, but there was nothing. Not a word. He must have been found, so why were the police keeping it quiet? Was it to rile him? Were they trying to make him come forward and show his hand? If that was the case they were out of luck. He would never dance to their tune.

He switched the television off and climbed into bed. He had Jessica Carter's appointment to look forward to, but there was an extra little job he had to carry out before then. All he needed to do was pick the day.

CHAPTER TWENTY-FIVE

Paolo arrived at the station on Tuesday wondering if the break they needed was ever going to come. As he entered his office, his mobile rang and he recognised the ring tone he'd set for Lydia. Juggling papers and phone, he made his way to his desk and managed to put the papers down safely before taking the call.

"Hi, Lydia, what can I do for you?"

"I think you've lost your tiny little mind."

"Hmm, now that's not friendly and nor is it enlightening. What have I done this time?"

"Katy tells me you've met this boy she's infatuated with. Not only that, apparently you're now helping his criminal brother get a better deal. Isn't locking people up supposed to teach them the error of their ways?"

"Whoa, when did you become Miss Angry of Bradchester? You'll be demanding the death penalty for parking offences next."

"That's not funny."

Paolo sat down. "Sorry, you're right, it isn't funny, but when I get torn off a strip before I've even had chance to grab a cup of coffee my rapier wit tends to be a bit blunt. Shall we start this conversation again? What is it that I'm supposed to have done that has got you so riled up?"

"Encouraged Katy to defy me, as usual."

"Don't be ridiculous. I haven't encouraged her to do anything. Katy brought Danny to ask if I could do anything to help his brother. That's all."

"All? She now thinks you approve of him."

Paolo thought for a moment before answering. Approved was a bit strong, but he didn't disapprove.

"He seems a nice enough lad. He volunteers at the local homeless shelter. That's where he and Katy met."

"Yes, well, I've told Katy I don't like the idea of her being with all those down and outs."

Paolo took a deep breath. "Do you know something, Lydia? I've never realised until today that I don't like you very much. I'm sure you used to have a much kinder heart. Katy and Danny work together at the shelter because they are two nice kids who want to help those less fortunate than themselves."

"That's all right for you to say, but—"

"Just stop right there. Let Katy be. She knows what she's doing."

"When she gets mixed up with the drug-dealing brother you'll change your tune. You're supposed to be on the side of law enforcement, Paolo, not teaching our daughter that there are no penalties for bad behaviour."

"Lydia, I believed Danny and his brother when they said Mark was set up. I've met the stepfather and he is exactly the type who would do something like that. All I've done is arrange for him to stay in the youth hostel here under supervision. He's being watched, but really doesn't seem the type to do drugs."

"Just deals them," Lydia snapped.

"I give up! It doesn't matter what I say, you've decided the two boys are the dregs of society. I've met them. You haven't."

"I don't want to meet them. I want you to tell Katy to stay away from both of them."

Paolo sighed. "I'm not going to do that. You should know better than this, Lydia. I trust Katy; why can't you?"

"It's pointless talking to you, Paolo. I don't know why I bothered to call. Just don't blame me if Katy ends up as a drug-addicted dropout."

Before Paolo could answer, the dialling tone buzzed in his ear.

He was still sitting glaring at the phone when Andrea stuck her head round the door.

"You'll never guess what I've just picked up, sir."

It took a massive effort, but Paolo managed a smile.

"How many guesses do I get?"

She stepped into the room carrying a thick bound document and held it up for him to see.

"Just one, sir."

"The trial transcript. At last."

She grinned and pretended to collapse under its weight. "It's going to take me a while to get through this."

"Take as much time as you need. I'll move your case files onto other officers. I'm convinced the answers we need are in that file."

***

Jon came into work on Tuesday morning feeling that his life was finally turning a corner. At last something was going right for him. He'd spent six nights in the B and B and had hated every one of them. But tonight was the last one where he'd have to share a bathroom with a bunch of strangers. The bedsit he'd gone to view the night before was small, but he could make it into somewhere to call home.

As he hung up his jacket and reached back into the locker for his work clothes, he saw Iain approaching. If he could only get Iain off his back, life might be worth living again. He decided to face up to the man and find out once and for all what it was the idiot had against him. He shut his locker door with a bang and turned to face him.

"Shall we sort this out? I'm sick to death of your bullying. Tell me what I'm supposed to have done all those years ago."

"Like you don't know," Iain said.

Jon slammed his fist against the nearest locker, sending metallic reverberations around the room.

"Sandra Milligan," Iain said.

"Who? What? I've no idea who she is."

Iain came closer and leaned forward. "That's my point, you little shit. You don't even remember her, but thanks to you she's in a mental home."

Jon felt as if he was caught in a B movie, but he was the only one who didn't know the script.

"Iain, I have no idea who the hell Sandra Milli...oh God, you mean Sandy. I haven't seen her for years."

"No, because you dumped her when she needed you most."

"I didn't dump her. We'd only been out a couple of times and then...well, and then my life took a turn for the worse. I lost touch with her."

"That's not the way her mum tells it."

Jon sat down next to his locker. "Look, I've still no idea what you're on about, but clearly you think I did something dreadful to Sandy. If that's the case, how come you were all right with me when we first worked together?"

Iain sat down opposite, but Jon could see by the way his fists were clenching and unclenching that he was ready to lash out on the smallest provocation.

"I didn't know who you were back then," Iain said. "It was only when my aunt Vera saw you outside one day that she told me you were the prick who'd ruined Sandra's life."

"Iain, I swear to you, Sandy...Sandra, I mean, we weren't a couple, no matter what your aunt says. We went out three times, max. Sandy was nice, but she was a bit too clinging for me, almost as if we were planning wedding bells instead of someone I barely knew. Then the accident happened and I got caught up in all that shit and—"

"What accident?"

Jon wondered if Iain was putting him on. If his aunt knew who he was, surely she must have mentioned the accident. It had been big news back then.

"You really don't know?"

"No, when did it happen?"

"About ten years ago. Round about the time your cousin and I split up."

Iain looked disbelieving. "How convenient."

Jon stood up. "There's no point in talking to you. It wasn't fucking convenient. It was horrific, a woman died, my brother was in hospital for months and I almost went to prison. If you thing that's *convenient*, you're off your fucking rocker."

Iain waved a hand towards the seat. "So, explain it to me."

Jon sat down again. "There's not much to explain. I told you, Sandy was just someone I'd had a few dates with. She wanted it to be more than that. I can't remember now what I wanted, but I ended up crashing my car and all the other stuff I've told you about. I didn't give her another thought. I was either at the hospital with my brother, or talking to my solicitor. It was a nightmare year. By the time it was all sorted, I'd forgotten Sandy even existed. If that makes me the villain in your eyes, there's fuck all I can do about that, but I didn't mean to hurt her."

Iain sat silently for a couple of minutes, staring at the ceiling, and Jon wondered if he should get up and get back to work, but then Iain looked back at him.

"I was away when Sandra tried to kill herself. I only came back to Bradchester three years ago. I've been travelling all over and had no idea what was going on with the family. I stayed with Aunt Vera when I first came back, my parents moved down south when Dad retired. All I heard was about this arsehole who'd driven Sandra into the asylum. I remember her as a sweet kid. We lived in the next street and as she grew up she used to follow me around."

Iain stood up.

"I couldn't give a shit about you or your life. It's all boohoo poor fucking me." He leaned over Jon. "You wound her up and convinced her she was the best thing that had ever happened to you. Don't bother to deny it because I don't believe you. I've seen you pretending you don't know people when they talk to you. Then the next time you see them it's all hello how are you? Acting as if you hadn't blown them out the last time you met. Well that shit won't wash with me. You see, Sandra was a lovely girl. She isn't now, of course. Now she's a trembling wreck who begs anyone who comes to see her to bring enough pills so that she can die. That's what you did to her. Now fuck off out of my sight before I wring your scrawny neck."

CHAPTER TWENTY-SIX

On Wednesday morning, on the way to his own office, Paolo stopped by Andrea's desk.

"How's it going?" he asked, pointing to the pages she was poring over.

"Heavy reading, sir. There's pages and pages of stuff that just goes over and over the same old evidence. How can barristers get excited about this stuff? It is so deadly dull and boring."

Paolo smiled. "It's just as well you didn't go into that side of the law. I can imagine the judge's face if you jumped up and told the defence to get on with it because you're bored stiff."

Andrea laughed. "It's not just the defence, sir. The prosecution's as bad. He says blah, blah, blah and then the witness says the same thing and then the defence says blah, blah, blah, but tries to make it sound like a different thing altogether. They just repeat themselves. I pity the poor court stenographer who had to type up this lot. She must have needed gallons of coffee to keep her awake."

"So there's nothing in there to help us?"

She shook her head. "Nothing we don't already know, so far, but I'm going through it slowly to make sure I don't overlook anything."

Paolo wished her well with it and passed on to his office. He was surprised to find Barbara waiting for him.

"I hope you didn't mind me coming in, Paolo, but I wanted to make sure I caught you before you went out anywhere."

He came in and shut the door behind him.

"No, I don't mind at all. Is everything okay? Is it to do

with Friday?"

She smiled. "I'm as ready as I'll ever be for the op on Friday. No, it's nothing to do with that. I've noticed something in autopsy yesterday that I think might interest you."

He sat down and gestured for her to continue.

"I conducted an autopsy on a vagrant yesterday afternoon. He'd been found in a shop doorway on Saturday morning and was believed to have had a heart attack. The autopsy should have been routine, but you'd requested a tox screen on all bodies found on Saturday."

Paolo sat forward. "And?"

"The test came up positive. He'd died as a result of insulin overdose."

"And he was definitely found on Saturday?"

Barbara nodded.

"Any ID?"

This time she shook her head. "I'm afraid not, but he has old scars on his wrists. Suicide type scars, which might make it easier to identify him."

Paolo felt a shiver run through his body. "Suicide scars? How old do you think?"

"It's impossible to say, but they look as if they've been there a number of years. Why? Do you know who he is?"

"I don't know for sure, but I have a hunch this might be the man we've been hunting for, Conrad Stormont. We know he tried to commit suicide by slashing his wrists. Could the insulin have been self-inflicted? Another suicide attempt, but successful this time?"

Barbara nodded. "It's possible, but there were no needles found anywhere near him. Although I suppose passing junkies might have taken anything that was lying around."

"I didn't think they shared needles," Paolo said.

"It depends how desperate they are."

Paolo picked up a pen and tapped it against the desk. "I wonder why there was no envelope with the numbers in it."

Barbara reached forward and took the pen away. "You have no idea how irritating it is when you do that," she said.

213

He grinned. "You sound just like my old English teacher. She used to take my pencil away when I did it and then still expected me to write an essay."

Barbara smiled, but kept the pen. "Maybe," she said, "there was an envelope and it blew away in the wind, or maybe someone saw it and thought it might contain money or drugs, so took it and ran."

Paolo nodded. "Everything's possible. We can easily find out if this is Stormont."

"How?"

"I happen to know both of his sons. I'm sure we can persuade one or both of them to provide a DNA sample to check against."

Paolo's smile faded as he realised what that would mean.

"If the body of the vagrant turns out to be that of Conrad Stormont, we're right back to square one with this case. We don't have any other suspects and the only thing that tied Fulbright in with the other three was Stormont."

"But surely if Stormont is a victim, that must mean the connection is still there, even if he isn't the murderer."

He reached across and retrieved his pen from Barbara's clasp. "The only thing I'm certain of is that I'm uncertain about every bloody thing to do with this case."

Paolo heard Katy's voice, chatting to Dave and introducing Danny to everyone in the office, long before she tapped on his office door. Considering he'd only called Danny an hour earlier, he should have been surprised to find she'd come in with him, but he wasn't. He remembered Lydia's words and contemplated suggesting Katy put a bit of distance between herself and the Stormont boys, but decided against it. He was convinced Lydia's approach was the wrong one and would, if anything, push Katy into seeing more of Danny, not less.

She stuck her head round the door and grinned at him.

"This is getting to be a habit," she said. "Maybe you should put me in one of your cells to save me having to get the bus all the time."

"Come in, both of you, but Katy, what I have to say to Danny is personal, so he might prefer for you to wait outside."

Paolo caught the look that passed between them. It was one of friendship and trust. Danny nodded and pulled out a chair for Katy before sitting down on the one next to it.

"I'm happy for Katy to hear whatever it is you've got to say. You were a bit mysterious on the phone."

"I know. I'm sorry about that, but I wanted to break this to you face to face. There isn't any gentle way to say it. Danny, I'm sorry, but I think we might have your father's body in the morgue."

Danny sighed. "I thought it might be something like that. Actually, I thought maybe you had him locked up, but if he's dead I'm not really surprised. From what Mark said when he saw Dad, he looked like he might be living rough." He frowned. "But that doesn't explain why you needed me to come in to the station. You could have come to the care home to tell me."

"The thing is," Paolo said, picking his words with care, "we don't know for sure it is your father. As you know, Mark's DNA is on our database and we are going to cross match his against the unknown man's. But I wondered if you would be able to give a visual identification."

Danny's face blanched. "You mean look at a dead body?"

Paolo nodded. "Yes. We can wait for the DNA results to come back, but in the meantime there is a murderer on the loose who could strike again. It's really important for us to establish the man's identity as soon as possible."

"Murderer? Are you saying my dad, this man, was murdered?"

"It looks that way. I'm sorry. Do you think you would recognise your father after all these years?"

Danny shrugged. "I don't know. I think I'd know if it *wasn't* him, if you can understand that. Why didn't you ask my mother? No, don't answer that. You did ask and she said no."

Mrs Hunt's foul-mouthed tirade when he'd phoned still rang in his ears, but he had no intention of sharing that with Danny.

"Will you do it?"

Danny swallowed and nodded. "Now?"

Paolo stood up. "I'll come down with you."

"Me, too," Katy said. She stopped and took Danny's hand. "As long as you want me to."

"Yes, please. It'll be easier with you there."

After the viewing Paolo went outside to say goodbye to Danny and Katy before heading back to his office. Danny had taken one look at the body and broken down in tears. Just looking at the man and boy in profile, had told Paolo all he needed to know. They were almost identical.

"You will find the killer, won't you?" Danny said, a catch in his voice.

"I'm going to do my best, Danny. I promise you that."

To his surprise Danny nodded. "That's good enough for me. You said you'd do your best for Mark and you did. I trust you and I never thought I'd say that about a policeman after what happened with my brother."

"We will still need to carry out the DNA match, just to be certain, but from the point of view of our investigation, we are now looking into the murder of Conrad Stormont."

"I don't understand," Danny said. "Why would anyone want to hurt my dad? He was a wreck and had nothing. He didn't even have a home. Why kill him?"

"I don't know yet," Paolo said, "but I'm going to find out."

***

Paolo headed back into the station after waving off Katy and Danny. He smiled. No matter what Lydia said, he liked Danny and wasn't going to do anything that might interfere with their friendship. A tiny voice in his head asked how he would feel if it went deeper than friendship, but fortunately, the desk sergeant called out to him, preventing him from having to walk that particular path.

"Call just in, sir. I think it's one for you."

"Thanks," Paolo said, taking the receiver.

He listened to the details and asked for the address. Handing the phone back to the sergeant, Paolo headed for the stairs. Slightly out of breath by the time he'd climbed to the right floor, he pushed open the central office door.

"Dave," he yelled. "Grab your things. We've got another body."

He noted the looks of interest on the faces of his team.

"I'll fill you in when we get back. I don't know if this is one of ours or not, but the investigating officers found insulin hidden on the premises."

In the car Paolo gave Dave the address and then outlined what he'd been told on the phone.

"Apparently, the upstairs neighbour found the body and called for an ambulance. The victim was dead when they got there and they called us in. Probable cause of death is insulin overdose."

Dave flicked on the indicator and turned right. "How could they tell so quickly?"

"Because the syringe and the vial the insulin had been drawn from were left lying next to the body."

"But that doesn't sound like our man. He hasn't done that before."

"No, I know, but he also hasn't killed on a Tuesday before, either. From what I was told on the phone the body has been there for at least twenty-four hours. The only definite connection is the fact that insulin has been used. However, the victim's name is Andrew Miller, which just happens to be the same name as the brother who was paralysed in the accident which seems to connect to so many strands of our case. I don't know if it's the same person, or a coincidence, but it seems a bit of a stretch to believe in a coincidence that huge."

Dave pulled up near to the police tape cutting off access to the street. As Paolo got out of the car, he looked at the crowd gathered and tried to spot any familiar faces from the previous crime scenes, without any luck. While in the car he'd called for a photographer to take images of the onlookers. So far they hadn't picked up the same person appearing at more than one event, but it was still worthwhile taking the pictures, just in case.

As they entered the flat, the stench of decay hit full force. Paolo didn't think he'd ever get used to the slightly sweet smell of rotting flesh. A young uniformed officer came forward.

"The gentleman who found the body has gone back up to his flat with a constable, sir. I've told him to expect a visit from you. It's the one directly above this one."

"Yes, thank you. Dave, you go up and keep the witness company. I just want to have a word with the pathologist and I'll be up."

Paolo was surprised to see Barbara on duty. With her surgery programmed for Friday, he'd expected her to take a few days off to prepare. She looked up as he came in and frowned.

"There's something not quite right about this one, Paolo."

"You mean apart from him being dead?"

She laughed. "You know that's not what I meant. Our victim this time was pretty badly beaten before death. The positioning of the syringe points to the same killer, or someone who knows the way the killer works, but there was quite a scuffle that took place here prior to the murder. The attacker was really angry. Look at all the bruising on the victim's face."

"So you think—"

"Just stop right there, Paolo. I won't know what to think until I've had chance to do a proper examination of the body. All I know is that these bruises are pre-mortem. That's as far as I'm prepared to go."

"Can you at least give me an approximate time of death?"

"The best I can say at the moment is sometime between

nine in the morning and midday yesterday."

Paolo smiled. "Thanks. See you on Friday," he whispered.

Barbara nodded. "Not sure I'd be able to go through it without knowing you'll be there when I wake up," she said so softly he had to lean forward to make out her words.

Paolo touched her arm. "You would. You're a strong woman, but I won't let you down. I'll be there."

Upstairs the flat was an exact replica of the layout down below. The only difference was in the décor and choice of furniture.

Paolo smiled at the police constable. "Thanks. You can go downstairs and help keep the crowds back."

When he'd left, Paolo took a seat on the sofa next to Dave, facing the man who'd reported the death. He waited for Dave to get his notebook ready.

"I'm Detective Inspector Paolo Storey. I take it you've already been introduced to my detective sergeant?"

The man nodded.

"And your name is?"

"Gordon Fairbairn. I'm Andy's friend."

"Could you tell us what happened today?"

Gordon shuddered. "I've been away for a couple of days. I went to visit my mum in Nottingham. When I got back today I thought it was odd that I couldn't hear the television coming from downstairs. Andy always has it on. Anyway, I had something to eat and then went down there to have a chat."

"And the door was open?" Paolo asked.

"No, I've got a key. Andy gave me his key months ago and asked me to make a couple of copies to keep safe because he was always losing his. They'd fall off his lap when he was out in his wheelchair and he wouldn't always notice until he got home and couldn't get in."

"So you used the key to let yourself in? Do you often do that?"

Gordon shifted in his seat as if trying to find a

comfortable spot. "Yeah. We were good mates, Andy and me. We used to watch…um, films together and play video games. I used to keep him company while his brother was at work."

"His brother being?"

"Jon, Jon Miller, but Jon and me, we don't really get on. He didn't get on with Andy either. In fact, it wouldn't surprise me if he did Andy in. He was always threatening to."

Paolo raised his brows. "Really? Do you know why?"

Gordon snorted. "I couldn't help but know. Every night until Jon moved out they'd go at it hammer and tongs. I bet the whole street knew why they hated each other. Jon was driving and caused an accident. Poor Andy ended up in a wheelchair and Jon walked away without a scratch. That's not fair, is it? Jon acts as if none of it was his fault. Always on about how hard he works to support Andy, as if he's some high-flying businessman."

"What does he do?" Paolo asked.

"He's got some dead-end porter's job at the hospital. Such a loser."

Paolo looked to Dave, who nodded. He'd picked up on who the brothers were.

"Let's get back to the discovery of your friend's body. You opened the front door and then what happened?"

"I could smell something dreadful. I called out Andy's name, but he didn't answer, so I opened the door to the lounge and there was like this black thing. It was shimmering and the smell was horrible. It made me heave and when I did, oh Jesus." He stopped and put his hand over his mouth as if to prevent himself from throwing up. Eventually he seemed to regain control. "When I heaved, the black thing moved and it was like millions of flies in the air all at once. Buzzing all angry, like."

"What did you do then?" Paolo asked.

"Chucked up, didn't I. Couldn't help it. Then I sort of staggered outside and called for an ambulance, cos when the flies went up in the air I saw it was Andy underneath."

"And, forgive me, I have to ask this, but can you prove where you were yesterday?"

Gordon nodded. "Like I said, I went to visit my mum. I left in the morning and spent all day with her. I stayed overnight and came back today."

"What time did you leave here?"

Gordon thought for a moment. "I caught the 11.05 train, so I must have left here at about half ten."

That keeps him in the frame, Paolo thought, but smiled, encouraging Gordon to continue.

"My mum had invited half her street to come over. I should think at least twenty people saw me at Mum's yesterday."

Paolo stood up and held out a card. "If you remember anything from yesterday, no matter how insignificant you think it might be, please call me."

Gordon took the card and stood up, putting it in his trouser pocket.

"Are you going to arrest Jon? I bet he did this. He's a right weird one. Sometimes he acts like he doesn't even know me. Walks right past me in the street as if I don't exist, he does."

"We'll certainly look into Mr Miller's whereabouts for the time of the crime. Thank you, you've been very helpful."

Paolo waited while Dave put his notebook away and then headed downstairs.

"What did you make of him?" Paolo asked, as soon as he was sure they were out of earshot.

"He's certainly got it in for the brother, but maybe he has good reason. Sounds like these two are definitely the ones in the trial Andrea is reading up on."

Paolo nodded. "There's no doubt about it. We need to track down the brother."

"That shouldn't be too difficult, sir. There can't be many porters at the hospital called Jon Miller."

A uniformed officer tapped Paolo on the shoulder.

"Sorry to disturb you, sir, but I think you should see

this."

They went back into the lounge to see the sideboard had been moved. On a sheet of plastic, the contents of a parcel lay exposed. Several vials of insulin lay in a small heap. The label showed the parcel was addressed to Jon Miller.

"I swear this case gets weirder by the day," Paolo said. "If he killed his brother, why leave this sort of evidence behind? It's like Conrad Stormont all over again."

"Sir?" Dave said, a look of confusion on his face.

"The evidence pointed so strongly to Stormont that it made me think it couldn't possibly be him. Then he turns up as one of the victims. Now the finger is pointing so firmly at Jon Miller, I'm not sure I believe it."

"Maybe the other killings were planned, but this one was done in anger. Maybe he killed his brother and ran off, forgetting about the insulin he'd stashed."

Paolo sighed. "Now that I can believe, but does that mean this is the final killing? Is this number six, or is there still one more to go? Let's get back to the station and let CC and Andrea know what we've found."

As they stepped outside, Paolo heard a window being opened above and looked up. Gordon Fairbairn's body appeared and he was pointing into the crowd on the other side of the tape barrier.

"There he is," he yelled. "That's the bastard who killed my friend."

Paolo looked to where Gordon was pointing just in time to see a man turn and run.

CHAPTER TWENTY-SEVEN

Paolo put down the phone and went to double-check with Andrea that the man they'd caught running from the crime scene was the same as the person involved in the court case she was studying. Dave and CC were with Andrea, looking over some paperwork on her work station.

She looked up as he approached. "I was just showing the others, sir. All the victims' names have appeared in the transcript, even the brother's. The only exception being the surgeon, Edwin Fulbright."

"Can you give me the full name and date of birth of the young man at the centre of the case and that of his brother?"

"Yes, sir, I've written down all the principal players and their details. Jon Miller's date of birth is 24th June 1978. His brother, Andrew, was a couple of years younger. He was born on 12th January 1980."

Paolo jotted down the dates. "We've got Jon Miller in interrogation room three. According to the upstairs neighbour he frequently threatened to kill his brother. Certainly running away as he did makes him look guilty, but let's see what he's got to say. It will be interesting to hear his views on the parcel behind the sideboard containing the insulin."

Dave grinned. "You think he'll come up with a convincing story?"

"Not really, but he's going to have to tell us something. Dave, you come with me while I have a chat with Mr Miller. Andrea, carry on with the transcript. If you find anything that might be useful while we're questioning Jon Miller, bring it down."

"Yes, sir," she said, "but I'm only about halfway into the

trial at the moment. It's going to take me a couple of days to get to the end."

"No problem," Paolo said. "Judging by what we have so far, holding Jon Miller for as long as we need isn't going to be a problem."

Paolo and Dave entered the interrogation room to find Jon slumped face down on the table. Paolo had been expecting to see a solicitor at his side, but he was alone.

Paolo turned to the officer on duty. "Has he been offered the services of a legal adviser?"

"Yes, sir, but he says he doesn't want one."

Jon looked up at that, his face was white and haggard, making him look much older than the thirty-five years of age Paolo knew him to be.

"I don't need a solicitor. I haven't done anything wrong. I went to collect my stuff and couldn't understand why the police were there. Then that idiot upstairs starting yelling that I'd killed Andy. I didn't kill him. I haven't been back to the flat for days."

Paolo pulled out a chair and sat down. Dave leaned against the wall, arms folded.

Flicking the switch on the recorder, Paolo gave the date, time and names of those present.

"For the record, Mr Miller has declined legal representation. Could you please confirm that for the tape, Mr Miller?"

Jon nodded.

"In words, please, sir."

"I don't want a solicitor," Jon said. "I don't even understand why I'm here. Someone's killed my brother and you're wasting time talking to me."

"We have a few questions we'd like to put you to, that's all. After you've given us your answers, you'll probably be free to go home."

"Probably?"

Paolo smiled. "It depends on how helpful you are. Let's start with why you ran away."

Jon shrugged. "I don't know. It was the police tape and Gordon yelling. I took fright, that's all."

"But why?"

"I just said, I don't know."

"Okay," Paolo said, "would you like to explain the insulin you had hidden behind your sideboard?"

Jon frowned. "What insulin? I don't know what you're talking about."

Paolo nodded and the police officer placed a plastic evidence bag on the table.

"I'm showing Mr Miller the parcel and its contents uncovered during a search of his home. The parcel contains several vials of insulin."

"That's nothing to do with me," Jon said.

"But it's addressed to you and paid for on your credit card," Paolo pointed out.

"Then I expect Andy ordered it. He was always buying stuff on my card."

Paolo looked down at his notes. "Was he diabetic?"

"What? No, not as far as I know."

"I thought you lived together," Paolo said. "You must know if he was or he wasn't."

"He wasn't," Jon said.

"But you think he bought insulin anyway? Why?"

"I don't know and I don't understand why you're going on about it. What has that got to do with Andy's death?"

Paolo tapped the file on the table. "Because it seems very likely your brother was killed by an overdose of insulin. Now perhaps you can see why we are very interested in the insulin we found addressed to you and paid for by you."

Jon sat back. "I didn't order it and I didn't kill him."

Paolo took out a sheet of dates. "Perhaps you could tell us where you were yesterday morning?"

"I was at work."

"Is there anyone who can vouch for that?"

"My supervisor, Iain, but…"

"But?" Paolo prompted.

"He might not tell the truth."

"Why not?"

"We haven't always got on. He blames me for something that happened to his cousin years ago."

Paolo made a note of the man's name. "Did no one else see you?"

Jon shook his head. "No, we had a big row and I stormed out."

"I see," Paolo said. "Where did you go after that?"

"I just walked around thinking about stuff. I went to the park."

"Can anyone there vouch for you?"

Jon shook his head. "I wasn't feeling very sociable."

"Okay, let's move on. Can you tell me where you were on these dates and times? For the record, I am passing Mr Miller a sheet with five dates and times."

As they went through them one by one, it became apparent that Jon didn't have alibis for any of the murders apart from the first when he'd been in Leicester for a job interview. Paolo noted the details and passed the piece of paper to the officer.

"Take this to my team and ask one of them to look into it for me, please."

Paolo waited until the officer closed the door behind him and then turned back to Jon. "Do you still hold a grudge against Conrad Stormont?"

"Who?"

Paolo pointed to the file again. "Don't be smart, Mr Miller. We know all about the accident and who gave you the medication which caused it. There's no way you would forget the psychiatrist who put you in that situation."

"I'm sorry, I really don't understand. I had forgotten his name, but now you've brought it to mind, it's come back to me. What's he got to do with Andy?"

Paolo smiled. "Well, he's also dead as a result of insulin poisoning. As is Professor Edwards who was your consultant, Peter Bishop, your solicitor and Marcus Wittington-Smythe the barrister who acted for you in court.

All dead and all killed by an overdose of insulin. Do you still feel Andy's death isn't related to these others?"

Jon shook his head. He looked so dumbstruck Paolo was almost tempted to believe he knew nothing, but he'd seen too many criminals able to put on a convincing show of innocence to be taken in without solid proof.

"What can you tell me about Edwin Fulbright?"

"I don't even know who he is," Jon said. "You're just making up names now."

"No, I can assure you I'm not," Paolo said. "Did you set out to kill those men, including your own brother, and set up Conrad Stormont as a suspect?"

"No," Jon cried. "I didn't kill anyone. I couldn't. I…" he stopped and Paolo watched as his face showed a thought had occurred to him so fantastic he couldn't quite believe it.

"What have you remembered?" Paolo asked.

"It's not that I've remembered anything," Jon said, "but I've just realised who could have killed them, but not to point the finger at that psychiatrist. I think it was to set me up."

Paolo smiled. "That's a bit far-fetched," he said. "Who do you think was the master criminal working behind the scenes?"

"My brother," Jon said.

"So you think a man in a wheelchair—"

"No, you don't understand. He could walk. It was when I found out that he'd been fooling me for over a year that I threatened to kill him."

Almost as if he'd realised what he said, Jon subsided. Paolo watched as his shoulders slumped and an air of defeat swamped him.

"And did you?" Paolo asked. "Did you realise what your brother was doing and murder him in the same way as he'd killed the others?"

Jon shook his head. "I've already told you. I didn't kill him."

There was a tap on the door and the uniformed officer came back in. He handed Paolo a sheet of paper. Paolo smiled.

"It seems there was some mix up with your interview time in Leicester. You turned up several hours too early. That was on the day Professor Edwards was killed. My colleague upstairs has checked with the hospital in Leicester. It seems you called to change the appointment from the morning to the afternoon, but claimed to know nothing about it when you got there."

"I didn't change it," said Jon. "Someone else did."

Paolo put the paper down in front of Jon. "But, you see, that left you with four to five hours unaccounted for. Plenty of time to come back to Bradchester, kill the professor and then get back to Leicester for your interview."

"How many times do I have to tell you? I didn't kill anyone. Can I go home now?"

Paolo stood up. "Not yet," he said. "We'll be back with a few more questions."

"In that case, I've changed my mind," Jon said. "I want a solicitor before I say anything else."

"Of course, that's your right," Paolo said. "This interview is terminated."

He added the time and then switched off the recorder.

Outside in the corridor, Paolo turned to Dave. "What do you think?"

Dave shrugged. "I really don't know. Even if his supervisor gives him an alibi for his brother's death, he could still be in the frame for the others."

"I agree, but why did he order the insulin? If he didn't buy it, did his brother use his card to do so? Why? Too many bloody questions and not enough answers. I know I threw those other names at Jon Miller, but two out of the four actually helped him. His solicitor and barrister must have done a good job to get him off all charges. And we can't find any connection between him and Edwin Fulbright. The big question now is who killed Andy? It doesn't fit the pattern of the others, but I still feel it's part of the same case."

"Well, Andy was mentioned in the trial, sir."

"Yes, but as a victim. He didn't have a part to play other than being named as a passenger in the car. As far as Andrea has discovered, Andy didn't even appear in court. He was still recovering in hospital."

"I'm going to call Barbara to see if she can give us a smaller window on time of death. We can't do too much more until Miller's solicitor gets here, so see if you can get hold of the supervisor. It will help to know if his alibi for the time of his brother's death holds water. I'll see you back here in about an hour."

Paolo entered his office as his mobile rang. Lydia again. They spent more time talking to each other now than they did when they lived together.

"Lydia, I'm in the middle of an investigation. If you want to yell at me, can you make it quick or call me at home this evening?"

He heard her laugh. "Do I only call to yell at you?"

Before he could think of a tactful way of saying yes, she continued.

"Actually, Paolo, I won't keep you long. I just wanted to say thank you."

"Really? What for?" he asked, kicking the office door closed behind him.

"For making me realise that I'd gone the wrong way to work with Katy. I took your advice and told her she could bring Danny round this afternoon. He seems to be a nice young man. Not at all what I expected."

Paolo sat at his desk, put his feet up and smiled. "I am so pleased to hear you say that."

"They told me what you'd done for his brother and why. Anyway, Paolo, I won't stay on. I just wanted to say sorry for being a bitch and thank you for everything."

"Any time. Does this mean I'm allowed to come into the house again? I thought after your last call I might need to wear a bulletproof vest when I faced you."

"Very funny. Don't push it or that might still be the case. Come for lunch on Sunday if you're not doing anything.

229

Katy and Danny are coming and they're bringing Mark, too, if he can get permission."

"I'd love to, but I can't make any promises. I might need to work."

"I'll keep a plate of food for you in the microwave. Come over when you're free."

"Will do," Paolo said, ending the call.

He sat for a while, staring up at the cracks in his ceiling. When Lydia was nice, being in her company was a delight, but when she lost her temper there wasn't enough room in the world to put the right amount of distance between them.

Paolo made his call to Barbara, but she wasn't able to be more precise, so he headed back into the main office. Dave fell into step beside him.

"The supervisor had already left the hospital," Dave said. "They gave me his home number, but I get the answering machine. I've left a message for him to call me."

"And Barbara couldn't add to what we already know, so we're not exactly going in there with much ammo."

Paolo opened the door to the interrogation room to see a smartly dressed man sitting next to Jon. The man stood up and held out his hand.

"Good evening. I'm Sebastian Phipps, representing Mr Miller. I have to tell you that no interview will be taking place this evening."

"Oh," said Paolo, "and why is that?"

"Because my client suffers from dissociative identity disorder and I insist on a psychiatric report before you question him any further."

CHAPTER TWENTY-EIGHT

On Friday morning, Paolo called his team together. Their frustration was evident, but it was nothing compared to the way he felt. Jon Miller's supervisor had backed up his alibi, even though it was evident he hadn't wanted to, but that only cleared Jon of his brother's death. He didn't have an alibi for any of the others and, as Andy's death followed a different pattern to the others, it was possible that someone else had murdered Andy, but used the same means to do so.

"Okay, listen up, everyone. Jon Miller's solicitor is doing his best to make it difficult for us to keep Jon in custody. He's pressing for us to either charge Jon or release him. We're not in a position to do either at the moment, so we desperately need something to help us out."

He looked round. "Where's CC?"

"She's gone to the hospital, sir," said Andrea. "She wants to try to shake up the person who was looking into Edwin Fulbright's cases. CC called the department yesterday and got the run-around, so thought the direct approach might achieve more."

"Good thinking on her part. Let's hope she comes back with some solid information. How are you doing with the trial transcript?"

"I'm about two-thirds of the way through it. I've just got to the part where they are talking about Jon's brother and the woman who died. You know, position of car at point of impact and estimated speed. The woman was a pedestrian. Her husband says she was on her way to the hospital for a routine check-up when Jon Miller's car ploughed into her. She suffered a great deal of internal damage, apparently, and died the same night."

Paolo smiled. "I know it's tedious, but keep reading. I am certain the clue we need is in that transcript."

The door swung open and CC burst in. "You'll never believe what I've got. Fulbright didn't just save Stormont's life; he was also the surgeon who operated on Andy Miller after the accident and he looked after the woman who was knocked down as well, but she didn't survive."

Paolo looked across at Andrea. "How's that for synchronicity?"

"Sin what, sir?"

"Synchronicity. It's when two events are meaningfully related. You've uncovered the woman in the trial transcript and now CC has discovered she was Fulbright's patient. Tell us more, CC."

She slipped off her jacket and sat down. "It makes for interesting reading, sir. As you know, Edwin Fulbright operated on Conrad Stormont's wrists to save his life, but that was some considerable time after the accident we're looking into. Andrew Miller and Grace Simmonds were both admitted at the same time. Andrew Miller eventually recovered, although he was left paralysed. Grace Simmonds wasn't so lucky. Fulbright operated on her and she was expected to pull through, even though she'd suffered terrible internal injuries. Apparently, Mr Fulbright was a brilliant surgeon. Anyway, she suffered a massive heart attack during the night and she died."

"Do you have the husband's details on record?"

CC shook her head. "Unfortunately, no. The accident happened on the same day as that terrible train crash and the hospital was overrun with cases. In the chaos, the staff neglected to take down the husband's address or phone number. I presume that's why he didn't find out until the next day that his wife had passed away."

"How do you know he wasn't told until then?" Paolo asked.

CC showed him a photocopy of the hospital records. "Because the nurse on duty noted it down. Oh my God!"

"What?" Paolo asked.

"Look, sir. She was admitted on a Friday and died overnight, but her husband only found out on the Saturday. That fits the pattern of the first five murders."

"You're right. We need to find out this man's name and address."

"I can help you with that, sir," Andrea said. "All those details are here in the transcript. His name is Bradley Simmonds and the address given is 43, The Pallisades, Riversmead. That's over the other side of town, isn't it?"

"It is. I don't suppose there's a phone number listed?"

Andrea shook her head. "I'll see if I can find one."

"Do that," Paolo said, "but don't call him. I don't want him warned. Dave and I are going to pay him a visit."

Dave pulled up outside the house and Paolo was relieved to see it looked well cared for. That meant someone was living there. He could only pray it was Bradley Simmonds. He got out of the car and waited for Dave to lock it. They walked along the path next to a well-tended flower bed. Paolo had barely lifted his hand to ring the bell when the door opened.

A young boy of about eleven, hand clasped around a football, stood in front of him. Before Paolo could speak, the boy turned and ran back into the house, still clutching the football.

"Mum, there's two strange men at the door."

Paolo saw him disappear into the room at the end of a short hallway. Soon afterwards, a woman came out who bore such a striking resemblance to the boy that she had to be his mother. She walked forward slowly, as if she wasn't sure it was safe to come to the door.

Paolo held out his warrant card. "Sorry to disturb you, madam. I'm Detective Inspector Paolo Storey and this is Detective Sergeant Johnson. We're looking for Bradley Simmonds. Is he in?"

The woman visibly relaxed. "I'm afraid he doesn't live here."

"Do you have an address for him?"

She shook her head. "No, we've only been living here for six months. Maybe the people we bought from have his address."

"Do you know how long the previous residents lived here?"

"I think they said for about five years. I don't know who had it before that."

"I see," said Paolo. "Could you give me a contact number or address for the people you bought the property from?"

"Sorry, I've no idea where they moved to. Up north somewhere it was."

Paolo smiled at the boy who had reappeared and had come to stand next to his mother.

"I'm sorry I startled you."

The boy gave a sheepish grin. "I wasn't expecting anyone to be standing there when I opened the door." He looked up at his mother. "Can I go now?"

"Yes, but come straight back after practice."

"I will," he yelled as he ran down the path.

The woman turned back to Paolo. "I'm sorry, I haven't been much help."

"Not a problem. We can find out all we need to know from the public records office. Thank you for your time," he said.

Back in the car, Paolo thumped the dashboard. "Every time we get a step closer, it seems we get knocked back again. Still, it shouldn't be too difficult to track down Bradley Simmonds."

"You think he could be our man?"

Paolo nodded. "Bradley Simmonds would have good reason to hold a grudge against the solicitor and the barrister who acted for Jon Miller. He has a valid beef against both Conrad Stormont and Professor Edwards because it was their combined act that provided Jon Miller with the wrong medication. Edwin Fulbright saved Andy Miller, but didn't save his wife, Grace Simmonds. It all fits better than some of the other avenues we've explored, with the exception of

Andy Miller's death." He smacked the dashboard again. "Why is it that there always seems to be one death that falls outside the rest?"

As Dave pulled away, Paolo's mobile rang.

"Storey."

"Sir," CC said and Paolo could hear the excitement in her voice. "I've been checking into Grace Simmonds's medical history. You'll never guess what her appointment was for on the day she was knocked down. It was to have her insulin levels tested. She was a diabetic!"

"So her husband would have been familiar with the risks of insulin overdose. Great work, CC. Listen, while you're on, do me a favour and see if you can find any records for Bradley Simmonds. He sold his home some years back, but not to the current owner. Check every database you can to see if he pops up anywhere."

"We've had the six bodies he promised in his notes, sir; do you think he's finished?"

"No, something tells me that last murder wasn't part of the pattern. Apart from the element of rage involved, why didn't he leave us his usual note?"

"He didn't leave one on Stormont," CC pointed out.

"I'm not so sure about that," Paolo said. "I think he probably did and someone saw what they thought was a drunk or druggie passed out in a shop doorway with an envelope on his chest. I think a passer-by whipped it away in the hope of finding a few quid inside." He sighed. "We're on our way back to the station. We need to find Bradley Simmonds before he strikes again because someone is going to be in danger tomorrow."

By the time Paolo and Dave reached the station, CC and Andrea had reams of information for them to go through, but none of it very helpful.

Paolo looked through the notes CC gave him. "Okay, so he dropped off the electoral roll eight years ago round about the same time as he sold his house. He resigned from his job and didn't take another one, but neither did he sign on for benefits, so what's he been living on for the past eight years?"

"And where?" Dave said.

That evening, nestling next to Jessica on her couch, Paolo felt the tension of the day finally leave his body. They'd barely spoken since he'd got there two hours earlier, but it felt one of those rare comfortable silences where no one has to say anything because everything is understood without words.

"Would you like to watch a film," Jessica asked, smiling up at him.

He pulled her in closer. "No, thank you. I'm quite content just sitting here with you. How was your day?"

"Okay. Interesting. Yours?"

"Frustrating. We spent most of it following up what looked like promising leads, only to find each one ended in a brick wall. We're fairly sure now we know who we're looking for, but not where to find him. He's going to strike again tomorrow. I'm sure of it, but I don't know who he has in his sights this time."

"Why are you so sure there'll be another murder? You said all the notes pointed to six victims."

Paolo shook himself. He was here with Jessica and should be enjoying the moment, not trying to second guess a madman. He turned to face her.

"I can think of much nicer ways of spending our time than talking about my work or even watching a film," he said.

She grinned. "What could be better than watching a film?"

"This," he said and pulled her to him.

CHAPTER TWENTY-NINE

Week Six – Friday 29th August to Thursday 4th September

Paolo picked up Barbara's overnight case and carried it out to his car. He held the passenger door open and Barbara slid in.

He thought she looked more fragile than ever, but that was hardly surprising considering what she been through just to get to this point.

"Thanks for doing this, Paolo," she said.

"Nonsense, that's what friends are for."

She tried to smile, and Paolo thought he'd never seen such a feeble attempt from someone who was usually so strong minded she terrified all the male staff on her team.

"Anyway, you'd do the same for me," he said.

"I hope I never have to, but yes, I would."

They drove to the hospital in silence. Paolo pulled into the car park and found an empty space.

"I'll stay with you as long as they allow me to. Okay?"

Barbara nodded. "And you'll be there when I come back to the ward after the operation? Promise?"

"I promise," he said.

Paolo stood at the front of the central office, his mind still on Barbara, but he knew he had to put thoughts of her to one side. Someone was going to die today unless he figured out a way to prevent it. Of that he was absolutely certain.

He tapped the board to get everyone's attention and the room went quiet.

"I've been summoned upstairs to see Chief Constable

Willows and I need something to tell him. Have any of you managed to track down Bradley Simmonds since he disappeared eight years ago? Please don't tell me this is Conrad Stormont all over again and he'll only turn up when someone kills him."

The room remained silent.

"Nothing? One of you must have something."

His mobile rang.

"Saved by the bell," someone called out.

"Storey," Paolo said.

"Are you the copper who came upstairs when Andy died?"

"Yes. That's Gordon, isn't it? What can I do for you?"

"Look, I don't know, it might be nothing, but it's the barman from our pub."

Paolo sat on the edge of the closest desk. "What about him?"

"Well, I saw him, see. I mean it's probably nothing. I shouldn't have bothered you. Sorry."

"No! Wait," Paolo said. "It's often the things that people think aren't really important that turn out to be crucial to solving cases. Now, as calmly as you can, tell me what it is that bothered you about your barman."

"It was the morning I went to see my mum. You know, I told you I walked to the station to catch the train."

"Yes, I remember you telling me that."

"Well, that's the point. I saw him going in the opposite direction, but I didn't think he lived out our way. But I've just realised, he was probably visiting a friend or something. I've wasted your time, sorry."

"Gordon, don't go. This is really important. Are you saying you saw your local barman heading towards where you live, but you've never seen him in the area before?"

"Yeah, that's right. I think he lives over by the river, so it's the opposite direction from the pub to us."

Paolo could feel his heart beating so fast it felt like a beginner drummer had let rip with an extended drum solo.

"What's the barman's name?"

"I don't want to get him into trouble. I mean, I didn't see him do nothing."

Paolo forced his voice to remain calm. "I understand that completely. Don't worry; he won't be in any trouble unless he's done something wrong. We just need to eliminate him from our enquiries. What's his name, Gordon?"

"Brad. Brad Masters."

"I see, thank you, and which pub is it?"

"The one down the road."

"I meant, what's it called?"

Gordon laughed. "Sorry, I'm such a dickhead at times. It's the White Horse."

"That's great. Gordon, if you should see Brad before we do, please don't mention that you've told me you saw him that day. He might think he's in trouble and get a fright."

"Oh, okay. No, I won't say a word. He doesn't like me much anyway, so we're not exactly on buddy terms."

Paolo ended the call and turned back to the room. Every face was intent on his. They all looked as if they'd been hanging on every word.

"We've got a name to chase up. Find out what you can about a Brad Masters. He's the barman at the White Horse. Dave, let's get going. We should get there just before opening time with a bit of luck."

Dave drove to the pub and slowed to look for somewhere to park.

"Just pull up outside and park on the double yellow lines," Paolo said. "We haven't got time to waste looking for the perfect parking spot."

He reached into the back and grabbed the police sign, slinging it on the dashboard before getting out.

The pub was still locked up, but Paolo hammered on the front door. After a couple of minutes it was flung open.

"For Christ's sake, keep your bloody hair on. I'm only five minutes' late opening."

Paolo flashed his warrant card.

"Bradley Masters?"

239

"No, I'm bloody not, and if you're looking for him, you're out of bloody luck. The bastard hasn't turned up for work since he left on Monday night. I've had to do it all myself, haven't I, which is why I'm late getting the doors open. What d'you want him for anyway? I went round to his gaff but he didn't answer the door. I don't know if he's done a bunk or what. If *you* find him, smack him around the head for me, will you."

He paused to draw breath and Paolo seized his chance.

"Could you give us his address, sir? It's very important."

"Yeah, come in. I've got the fucker's phone numbers, too, but a fat lot of good that is. He's not answering his landline or his mobile. If he's sick I hope he dies, leaving me in the lurch like this with no warning."

As he was ranting, he'd made his way to an office behind the bar. Paolo and Dave followed him in and watched as he scrabbled through the piles of paper scattered over a battered old desk.

"Where did I put it? I had it here yesterday. Called on and off all bloody day, I did. The kitchen staff'll be here in a minute and I'm nowhere near ready with the bar even. Here it is, no that's not it. Aha!" he said, holding up a sheet of paper as if it was the crown jewels.

In Paolo's eyes, if it led them to Bradley Simmonds, or Brad Masters as he now was, it was worth more than any jewels. He took it and thanked the man before he could start on another rant.

As he and Dave left the pub, the man's voice was still ringing out.

"Don't forget. Smack him one for me when you find him."

"Do you know how to get to this address? Flat three, 78, Cooper Street," Paolo asked.

"I don't," Dave said, "but the Sat Nav will. I don't think it can be far from here."

Paolo waited with mounting impatience for Dave to key the address into the Sat Nav, but was rewarded with the information that the street was only a couple of roads away.

"I think it'll be quicker to run there than move the car," Paolo said. "I'll call in for back-up, just in case."

He fished the mobile from his pocket and gave the address to the operator.

"Right, let's go," he said. "There's a car on its way. They'll meet us there."

As they ran, Paolo's conviction that Bradley was already out, possibly even with his next victim, grew even stronger. They turned the corner into Cooper Street, looking for number 78.

"Over there," Paolo said just as a police car swept past them and pulled up outside a terraced house. There was a single front door, but a panel at the side contained four buzzers, showing the house had been converted into flats.

Slightly out of breath, Paolo was glad of a chance to recover while he waited for the uniformed officers to get out of their car.

"What would you like us to do, sir? We've got an enforcer in the car if it's needed."

"Let's see if anyone is at home first."

Paolo rang the bell for flat three and listened. He thought he heard a noise and waited, but when the door opened a young woman in her early twenties confronted him.

"My baby's asleep upstairs. Can't you keep the noise down?"

"I'm sorry," Paolo said. "Are you from flat three?"

"No, next door to him, but his bell is on the party wall. It's fine if someone just presses it and lets go, but you're standing there like you're planning to wait all day if necessary and you'll wake my baby if you keep it up. Anyway, I don't think he's in. I haven't seen him for a few days."

"Do you have a key to his flat?"

She looked horrified. "Why would I? I barely know him other than to say hello. Try Mrs Jenson at number one. She's our landlady. I know she's got a spare key to my place because she watches Jamie for me sometimes and lets herself in."

Paolo thanked her and promised to try not to disturb her more than they already had.

He followed her into the entrance hall. There was a door on either side of the space. The young woman ran up the narrow stairs leading to the floor above. Paolo knocked at flat one. The door opened a crack and dark eyes peered out at him.

"Who let you inside?"

Paolo showed his warrant card and introduced himself.

The door opened a little wider and the dark eyes were matched by mahogany skin. The bright orange hair didn't seem to fit the face, but Paolo was so used to CC's wild colour choices that he barely noticed.

"What do you want?" she asked.

"Mrs Jenson? I believe you have a key to number three."

"What of it?"

"It's very important that we have access to that apartment."

"Do you have a warrant?" she asked.

Paolo shook his head. "No, but it really is very important we get inside."

She grinned. "I'm sure it is, but you aren't getting any key from me without you show me a warrant."

"Okay," he said. "You win. Officer, we'll use the enforcer."

The door opened fully and she strode out. "What's an enforcer? You can't go bringing that thing into my house."

"I'm sorry, Mrs Jenson, but I'm trying to prevent a murder taking place. If you won't open the door for me, we'll have to use that," he said, pointing to the mini battering ram cradled in the arms of the uniformed men.

"But that'll break the door all to bits."

Paolo nodded. "It will, but don't worry, you can claim for damages. I'm sure you'll be reimbursed eventually. Off you go, men."

"Now just you hold on," she yelled. "I'm not having my doors broken down. I'll get the key, but I'm coming in with you. I don't trust you lot not to plant stuff on that poor man."

Muttering under her breath, she went back inside and soon reappeared with the key.

"Just you and him," she said, pointing to Paolo and Dave. "I don't want them up there. If my poor husband knew I'd even let you in the house he would be spinning in his grave, except I had him cremated and scattered his ashes, so it'd be hard for him to spin."

Paolo and Dave followed her up to the first floor where the young woman was standing outside her apartment door.

"Will you please keep the noise down?" she hissed.

The words were no sooner out than a baby's scream pierced the air. The woman threw them a look of pure venom.

"Now look what you've done," she said, going inside and slamming the door.

"I don't think this is the place to sell police raffle tickets somehow, sir," Dave said. "We don't seem to be very welcome here."

Paolo shrugged. He didn't care if every resident in the house hated them as long as he could get inside Bradley's flat. Mrs Jenson made a big performance out of unlocking the door. When she'd turned the key she took it from the lock and put it in her pocket.

"And there it stays," she said. "I've opened the door under protest, but you're not getting your hands on the key."

Grudgingly, she moved to one side to let Paolo and Dave enter. Immediately, Paolo knew they'd come to the right place. The walls were covered in articles taken from the local papers showing group images taken at social events. In all of them, either the professor, Wittington-Smythe, Peter Bishop or Edwin Fulbright was present. Paolo moved over to a chest of drawers, pulled on some gloves, and opened the top drawer. There was nothing of interest to find, just clean underwear and socks.

The next drawer down contained tee-shirts, but the third held the jackpot. Boxes of syringes and vials of liquid filled one side of the space. Notebooks were stacked in the other half.

"Look at this, Dave," he said, moving so that his back shielded the contents from Mrs Jenson's view.

"Bloody hell, sir. We've found the right man, but where is he?"

Paolo reached down for the top notebook. Marcus Wittington-Smythe was neatly printed on the front. Inside the pages were full of information about him, his wife and his missing son. Ideas on how to approach him were written and then crossed out. The only one not scratched through was a detailed plan to use the barrister's love for his missing boy as bait.

He put the notebook on top of the dresser and picked up the next one. Peter Bishop's name was printed on it. As with the first book, it contained pages and pages of details about the solicitor's life and movements.

Professor Edwards's name was on the third and Edwin Fulbright's on the notebook under that one. Paolo placed them with the other two on top of the dresser and reached down to pick up the next notebook. As he did so his phone rang.

"Storey," he said.

"Sir, it's Andrea. I've almost reached the end of the transcript."

As she spoke, Paolo stretched out his left hand to lift up the next notebook and wasn't surprised to see Conrad Stormont's name printed on it. The final notebook had Jon Miller's name on the cover. So that's who the last victim was going to be! Not what Paolo had expected.

"Yes, sir, and there's another name mentioned right near the end as an expert witness."

Paolo rested the book on the dresser and turned the page, seeing that this one was different to the others. It detailed ways in which it could be made to appear as if Jon was the murderer.

"Sir, I feel I have to warn you."

Paolo felt the room spin around him. On the second page was a list of intended victims. The first five had ticks against them. As the sixth name registered, he knew exactly what Andrea was going to say and heard the words as if from the end of a long tunnel. Her voice seemed to echo and reverberate.

"It's Dr Jessica Carter, sir. She gave evidence in favour of Jon Miller."

CHAPTER THIRTY

Paolo hit speed dial again. "Come on, Jessica, answer your bloody phone."

Her recorded message clicked in and he left yet another message.

"Dave, can't you drive any faster?"

Paolo knew he was being unfair. Dave was already endangering himself and other road users by driving too fast on crowded roads. He was weaving in and out of traffic, often missing oncoming vehicles by inches.

Paolo dialled again, this time getting through to Jessica's secretary at the hospital.

"At last," he said. "Your line has been solidly engaged for bloody ages."

"Can I help you?"

Paolo forced himself to behave rationally. "I'm sorry; I didn't mean to be rude. This is Detective Inspector Storey. It is essential I speak with Dr Carter. Do you have more than one number for her at her office?"

"No, sir, I'm afraid not. She just has the one line over there, but she has a new patient today, so she won't answer the phone until he has left."

"New patient? What's his name?"

"I'm afraid I cannot tell you that, sir."

"Why is she seeing a patient today? I thought she used Fridays to catch up on her cases?"

After a brief silence, the secretary must have decided answering wouldn't breach client confidentiality.

"Because the new patient wanted to see her on a Friday. He was quite insistent about it."

"What time is the appointment."

"I, er, I don't think…"

"What time is the bloody appointment? For Christ's sake, I wouldn't ask if it wasn't necessary. Dr Carter could be in serious trouble, now what time is the appointment?"

"It's at two-thirty."

Paolo looked at his watch. They had five minutes to get there.

"If Dr Carter should contact you, please tell her she needs to listen to the messages I've left as a matter of urgency. She must listen to them *before* she sees her patient. It's a life or death situation. Have you got that?"

"Yes, sir," she said.

Paolo ended the call and tried Jessica's mobile again, only for it go straight to voicemail. He was about to dial her office number when the car swung violently to the left and Dave drove into the car park. Paolo didn't wait for the car to come to a complete stop before jumping out. He was vaguely aware of Dave's footsteps thundering behind him as he pushed the glass door open and ran for Jessica's office.

The waiting room was empty. Had Bradley arrived early? Was Jessica alone? He didn't hesitate. He tried the handle, it was unlocked. Throwing open the door he burst into the room. There was a man standing next to Jessica, pointing to something on the desk. Paolo launched himself across the room and tackled the man to the floor.

Jessica stood up. "What the hell is going on?" she yelled. "Paolo, have you lost control of your senses? That's my patient."

Paolo forced the man's arms up behind his back. "No, he isn't. He's a killer. This is the man who murdered Professor Edwards and Conrad Stormont, amongst others."

"Have you got him secure, sir?" Dave asked. "I've got my cuffs here."

Paolo moved slightly to one side so that Dave could reach down and slip the cuffs on. He stood up and then pulled the man to his feet.

"Bradley Simmonds, I am arresting you on suspicion of the murder of Professor Edwards, Peter Bishop, Marcus

Wittington-Smythe, Edwin Fulbright, Conrad Stormont and Andrew Miller. You don't have to say anything but it may harm your defence if you do not mention, when questioned, something you later rely on in court. Anything you do say may be taken down and given in evidence. Do you understand?"

Bradley nodded. "You got here too soon."

"No," Paolo said, "I got here just in time."

Paolo looked over at Jessica. She hadn't said a word since he'd rushed in. He guessed she must be in a state of shock.

"Jessica, why don't you sit down? I have to take Bradley Simmonds to the station. Is there someone I can call to be with you?"

She shook her head, but still didn't speak.

"Jess, talk to me. I can't leave you like this. Let me call one of your friends."

She looked at him and Paolo felt as if he'd been slapped.

"How dare you? How dare you burst into my office when I have a patient with me?"

"Jessica, he was here to kill you."

"So you say, but he hadn't shown any sign of aggression. In fact, the only aggressors in this situation are you and Dave."

Paolo knew she'd only believe the danger she'd been in if he could show her evidence of it. He patted Bradley's pockets and felt the outline of a syringe.

"Hold him steady for me, please, Dave."

Dave stood behind their prisoner and linked his arms through Bradley's to stop him from lunging forward.

Paolo held the pocket open with one hand and carefully extracted the syringe with the other. As he dropped it into an evidence bag, he turned and smiled at Jessica.

"This was intended for you."

As she began to tremble, he moved towards her and gently eased her back until she sat down.

"Who can I call to be with you?"

She shook her head. "I'm fine. It just hit me I'd be dead

if you hadn't arrived in time." She glared at Bradley. "Take him away," she said. "Take him and do whatever it is you have to do."

Paolo dropped a kiss on her forehead. "You sure you'll be okay on your own?"

She nodded. "Really, I'm fine."

"I'll be over this evening as we'd arranged. Okay?"

He hated to leave her sitting all alone in her office, but had to accept that she didn't want him to call anyone. Forcing himself to remain calm and not lay into the man, as all his instincts urged him to do, he took hold of Bradley's arm and led him outside.

Paolo switched on the recorder and stated who was in the interrogation room, the date and time.

"For the purposes of the tape, would you please repeat your assertion that you do not wish to have a legal representative at this time?"

Bradley shrugged. "I don't want anybody. Can we just get this over with?"

"Do you realise the severity and number of charges against you, Mr Simmonds?"

"Call me Brad. Yes, and I freely admit to killing Edwards, Fulbright, Bishops, Wittington-Smythe, Stormont and Miller. If you hadn't come bursting in, you could have added Carter to the list."

Paolo pulled the file towards him, but before he could speak, Bradley tapped on the table.

"You don't have to get clever with the questions. I'll tell you why I did it. I just wish I'd managed the last one as well." He smiled. "You should have seen my Grace that morning. If ever anyone had a name to suit their personality, it was her. She was beautiful. Oh, not in the conventional sense. I don't suppose many would have given her a second look, but that was their loss. She glowed, Detective Inspector. She was full of grace and had her whole life ahead of her."

He stopped speaking and pulled a tissue from his pocket

to wipe his eyes.

"Do you know why she had that hospital appointment?"

Paolo shook his head. "No, was it for a special reason?"

"You could say that. We were going to start a family, but my Grace was diabetic. She'd arranged to see someone who was going to advise her on diet and such like if she fell pregnant. She said, 'I'm off to the hospital. I'll see you later.' Then she left. That bastard Miller ran his car into her. She went to the hospital all right, but she never came home again."

He sat forward. "I tried to come to terms with what had happened to her, but the hospital didn't even tell me she'd died until the next morning. I went there expecting to find her in the ward, but she was already in the morgue."

He wiped his eyes again. "They saved Andy Miller, but couldn't save my Grace. I went to the court every day, you know, thinking I'd see justice done. But it doesn't work like that, does it? All those people saying poor Jon Miller, it wasn't his fault. Well, it sure as hell wasn't Grace's fault, but no one cared about her."

"So you were angry when Jon Miller was found not guilty?"

Bradley shook his head. "Not then, I wasn't. I didn't really feel any emotion. I've read up on it. I must have been in a state of shock, because I stayed that way for years."

Paolo leaned his arms on the desk. "Where did you go? We couldn't find any trace of you after you sold your house."

"South Africa," Bradley said. "There was an advert in the paper for Chartered Accountants. I thought maybe it was a sign I should start a new life. I went for a couple of interviews at South Africa House and they accepted me. I moved out to Cape Town, lived in Claremont at first and then moved to Camps Bay. It was a good life while I was there."

"But you came back," Paolo said. "Did it not work out?"

Bradley smiled. "It worked out very well. I thought I'd stay, but a couple of years ago something called me home."

"What was it? Your plan to commit murder?"

Bradley shook his head. "No, not at all. I had come to terms with my loss and thought I'd moved on. When I landed at Heathrow, I had no job and nowhere to live, but I had earned a good salary in SA and hadn't spent much of it over the years, so didn't need to work for a while. I came back to Bradchester because it's where I was born. Where I got married and lived with Grace. Where I'd been happy."

"Then I don't understand," Paolo said. "If you were so at peace with yourself and the world, what happened to change all that?"

"Edwin Fulbright got married to that young woman."

Paolo thought he must have misheard, but the look on Dave's face told him he was confused, too.

"I don't understand."

Bradley sighed. "I'd only been in Bradchester a few weeks, staying in a B & B while I looked around for somewhere to rent. The local news came on the television and there was Edwin Fulbright beaming with happiness on his wedding day. It did something to me. Hurt in a way I can't describe."

"So you decided he should die for being happy?" Paolo asked.

"No, not straight away, but that same weekend, Wittington-Smythe and his wife were in the paper attending some charity event. The photographer caught them in one of those poses where they are looking at each other with the kind of look only people who've been married for a while can share. It showed how close they were and I hated them for it."

Bradley sat up straighter in his chair. "That's when I decided to look into the lives of all those I felt had let Grace down, or had been party to the accident. I discovered they all seemed to be living good lives. All apart from Conrad Stormont. It took me ages to find him. When I realised he'd dropped off the face of the earth, but wasn't dead, I hit on the idea of him living on the streets, so went round all the shelters and soup kitchens until I struck lucky."

He sighed. "He was supposed to have been the final one, but when I tried to get an earlier appointment with Jessica Carter, she wasn't in Bradchester. She was the last person to testify on Miller's behalf. Did you know that? That's what made me think it was meant to be. You know, it started when a woman died, so maybe it was fate for it to end with the death of another one." His voice broke and tears streamed down his face. "I loved my Grace so much. You'll never know how much. She died on the Friday night, but I only found out on Saturday morning." He wiped the tears away and sniffed. "When I decided to kill them all, I wanted it to be like with Grace; they die on Friday, but only get found on Saturday. Then I took it a stage further and thought it would be poetic justice to kill them with the stuff Grace used to have to inject herself with. Have you any idea how easy it is to buy insulin from the internet?"

Paolo shook his head. "I've never looked into it, but it frightens me to death to realise just what is available online. So you began following them?"

Bradley nodded. "I knew I'd need to be able to get close enough to inject them. That would mean setting up a situation where they trusted me, so I found their weak points. Then I pretended to be someone they would allow to get close."

Paolo nodded. From looking through Bradley Simmonds's notebooks, he already knew the answer to the next question he intended to ask, but wanted to get it on record.

"So why was Jon Miller not on your list of victims?"

"I planned to make it appear he'd killed them. I wanted him to go to prison for murder, because that's where he should have gone when he killed Grace. I killed them all at a time when I knew he'd have trouble proving his alibi."

"Was it you who called the hospital in Leicester and changed the time of his interview?"

Bradley nodded. "I took the job in the pub because I knew he used to go in there at least three or four times a week. I thought it was the easiest way of finding out what was going on in his life. It wasn't hard to get him to confide in me about wanting to move away from his brother. When he told me he had an interview on a Friday, it felt like fate was on my side."

"I take it you ordered the insulin on his card to incriminate him?"

Bradley nodded. "I thought that would convince a jury."

"How did you get his credit card details?"

"I copied them down when he paid for meals in the pub. Once I had the three digits on the back of the card, I knew I could use it online."

"I can understand your motives for the professor and Conrad Stormont. At a stretch I can see why you'd blame Jon Miller's legal team and Dr Carter, but Edwin Fulbright did all he could to save your wife."

Bradley looked across the table and Paolo was stunned by his bleak expression of loss and loneliness.

"But he didn't save her, did he? He saved Jon's miserable brother, but not my lovely Grace."

"Did you kill Andrew Miller?"

Bradley smiled and nodded. "Beat him to a pulp first and then killed him."

"But why?" Paolo asked. "He wasn't on your list."

"I told you, Jon Miller used to come in and whine about his brother. One day last week, he told me Andy had been able to walk for over a year, but had kept it quiet so that he could keep claiming the benefits. Jon thought it was also so that Andy could continue to play the guilt card." Bradley's eyes flashed with rage. "All the time I thought he was a victim of his brother's crime, I felt sympathy for him. When I discovered what he was doing, I decided to go round there and wipe him out. He was no use to society, and I thought Jon would probably get the blame."

"How did you get into the flat?" Paolo asked.

"I used a key. Jon had dropped one in the bar some time ago. I pretended to look for it, but stuck it in my pocket instead. I told him I'd given it to his upstairs neighbour."

Paolo checked his list of questions, but was already

pretty sure he'd covered everything. He glanced at his watch. Barbara would be coming out of the operating theatre soon. It was time to keep his promise to her.

"Do you have anything you would like to add?"

Bradley shook his head. "Just that I'm sorry I didn't manage to get justice for Grace. If you'd arrived ten minutes later, I would have succeeded."

Paolo shuddered at the thought of what would have happened to Jessica if he hadn't arrived when he did. He looked again at his watch and read out the time.

"This interview is terminated," he said.

***

Paolo sat next to the bed waiting for Barbara to wake up again. She'd opened her eyes briefly when she'd been wheeled in from the recovery room, but then had fallen back into a deep sleep. His gaze wandered around the room, taking in the fact that there were no cards or gifts. How she'd managed to keep her illness and this operation a secret was beyond him. One thing he had expected was for her friend, the giver of the special coffee machine, to be here for her. He wondered if that little romance had died a natural death and hoped for Barbara's sake that it hadn't. She deserved someone good in her life.

He heard a murmur and looked back towards the bed. Barbara's eyes were open. He stood up and walked the three paces separating the visitor's chair from the side of the bed.

"Hey," he said. "How're you feeling?"

"Okay," she whispered. "Funny. Groggy. Thank you for being here."

He held her hand, taking care not to disturb the needle connecting her to the various liquids being fed into her system from the drip support.

"The nurse who was here earlier said for you to press this buzzer if you have any pain."

"Okay."

Paolo smiled. "She also made it quite clear that I should

only stay for a few minutes after you wake up."

Barbara nodded. "Did you catch the killer?"

He smiled. "I did, but I'm not going to tell you about it now, except to say Jessica was his next target. Fortunately, Dave and I got there in time."

She laughed, but the spasm that followed showed it must have hurt.

"Got there in the nick of time, like a superhero. We'll have to set you up with a phone box to keep your superhero outfit in. Jessica is lucky to have you."

Paolo thought about the way Jessica had looked before he took Bradley to the station.

"She's pretty shaken up at the moment," he said.

Barbara's eyes closed. Paolo decided to go and turned towards the door.

The merest hint of a whisper reached him as he put his hand out for the handle, but surely he must have misheard? He looked back at the bed. Barbara was in a deep sleep.

As he moved along the corridor towards the lift, he tried to convince himself he hadn't heard her say anything at all, but deep inside he knew he had. Walking from the lift to the hospital's front entrance, he told himself he should go directly to Jessica's, but Barbara's whisper had left him feeling unsettled. He needed to sort out his thoughts before he went to Jessica's flat.

He'd never tell another living soul, not even Barbara herself, but he was certain he'd heard her say, "I love you."

He opened the door and walked out into the chill of a September evening. It seemed autumn had finally arrived to take away the warmth of summer.

THE END

Fantastic Books
Great Authors

CROOKED
CAT

Meet our authors and discover
our exciting range:

- Gripping Thrillers
- Cosy Mysteries
- Romantic Chick-Lit
- Fascinating Historicals
- Exciting Fantasy
- Young Adult and Children's
  Adventures

Visit us at:
www.crookedcatbooks.com

Join us on facebook:
www.facebook.com/realcrookedcat

Printed in Great Britain
by Amazon